IN AT THE DEEP END

HANNAH LYNN

B

First published in 2019 as *Fiona and the Whale* and in 2020 as *Treading Water*. This edition published in Great Britain in 2024 by Boldwood Books Ltd.

Copyright © Hannah Lynn, 2019

Cover Design by JD Design Ltd.

Cover Images: Shutterstock

A CIP catalogue record for this book is available from the British Library.

Paperback ISBN 978-1-83603-881-8

Large Print ISBN 978-1-83603-882-5

Hardback ISBN 978-1-83603-880-1

Ebook ISBN 978-1-83603-883-2

Kindle ISBN 978-1-83603-884-9

Audio CD ISBN 978-1-83603-875-7

MP3 CD ISBN 978-1-83603-876-4

Digital audio download ISBN 978-1-83603-878-8

This book is printed on certified sustainable paper. Boldwood Books is dedicated to putting sustainability at the heart of our business. For more information please visit https://www.boldwoodbooks.com/about-us/sustainability/

Boldwood Books Ltd, 23 Bowerdean Street, London, SW6 3TN

www.boldwoodbooks.com

For all the Marthas

1

Two suitcases, umpteen plastic carrier bags, and an oversized rucksack lined the hallway. Fiona stood on her tiptoes, wrapped her arms around her son and squeezed.

'Are you sure you don't mind us not coming?' she asked, releasing him and dropping down onto her heels. 'I'd have to rearrange a few things, but if you give me half an hour to ring the office and send a few emails...'

'Mum.' Joseph placed his hand on her shoulders. 'It's fine. I've got this. Everything's sorted. Dad'll drop me at the station, and I'll get a taxi at the other end.'

'You're sure?'

'Honestly. It's not like I'm going away forever.'

'Well it feels like it is.'

Casting an eye around the hall, she was filled with a mixture of pride, excitement, and sadness. Her baby was all grown up and heading off to university.

'You're sure you've got everything you need?'

'I'm sure.'

'I gave him a selection of pots and pans out of the kitchen

too,' Stephen appeared on the stairs, 'and a couple of pieces of crockery and cutlery to take with him.'

'You did?' She turned, a frown crossing her eyebrows. 'Which ones? Plates, that is? Nothing that was part of a set?'

'I don't think so. They were on their own.'

'Well can I check before you take them? I don't want to be left with a mismatched dinner service the next time we have people round to eat.'

Leaving her son, she crossed the hall into the dining room, where more bags overflowed.

'Which one did you pack them in?' she asked, to neither of the men in particular.

'I can't remember,' Joseph replied. 'One of the rucksacks, I think.'

Crouching down, she tugged at the zip of a red holdall.

'This one?'

'Maybe.'

'Fiona, is that really necessary right now?' Stephen's frown was almost a mirror image of hers. 'We need to get going.'

'Is it necessary to check that we haven't sent him off to university with part of my mother's Anna Weatherley dinner set? Yes. What colour were the plates he gave you?' She directed her question back to Joseph, while freeing the zip from whatever it had caught on.

'Yellow maybe? Or blue?'

'Fiona, please. I didn't give him your mother's china.'

'I thought you said you couldn't remember what it looked like?'

'I know what your mother's Anna Weatherley looks like. And it hasn't come out of the cupboard in over a year.'

The condescending edge to his tone rankled with her.

'We used it the last time Kat and Paul came over for dinner,' she corrected him.

'Which was over a year ago.'

Stephen fixed his eyes on hers. She raced through her memory, trying to recall the date. It was so frustrating when he did this, pushed a point so far, especially when he was almost certainly wrong. And now she had to come across as the pedantic one.

'No,' she pointed a finger at him, with the smug satisfaction that came with always being right. 'Your birthday. Eight months ago. We always use it on our birthdays.'

'Not last year,' Stephen replied, his face impassive. 'I had to head to Swansea and you had a conference to set up, remember?'

'And I ordered Chinese and you got pissed off at all the mess I left,' Joseph added, obviously feeling the need to join in.

The memory clicked into her mind. 'Of course, you did.'

How could she have forgotten? She'd arrived back home – after eighteen hours out of the house – feet throbbing, head pounding and desperate for a glass of wine. What she'd found in her exhausted state was an entire worktop covered in congealing patches of sweet-and-sour sauce, with fried rice strewn everywhere and a general smell of grease in the air. By the time she'd cleaned up and taken a shower to remove the stench of soy sauce and general grime of the day, it had been nearly three in the morning.

'And now someone else will have to deal with your mess.' She grinned.

'So, definitely no Anna Weatherley involved then,' Stephen said, the smallest of smirks playing on his lips. 'Now, we *have* to get going. I do have a job to get to you know.'

'If you'd rather I took him?'

'No, it's fine. I already said it's fine. I've got something I need to sort out, anyway.'

The clock in the hall ticked loudly, as if to remind them that time was passing. With a long sigh, she pouted, rubbed her temples, then smiled. 'I guess it's a good job we're going away next week.' She placed her hand on her husband's arm. 'We probably both need the break.'

After seeing her smile fleetingly reciprocated by her husband, she turned back to Joseph. 'Are you sure you don't want to come with us? It's Belgium. Chocolate and a spa hotel. It wouldn't be too late to get you a room.'

'And miss Fresher's Week?' he raised his eyebrows. 'No chance. It's fine. Just bring back a load of chocolate for when I come home with my washing.'

It was her turn to raise an eyebrow.

'If you think I'm still doing that, you've got me confused with someone else's mother.'

Joseph laughed and looped an arm around her shoulders.

'How did you grow up so fast?' she asked, causing him to laugh again. He had such a sweet laugh, the same as he'd had as a child, only deeper. It felt like only a week ago they'd been on holiday in the Seychelles, digging giant holes in the sand for him to bury himself in. And now he was towering over her, making her feel both incredibly small and incredibly old at the same time.

'Right, that's enough sentimentality for one day.' She blinked herself out of the moment. 'You'll miss your train, and your dad and I have got work.'

'I'll check the plates when I get there,' he said, his arm still around her. 'I'll bring anything I shouldn't have back with me next time I'm home.'

Nodding mutely, Fiona wrapped her arms around her son

and breathed him in for one last time. He hadn't even left, yet the house already felt emptier, as if part of its soul inhabited his belongings and now he was taking it with him.

'You're going to have so much fun,' she said. 'Just stay safe and work hard.'

'I know.'

'And it's going to be quiet around here,' she added.

'It is,' Stephen agreed, standing back and observing his son and wife. 'It's going to be very quiet indeed.'

* * *

The office was a comfortable six Tube stops away, with no line changes involved. It was a little farther out of central London than she would have liked, but what she'd lost in location, she'd more than made up for in space. And, despite being only a two-woman operation, space was paramount. Space and style.

It had taken more than a few tries to get the ambiance just right – and of course it all needed updating every couple of years to ensure it didn't start to look tired – but right now, Omnivents, Fiona's high-end, events-planning company, was at the top of its game. A large, silver name plaque greeted clients at the entrance and, inside, a small table offered goodies, ranging from retro sweets to French macarons, depending on who they were expecting that day. When not on offer, said sweets and treats were stored in the stock room, along with hundreds of empty presentation packs, over a thousand lanyards waiting to be filled, two portable mini projectors with built-in screens, and a whole host of other events paraphernalia. Hence the need for space.

On a second, small table, wooden diffusers heated essential oils, spilling citrus and lavender scents into the air, obscuring the unwanted smells that filtered through from the Lebanese restaurant downstairs. This juxtaposition was a double-edged sword; smelling shawarma chicken floating up from the kebab rotisseries at 8 a.m. each morning wasn't exactly pleasant, but having a falafel wrap with a side of hummus and pita delivered in less than five minutes could be a godsend when she didn't have time to leave the office for an actual lunch break.

In the twelve years since its inception, Omnivents had built up a client list that made her smile with pride every time she thought of it. Of course, she was small fry compared to the business Stephen worked for, but then most businesses were. (Alton Foods was run by the renowned entrepreneur John Orbiten and had been securely positioned in the top-five food producers in the UK for most of the eleven years Stephen had been there.) But, unlike her husband, who was at the beck and call of his boss twenty-four hours a day, Fiona answered to no one but herself. Omnivents was entirely her own.

During those years, it had gone through more than one reinvention. Back when she'd first started, she had taken any jobs she could get her hands on: sweet sixteen parties, book launches, not to mention weddings. God, she'd had fun with those weddings. But, somewhere along the road, despite the high-society christenings and elaborate twenty-firsts, she'd carved out a particular name for herself as the go-to person for bespoke, high-end corporate events. Now, some of the biggest names in marketing and business used her when it came to launches, Christmas parties, charity galas, and, most of all, seminars. Companies, she had discovered, liked nothing more than holding seminars.

'Soon you'll be earning more money than me,' Stephen had joked a couple of years back. He'd only said it in passing but, to her, it had become a target to aim at, particularly after one of his own company events led to her scoring three new clients.

Event planning as a whole, even being CEO of a company like hers, wasn't nearly as glamorous as people thought it was, though. It involved a lot of emails. And telephone calls. Not to mention the hours spent laminating itineraries and schedules. Fortunately, when it came to exciting jobs like loading up name tags and filling good-old corporate goodie bags, she had Annabel.

'Morning, Annabel.' Fiona placed a takeaway white-chocolate-strawberry-and-cream Frappuccino on her assistant's desk before reaching into her tote and pulling out a plastic bag. 'And, I know it's not your birthday for another month, but I saw this and couldn't resist it.'

'For me?'

'I hope it's okay.'

'You didn't have to do that!' Annabel bounced up and down in her seat as she spoke, causing her glasses to jump on the bridge of her nose. Mid-twenties and with more energy than a newborn lamb on a sugar high, the bouncing habit had almost cost her the job at her interview five years ago. Every question she'd answered had resulted in her bobbing further and further out of her seat. It wasn't that Fiona hadn't admired her enthusiasm, but to look at it every day? She was exhausted after the thirty-minute meeting. Even so, she'd decided to employ her on a trial basis. Three weeks later, she changed the contract to permanent and had never looked back.

Annabel pulled the T-shirt out of the bag and held it up against her chest, measuring it up for size. 'Oh, my goodness. I love it!'

'I didn't know which house to get you, so I got the one with all of them on instead.'

'It's perfect.' She ran her hand along the fabric. 'Personally, I always thought I was a Ravenclaw, but Pottermore says I'm Hufflepuff. Honestly, I'm not even sure how that's possible, given I was in the bottom set for—' She drew to a stop, closing her mouth in an embarrassed smile. 'Thank you.' She folded the T-shirt away and picked up her drink. 'How's Joseph? Did everything fit in the car? Did he get off okay?'

'I hope so. They haven't rung to say otherwise,' she replied. 'I guess I'll hear from him when he gets there.'

'He must be so excited.'

'I think he's been looking forward to this for the last two years.'

'Oh, he's going to have such fun.'

Thoughts of a son, out on his own in an unfamiliar city, far from home, would probably have made most mothers sick with anxiety. But Joseph wasn't like most boys. He had a good head on his shoulders.

'Is everything sorted for next week? No last-minute issues?' She brought herself back to the present.

'Nope.' Annabel sucked a mouthful of pink liquid through the straw. 'You are completely clear, but it means that it's going to be a bit of a crazy one when you get back.'

'Crazy's good. Crazy means we're making money. Which means a nice bonus to help you get that house deposit.'

'That would be brilliant. It seems every time we manage to save a bit more, the house prices soar and we still can't afford anything.'

'I remember that,' Fiona recalled, her fingertips resting on the handle of her office door. 'Stephen and I lived on beans and pasta for years. Or, at least, that's what it felt like. I'm not sorry those days are gone.'

'And now you're about to head off and celebrate your twentieth wedding anniversary. It's so exciting. Oh!' Another little jump. 'I forgot to say. Some of the promotional things arrived. I assumed they're for VertX, so I've put the boxes at the back of your office.'

'Fantastic. And you'll forward me the minutes from that last meeting by lunchtime?'

'I was about to hit send when you arrived.'

'You're an angel. Right, time to start the day then.'

Closing the door behind her, she sat down, shut her eyes and breathed in the aroma. Unlike Annabel, who was happy to start her working day with whatever combination of sugar, cream and additives she could get her hands on, Fiona's beverage of choice from the coffee shop was always the same: a triple-shot, full-roasted, Guatemalan espresso. Sitting back in her chair, she held the cup under her nose and inhaled the bitter scent. She had a coffee machine in the office, a mid-range number that could produce a good-enough result, particularly useful if clients were visiting, but this first one of the day was special.

This was the one moment when she could relax and not worry about anything. Not about clients, or home, or whether or not she was ever going to get to the gym again. (Despite the fact that she'd been paying sixty pounds a month on membership fees for the last two years, she'd only gone about once a month, if that.) She allowed herself to dream of the upcoming holiday, and of the holidays after that. Only after she'd tasted those last, flavourful tannins, followed by a small glass of water, did she actually feel ready to make a start on the mountain of jobs that preceded a week-long holiday.

Casting the cup into the bin, she turned her attention to the box on the floor. As was typical, half a roll of packing tape had been used to almost impenetrably seal the two foot by two foot container, and it was only after grabbing a letter opener and stabbing her way in that she managed to reach the contents.

'Excellent,' she said to herself, as she finally pushed aside the polystyrene beads.

VertX Wellbeing Assistance was her biggest client and had been one of the first corporate businesses to sign with her independently, as opposed to those who'd come through a connection to Stephen or the golf club. Back then, life coaching as a business was barely in the fledgling stage. A fresh and cocky upstart, Dominic Tan had been so full of outrageous and outlandish ideas that, new to the whole corporate conference world, Fiona had been hesitant about even working with him. Ten years later and he had taken the city by storm, turning VertX into the number-one life-coaching platform in the country, with centres across Europe and plans to venture further still. It had been Dominic himself who had convinced her to work with him, after she'd sat in on one of his group sessions. That was back in the day when he used to run them himself, rather than delegate to one of his underlings. There was no doubt, what he did was impressive. He was very impressive.

From out of the box, she pulled a large, plastic bag and from that a smaller one. She tipped out one of the items onto her palm. Dominic was a sucker for a top-notch goodie bag at his conferences. Goodie bags and branding. The name VertX from floor to ceiling. He wanted people to leave his events unable to forget the name. And she knew just how to make that happen.

USB sticks and chrome pens, with the company logo engraved on them, were well-seasoned staples. But it was those little extras that stood out, that told people they meant business. For example, baseball caps in summer and branded gloves in winter. Flight socks or good quality eye masks, if not both, if people had come in by plane. Mugs tended to get left behind, as did water bottles, but she had yet to see anyone turn down a stylish hoodie or portable charger. Better still, electronics kits, with adapters and cables added into the mix. She'd learnt the importance of quirky items too, like customised puzzle cubes. A marketing marvel, in her opinion. After all, you weren't likely to forget the name of a company after spending four hours attempting to reassemble its logo on six different faces.

'Go for it,' Dominic had said, when she'd run the idea by him. 'And make sure the brand's clear. Classy and clear. The brand is what sells us now, remember.'

'I'll send you through a prototype when it arrives,' she'd said. 'And don't worry. That's the only gimmicky thing. This conference is going to blow them away.'

'I trust you,' he'd assured her.

And go for it she had. With only three weeks until the big day, things were starting to come together. This was her favourite part, when all her ideas fell into place.

She pulled off the wrapping paper and turned it over in her hand.

'Shit!'

After the discovery of the mislabelled puzzle cube, the entire morning was lost searching for emails she'd sent months ago and then on the phone.

'It says VortX on them,' she spat down the line. 'The company name is VertX. *Vert* and then a capital X. VortX sounds like they're going to send you spinning into a whirlpool of misery.

'Annabel!' she called out. 'Please can you send me all the correspondence we've had on this. I wrote that order form myself. And I know it said VertX.'

'Coming through now.'

'Great. And can you dig out the contact and see who is in

charge there? This is why I hate dealing with salespeople.' The salesperson she was talking about was still on the line and could undoubtedly hear what she was saying. That was half the point.

By the time it was sorted – the company was going to expedite the new correct order, at no extra cost given that, as she already knew, the error was theirs – lunchtime had been and gone. Her head was buzzing from the caffeine Annabel had dutifully supplied her with and, despite the fact that she had, for the first time in years, indulged in a family breakfast that morning to mark Joseph's departure, her stomach was growling incessantly.

'Shawarma wrap it is then,' she said to herself.

* * *

Six hours later, the sky had adopted a dusky-pink hue. Dropping her bag to the ground, she turned her key in the front door and let herself into the house. Another emergency had come up only minutes after her wrap had arrived, meaning that when she finally got around to eating, all that was left was a half-disintegrating piece of bread, some drastically wilted lettuce, and a few pieces of cold, hardened chicken. As such, she'd taken one bite before dropping the whole thing in the bin.

'Stephen?' she called, kicking off her shoes.

She hung up her coat and headed to the kitchen. He was sitting at the counter, drink in hand.

'You're home. God, I need a drink.' She took a can of tonic from the fridge, cracked it open and swigged a mouthful before pouring the rest into a tall glass and topping it up with a generous measure of gin. She took a long gulp. 'Christ, I needed that.'

'So,' he said, watching her. 'Aren't you going to ask how my day went?'

She finished another mouthful. 'I assumed you'd have messaged if there'd been any problems?'

'What about Joseph? Have you called him?'

Removing the glass from her lips, she frowned at him. 'What's wrong with you today?'

'Nothing. Nothing's wrong. I just thought you might want to find out how our son was, on his first day away from home.'

'It's not his first day away from home. And, like he said, he'll probably be back again next weekend with his washing. Anyway, I was going to ring him later.'

Rolling her eyes, she headed back to the fridge which, being a Friday, was devoid of anything that could be assembled into a meal. She took out her phone, began to browse Deliveroo and was about to make the suggestion of Thai, when her gaze fell on two large suitcases.

'Did you pack for me?' she asked, suddenly realising that job had been on her to-do list all week. 'You didn't have to do that. When did you find the time? I was going to check the weather, anyway. You know I prefer to sort things out myself.'

'I didn't pack for you.'

'You didn't?'

It took a few seconds for her to think of another explanation.

'Shit,' she said. 'Have you rung Joseph? Does he know he's forgotten them?'

Her question was met with silence.

'Stephen, did you hear me? Does Joseph know he left these behind?'

'They're not Joseph's bags,' he replied.

She shook her head, confused. 'What do you mean, they're not his bags?'

'They're mine.'

She shook her head again and went back to her phone.

'That's ridiculous, Stephen, we're only going for a week. And we'll probably spend most of the time in the spa anyway. Why don't you take them back upstairs and see if there's something you can get rid of?'

Her suggestion was met with more silence, which hung there ominously.

'Stephen, did you hear what I said?'

With jaw clenched, he finally lifted his head and looked at her.

'They're not for the holiday, Fiona. I'm not going to Brussels. I'm leaving you.'

2

The hallway clock chimed and a peal of church bells sounded in the distance. But, to Fiona, it was all peripheral, as she struggled to understand her husband.

'What? You mean you're leaving for work?'

'No, I mean I'm leaving for good.'

'Where are you going?'

'I've made arrangements.'

She blinked, his words hitting a fog somewhere between his mouth and her brain.

'I don't understand.'

'I'm going, Fiona.'

'You're leaving me? Stephen, you're not making any sense. What are you talking about?'

He pressed his lips together, as if he were deliberating the top-prize question in a TV game show. When he opened his mouth to speak again, it came out in a rush.

'I can't do it any more, Fiona. I can't.'

'You can't do what?'

'This. Us.' He motioned between them. 'Pretending every-thing's okay. That this marriage works.'

'This marriage does work.'

'Perhaps for you.'

'What's that supposed to mean?'

'What do you think it's supposed to mean?'

Whether the question was rhetorical or not didn't matter; she wasn't answering it. Shaking her head, she tipped the glass and downed the rest of her drink in one go.

'You can't honestly kid yourself you *like* this, can you?' he questioned. 'We never see each other. We're like ships in the night, traversing entirely different bloody oceans.'

'Because we're busy. *We*.' She pointed back and forth between the two of them to ensure absolute clarity. '*We* are busy people.'

Putting her glass down, she crossed the kitchen and sank onto the stool beside him. They'd had fights before, plenty of them. Almost always at a time when one or both of them had an important deadline coming up. That was it. There was some-thing she'd missed. A conference, a big presentation, maybe a new line launch. It would be something she'd forgotten about, although she thought she'd checked both their schedules pretty carefully before booking the holiday.

'We're just tired, Stephen, that's all. It's been so busy lately, what with Joseph going off and you and me overloaded at work. It's not a surprise we're exhausted.'

'I'm tired of being tired.'

He lowered his eyes to the counter. She looked at the face she knew so well: the pitted marks from childhood chickenpox, the scar above his eyebrow where he'd walked into a cupboard door after a rugby team night out. She knew every inch of it, yet now there was a greyness to his skin.

'You'll see,' she said, brushing her hand across the scar. 'After the holiday. After some time together, things will seem better.'

'And then what?' His eyes came back up to meet hers. 'There's no spark any more. No fun. If we're not at work, then we're sitting in the living room, on our computers, hardly even speaking to one another, pretending that's what normal couples do.'

'That *is* what normal couples do.' She clenched and unclenched her fists. 'You really want to do this? After all we've been through, you really want to tear this family apart?'

'Joseph gets it. He understands.'

The words took a moment to register.

'Joseph knows?' Her voice was barely audible. 'Joseph knew that you were going to do this?'

A look, somewhere between shame and determination, crossed his face.

'I spoke to him on the way to the station.'

'You did what?' Her hands went to her head, her fingernails gripping her scalp as she tried to make sense of what she was hearing.

'He understands,' he repeated. 'He knows what it's been like.'

'*What it's been like?* Am I missing something here? Have I been living in some parallel universe? Because, from where I'm standing, life looks pretty damn good for us.'

'Fiona—'

'The house, the cars... you're delusional. You have to be.' Trembling with a mixture of fury and disbelief, she paced from one side of the room to the other. 'After everything we've done together. The life we've had. All the places we've been together.'

Her mind came back to the present. 'We're going away

tomorrow. Everything's booked. I've taken time off work. It's our anniversary, for Christ's sake! It's our twentieth anniversary.'

For the first time, his face showed a modicum of sympathy.

'I thought it would best to do it now. Give you a week away from people, so you didn't have the pressure of going into work.'

'Oh, how very thoughtful of you,' she spat, staring at her husband as he fiddled with the strap of his watch, light reflecting off the glass.

'Where did you get that?' she asked.

'What?'

'Where did you get that watch? What happened to the one with the leather strap I bought you last Christmas? The Patek Philippe? Why aren't you wearing that?'

Stephen pulled his jacket cuff down.

'It's just an old one.'

'Show me.'

'Fiona.'

'Show me!' She lunged at his arm, but he moved back out of reach, holding his wrist against him.

She dropped her hands and scoffed.

'There's someone else.' She could feel the bile rise in her throat. 'You've met someone.'

His eyes fell to the watch again. He traced a finger across the face and, for a fleeting moment, she thought he was going to deny it. Instead, he pushed his stool back from the counter and stood up. 'Don't do this, please.'

'You've been cheating on me?'

He crossed behind her, to where the suitcases waited.

'How long?' She could hardly recognise her own voice now.

He licked his lips.

'You owe me that much,' she insisted. 'Tell me. How long has it been going on for?'

Not able to meet her gaze now, he cleared his throat.

'*How long?*'

'About eighteen months.'

That was the moment her world fell away.

There had been a time in her life when she'd been a crier. Happy tears, sad tears, any emotional situation would elicit the same response; as a child, always erupting into floods at the slightest hint of reproach or injustice. When puberty hit, it had only become worse, earning her the label of *over-emotional* or *unsettled*. And while at university she'd got a slightly better grip on things, any form of confrontation would have her staring at the ceiling, desperately trying to blink away the tears before their escape ruined any chance she had of being taken seriously.

Then her mother got dementia.

When the person she'd loved and held dearest started calling her the most despicable and spiteful names under the sun, it became remarkably easy to ignore the unkind words of others. The cutting remarks from bitchy women or misogynistic men that she'd had to put up with in her first job were nothing compared to the blows her mother would deal out week after week. She became immune to it all. After a while, she didn't even bother thinking up witty retorts to fire back. When she moved on to her next position, she quickly got herself the reputation of someone efficient and no-nonsense, a hard arse.

Stephen knew the truth, of course. He had never witnessed the blubbering wreck she could once be reduced to, but she'd told him about it. On their wedding day, she had smiled through, calm and poised, without the slightest risk of ruining her mascara. Only at the arrival of Joseph had she felt that familiar prickling in her eyes.

Even now, desperately wishing she could find a way of

showing Stephen how he had ripped out her heart and squeezed it to a pulp in front of her, all she actually said was, 'I think you need to go.'

* * *

The next morning, Fiona packed a suitcase. It was probably a sensible thing to do, to escape a place that was full of memories: where they'd met; their first house; the roads they'd walked down so often, fingers intertwined, as they'd made time in their busy schedules to grab a hurried lunch together. Getting out of the city would be the best idea, Stephen had advised her before he left.

In the end, that was the very reason she found herself standing on the train platform watching the 12.02 pull away without her. Stephen didn't get to choose how she behaved any more, she thought, as people jostled around her. Not while he was behaving like this. That wasn't how it worked. Grabbing her bag, she marched outside to a waiting taxi, pulled out her phone and called the one person she knew she could face talking to.

'Fucking prick.'

Holly had always had a way with words. 'I'm going to be half an hour, is that okay? I'll come to you.'

'I've got some work I can do,' Fiona told her, having recounted the tale of the previous evening. 'It's probably best if I'm on my own for a bit.'

'Like fuck it is,' Holly replied.

'Only if you're sure.'

'I'll be half an hour.'

An hour and a quarter later, her best friend of nearly thirty years was at the door, with a bottle of gin and two tubs of ice cream.

Fiona smiled. 'I guess you'd better come in.'

* * *

'So, do you know who this other woman is?' Holly asked, topping up Fiona's glass yet again.

They were in the living room, where she and Stephen used to sit companionably, she'd thought, working on their laptops. It had always been her favourite room in the house, with its big bay windows and restored stone fireplace. She wished they'd found a better way of disguising the enormous television, though. After all, it wasn't like they ever watched it.

'Though maybe it isn't another woman,' Holly continued thoughtfully. 'You know I always thought he was far too eager to please that boss of his.'

'John Orbiten?'

'Is that him? The one he's always on the phone to? Maybe he's lured Stephen with a promise of a lifetime of free yogurts and frozen food. You know how he loves his yoghurt. God, imagine them smearing it all over each other's hairy chests.' She shuddered and Fiona let out a snort of laughter.

'I don't think it's him,' she said, swallowing a mouthful of gin and tonic and trying to banish the image of her husband and John Orbiten wallowing together in a tub of Alton organic yogurt. 'Though I wish I knew who it was. I swear, I've been racking my brains. I know a new partner moved into the firm last year—'

'He's always been a bit power crazed,' Holly added.

'And his old secretary left to go to law school...'

'The new secretary? No! Could you get any more clichéd?'

'But then I keep wondering if it's someone we *know* know. Like a friend. Remember Judith slept with Katherine's husband that time?'

'Yes, but Judith smells of Olbas oil. Stephen wouldn't go for that.'

'Well, he did go for someone.'

Their imaginations wandered as they sipped their drinks.

Smacking her lips, Fiona moved for the bottle again. She'd decided to abandon the tonic. It was only slowing down the inevitable. She needed to get drunk, inebriated to the point where she couldn't remember her address, or her age, or the fact that her husband had been sleeping with another woman for a year and a half. However, with drunkenness came the inevitable hangover. At forty-six, she considered herself well past the age of coping with that. Her thoughts drifted back to Stephen's bit on the side. She'd probably be too young to suffer a proper hangover, the sort that had you laid up in bed for forty-eight hours, craving salt-and-vinegar crisps and Diet Coke, and wincing at any sound above zero point four decibels.

'Eighteen months,' Holly mused, as if she were reading her mind. 'That's crazy. Eighteen months. That means he was seeing her when we all went to Judith's birthday party last summer.'

'Uh-huh.' She had now abandoned the gin for a bottle of sparkling water. 'And when we all went to Circus 21 for breakfast. And when we took Joseph to his leaving ball, and to pick up his A-level results. Not to mention the Alton Christmas party, and the massive fundraiser we threw for Stand up to Steroids or whatever that charity was called. I just can't believe I wouldn't have seen it, you know? You'd have thought I'd have spotted something was up. Some sign that things were amiss.

We've been married twenty years, for crying out loud. What did I do? Where did I go wrong?' She gulped the water.

'It wasn't you. It was definitely not you,' Holly replied.

Fiona pondered. It was true she worked a lot. Probably more than average. But that was something Stephen had always admired about her. Encouraged in her, even. Just last year, when she was umming and ahhing about taking on the Lovett–Rose–Rosenberg wedding, he had been the one saying how good the extra publicity would be for her company. And he'd been so pleased for her when she did take it on. She gazed down at her hand, at the eternity ring he had given her as a congratulations gift. Was it possible a person could switch his feelings on and off that quickly? Surely not.

'It must be something else. There must be more to it. Maybe this is a cry for help. Maybe the job's got too much for him. Perhaps it was Joseph moving out.'

Moving across the room, she picked up the bottle of gin, refilled Holly's glass and flopped down next to her. 'You know what, the more I think about it, the more that's what it has to be. A cry for help. Honestly, I don't know why I even called you. He'll probably be back tomorrow.' This explanation was making her feel somewhat optimistic.

'You think?'

'I do. I mean, obviously, there's something more going on here. Maybe he's had a bit of fun sneaking around with someone. But I know Stephen. Whatever this thing is, he's going to realise he needs me by his side for support. He'll be back within a week. Sooner, I expect.'

Feeling more assured, she stood up from the sofa.

'Do you want to stay the night?' she asked. 'The spare room's all made up. It'd save you having to get a cab.'

Holly yawned, covering her mouth for only a fraction of a

second before it ended. 'Actually, if you're okay, I should really head home. I've got a ton of deadlines next week.' Then, as an afterthought, she added, 'But I can stay if you need the company?'

'Don't be silly,' Fiona replied, collecting up the empties for the dishwasher. 'Go home. Get some sleep.'

'But I'll see you tomorrow? Or Monday?'

'You really don't have to mollycoddle me.'

'It's not mollycoddling, it's called being a good friend. Besides, if you're not busy with work or Stephen this week, it means we might actually be able to spend some time together.'

Fiona yawned now, breaking into a grateful smile partway through.

'Well in that case, how can I say no?'

As the front door closed, a hush fell on the house.

'He'll be back,' she said to herself. 'Just you wait and see.'

3

She had never really thought about how she would handle an existential crisis. Her father had been a drinker. He'd been that way before her mother died and only got worse afterwards. Her sister, after a messy relationship breakdown, had joined a sect who worshipped Mother Earth and the power of crystals, or some other such bollocks that Fiona avoided talking about whenever they saw each other. She, however, faced this trauma with her usual efficiency.

'Please, don't step on anything,' she said, leading Holly into the house, past the antique elm rocking chair that had once lived in Joseph's nursery but now stood in the middle of the hallway. 'It looks a little messy but, trust me, it's all organised.'

'What the hell's happened?' Holly asked, walking on tiptoes as she moved through the detritus. 'I've haven't even been gone a day. Is the *Antiques Roadshow* doing an episode here that you forgot to tell me about? Cos, I'm going to be honest, their venues are usually way bigger than this. No offence to your home or anything.'

Ignoring the comment, Fiona picked a path through to the kitchen. 'There's still a long way to go, but I'm getting there.'

That Sunday morning, she had needed something to occupy her mind. Reading hadn't worked; every other line, her mind would trip on a word and her thoughts would go spiralling into the past. The gym, while tempting, involved digging out sports clothes which were likely to be far tighter than she wanted to admit. And any thoughts she'd had about doing something work-related were quashed when she'd realised that everyone thought she was away on holiday for the week. Replying to emails – when she'd assured them she would be 100 per cent unplugged – would lead to questions she didn't want to answer. And so, she had been through every area of the house, including the attic and garage, opening boxes, cupboards and drawers, pulling the wrapping off long-forgotten gifts and wiping layers of dust from neglected heirlooms and keepsakes.

Currently, a large number of items, including the famous Anna Weatherley dinner service, had been removed from their normal homes and stacked all over the kitchen worktops. With a cloud of dust motes swimming through the air and towers of boxes four feet high in some places, it undoubtedly looked a little chaotic. But she knew exactly where everything was. And, more importantly, she had left a clear path through to the coffee machine.

'Latte?' she asked.

'Only if you've got a shot of something to go in it. What *are* you doing? Please don't tell me you're going to dump all this. Because if you are, I want first dibs on that candlestick thing over there.' Holly pointed.

Fiona dropped a coffee pod into the machine, clicked the

lever down and watched the sea of frothy foam fill the cup below.

'Don't worry, I'm not chucking anything out.' She passed her friend a drink. 'I'm doing the opposite.'

'Breeding antiques?' Holly questioned. 'Because that's what it looks like. Where has that painting come from? I swear I've never even seen it before.'

'It's a Tran Tuan.' She stopped bustling about and gazed at the vivid colours. White brush strokes shimmered in the light. A streak of orange burst from the canvas. It really was an incredible piece.

'A what?'

'A Tran Tuan.'

'I'll pretend I know what that means.'

'He's a Vietnamese artist.' She turned her attention back to her friend. 'One of Stephen's favourites. He's had this painting tucked away in his study for years. Since we bought it, in fact. I thought it might be nice if it got a more prominent place, on display. Like in the hall. That way, he'd be able to see it more often.'

'Who? Tintin?'

'No, Stephen.'

'Oh.'

'And I was looking online. I thought I might be able to pick up another one for him too. Of course, he'd probably prefer us to go to an exhibition together and choose himself.'

She continued to gaze at the picture, trying to remember the last time she and Stephen had been to a show. A few of her clients ran art houses. Alongside weddings, running exhibition openings had always been one of her favourite commissions when she'd started up. On the day, all her time would be spent with the client, leaving Stephen to wander around on his own, more often than not on the phone himself, trying to solve an issue with cheese deliveries or some other riveting aspect of his work. As he moved higher up the corporate ladder at Alton Foods, he'd eventually stopped coming altogether. Still, there was time to make up for it, she thought. Once they'd gotten over this bump. An art gallery a month. That was doable.

'So, have you spoken to him? Stephen, I mean, not this artist,' Holly added for clarity.

She shook her head. 'No, I'm giving him space. That's what he needs, so that's what I'm going to let him have.' She felt even more assured than she had before. 'He won't go through with this. Believe me, I know him. It's just a phase. Like the time he decided he wanted to take up the bass guitar. Or that course he went on, so he could start a home brewery. He does this from time to time, you know that. This is just one more example. And do you not remember that yachting kick? He'll come back. He will. And when he does, I want him to be surrounded by things that make him happy.'

'Like that Tintin painting?'

'Tran Tuan,' she corrected. 'Exactly.'

From outside, the sound of traffic drifted through, as they each stood with their thoughts. They had been friends long before Stephen had arrived on the scene, and shared silences were something they understood. They could tell the difference between a tired silence, a judgmental silence, or one that was simply two people enjoying each other's company, needing no conversation. A pissed-off silence sounded substantially more aggressive than one which meant *give me a minute, I need to think about this*. And then, of course, there was the overwhelming silence, when words were just too painful.

This one – which came with a repeated movement of the lips – meant Holly had something to say. Something awkward.

'What?' Fiona asked, conscious that she had a lot more sorting to do and procrastination of any kind wasn't helpful.

'What do you mean, *what*?'

'What do you want to say?'

Her friend's lips twisted again.

'For God's sake, Holly, just spit it out.'

'I just wondered if you'd spoken to Joseph?' she asked eventually. 'You know, if Stephen has told him stuff, he might be worried. You know how he gets.'

'I know. Don't worry. I spoke to him.'

'Really?'

'Really. I mean, we didn't say much; he was busy.'

'But have you spoken to him about Stephen?'

Avoiding eye contact, she turned her attention to the coffee machine and began cleaning the water filter.

'Fi-o-na?' Holly stressed each syllable of her name.

'What? I told you, I rang him, and he was busy but, yes, Stephen's name did come up. We just didn't have time to go into that much detail.'

Feeling as if she was undergoing an interrogation she didn't deserve, she hit a button, which flooded the machine's filters with steam.

'Are you going to tell me what he said? You don't have to but, you know, if you need to talk about it...'

'Look,' Fiona stumbled, 'he's fine. We're all fine. Like I said, he was busy. Cooking if you must know.'

It had been nearly midday when she had finally plucked up the courage to ring her son for the first time since he'd left. She'd already felt guilty about her lack of communication – putting her own needs for solitude above his to hear from home – although she consoled herself with the fact that, if he'd needed to speak to her, he would surely have rung. As it was, he'd answered immediately.

'Hey, Mum, I'm in the kitchen at the moment. I'm doing a Sunday roast for everyone. Can I ring you as soon as I'm done? Would that be okay? Maybe a couple of hours?'

'Oh, you're cooking. A roast. For people. Wow, that's a good way to make yourself some friends.' He had never been one for phone calls but, still, the abruptness had taken her aback.

'That's what I figured.'

She could see his grin at the other end of the line. Despite how much she and Stephen had shunned cooking, Joseph had developed a real love for the culinary art. They'd always joked that people would keep him as a friend, just for his roast potatoes.

'I'm in the middle of these Yorkshires. I don't want to stop, or the fat will cool down. I'm sorry, I didn't know you were going to ring. You didn't message or anything.'

'You're right. I should have text first. Checked if you were free. We can catch up another time.'

'I'll be all done in an hour or two. Good thing about doing the cooking is, I don't have to wash up.'

A pause had hung in the air between them, disturbed only by a half-hearted chuckle from Fiona.

'I spoke to Dad,' Joseph had said then, quietly. 'He told me.'

Heat had risen to her cheeks. When they did finally sort themselves out, Stephen was going to have to do some serious explaining, treating their son like this, for crying out loud.

'Things like this happen when people get older,' she'd managed, unsure where the calm in her voice was coming from. 'Midlife crisis. That's all it is. I think we just need a little time apart to realise how much we need each other.'

'Yeah, maybe...'

'You don't have to worry about us. You just sort yourself out there. Have you got your lecture timetable yet?'

'No, it's only Sunday, remember?'

'Of course it is.' Another awkward pause. 'Off you go then. Sort out your dinner. You won't impress anyone with flat Yorkshire puddings.'

'Mum, you know—'

'I love you.'

'I love you too, but—'

Before he could say anything else, she'd hung up the phone, her hands quivering and her heart drumming a tattoo against her ribs. Stephen had a lot to answer for.

True to his word, a little over an hour later, her phone had buzzed and Joseph's name flashed up on the screen. He was obviously ready to pick up the conversation where they'd left it. But she hadn't answered. She didn't know what else she could say. Besides, eighteen-year-old boys who've just started university should be spending their first weekend getting drunk, she'd told herself. Not on the phone to their mothers.

'How come the TV is on?' Holly called now.

During Fiona's moment of reflection, Holly had moved into the living room.

'I thought you hated watching television.'

'I do,' she replied, shaking her head and relocating wine glasses from the kitchen draining board to the cupboard beneath the island worktop. 'I find the voices so whiny, but there was a good programme earlier, on e-currency. I must have forgotten to turn it off.'

'Sounds thrilling.'

'It's good to know about the markets we're working in.'

When they'd managed to clear enough room to sit down, Fiona ordered takeaway.

* * *

'He just needs time, that's all,' Fiona repeated, as she scooped another spoonful of Tabbouleh salad onto a fine china plate she hadn't seen since the last move.

They'd talked about plenty of other things: Holly's current employment situation – somehow she managed to hop from one job to the next, with better hours and better pay each time, yet she never appeared to do any work; how Joseph would cope once university lectures started; and Fiona's big, society wedding coming up in the New Year. But it hadn't taken long for the conversation to roll back around to Stephen.

'He needs time to realise he misses me. You know how much I do for him. He'll be back.' She took a gulp of wine. 'You don't just walk out on someone like that after twenty years. Not when you've built a life together. Not when a child is involved. You don't throw it all away.'

Topping up her plate, Holly hummed thoughtfully. 'What are you doing for the rest of the week? You're not going into work, are you?'

She shook her head. 'I need to get this place sorted. I've still got all the upstairs rooms to do, and I don't think I've even opened some of the boxes in the backroom since Mum died. I can't believe how therapeutic this has been. I should take time off more often.'

'I'm not sure that this counts as time off.'

'It does to me.'

Her friend raised an eyebrow. 'But you will get out, right? You won't stay inside the whole time? I've got a yoga class Friday lunchtime; you could come too. Great male-to-female ratio!'

'I'm married.'

'*You* are. I'm not.'

Fiona forced her face into what she hoped looked like a genuine smile.

'Maybe,' she offered.

An hour later and the pair stood in the hallway, the elm rocking chair now safely back in Joseph's bedroom. 'You'll ring me if you need anything?' Holly asked as she hugged her goodbye at the door. 'Any time, day or night. I don't mind.'

'I know.'

'And tell me if you hear from him?'

'I will do.'

'And yoga on Friday?'

'I'll think about it.' She had no intention of thinking about it at all. 'I'll definitely think about it.'

Holly released the hug. 'I love you.'

'I love you, too. Now *go*, I need to sleep!'

The door clicked shut and sleep, she knew, was one thing she was unlikely to find.

4

A chill seemed to have settled on the house, accentuating the stillness. From downstairs came the sound of the television in the living room while, from outside, the hum of late-night traffic as it rolled along the street. There was something about a place without other people around, particularly at night time. Not so much the silence, more the absence of noise. She'd never before realised how audible the almost imperceptible movements of another person were, even of the air as they breathed. She moved from hall to kitchen and fixed herself a drink before heading to the table and flicking up the lid to her laptop. She couldn't reply to her emails, but she could still read them. Besides, it was too quiet to sleep.

At 2 a.m., she dragged herself towards the stairs and her bedroom, eyelids drooping, and muscles slow with fatigue. The slower she moved, she discovered, the more her thoughts drifted. But there was nothing she could do about that. Eighteen months, that was the thing that kept coming back to her. Eighteen months. That wasn't a fling. That wasn't some accidental lapse of judgement after one-too-many drinks. Eighteen months was an affair. How many times had he lied to her, to go to that other woman? How many times had he been in their bed messaging her, while Fiona was busy answering emails on her phone? She paused on the stairs. How many times had Fiona had sex with him since he'd started cheating on her? The thought made her gag, so much so that she had to sprint back down to the toilet. He was an idiot. A selfish idiot, she told herself as she wiped her mouth. Well, he'd be back grovelling in no time. And she wasn't going to make it easy for him when he did.

Dappled, grey light filtered through the curtains and merged with the dull glow of the television. With the fog of sleep not yet lifted, she reached across the bed, only to find her hand touch something hard and cold. She jerked awake, heart racing, and then realised where she was. She hated falling asleep on the sofa, if for no other reason than the discomfort it left her with for the rest of the day. Groaning, she swiped her fingers across her phone. 6.14 a.m. She groaned again and flopped back over. There would be no point going to bed now. She wouldn't sleep. The best thing she could do, she decided, would be to get up, get showered, and get on with the day. After all, it was Monday, the official start of her weeklong break from work and she needed to get her life organised, before Stephen came to his senses and returned.

The realisation that it was Monday brought with it the thought that it had been three days since he'd walked out of their house, with two full suitcases, containing everything from underwear to work clothes, plus his favourite 1970s Kiss T-shirt that she'd refused to let him wear but he'd refused to throw out.

She knew he had taken that, and a whole range of other things, because she'd gone through all his drawers. She also knew that he'd left plenty behind, like the penknife his father had given him on his eighteenth birthday and the novelty mug with the tie handle that Joseph had given him nearly a decade ago. That was how she was certain he would return.

A babble of voices from the television pulled her thoughts away from Stephen to the morning news programme, where the two presenters were discussing something in serious tones, not that it mattered. It wasn't on for viewing. The line she'd spun Holly about watching some documentary had been a complete fabrication. She hadn't watched so much as a single advert or weather forecast since she'd switched it on, on Saturday night. But now she couldn't turn it off. She'd even switched on the one in Joseph's room, too, to make the house seem less empty. She'd considered using the radio instead but, after a few hours, had changed her mind. Something about music didn't work well, especially if it was a song that evoked memories. She and Stephen had never had a special song of their own. That wasn't them at all. Even for their wedding reception, she'd chosen a first-dance song because the lyrics were appropriate for the occasion, rather than opting for anything personal. Twenty years later and she couldn't even remember what it was. Yet twice within an hour of switching the radio on, music had come across the airwaves that had caused her stomach to tighten. Television was safer.

Stretching her arms out and bending from side to side, she contemplated what to tackle next. There was still plenty of sorting to do before she went back to work.

It had turned out that the Tran Tuan was a little overbearing for the hallway, but looked perfect above the mantelpiece in the dining room. That meant shifting the large mirror out, but she decided it could add a little extra light somewhere else. This, in turn, created the problem of what to do with the seascape Stephen had commissioned of the cove in Cornwall where he used to holiday as a child.

By eleven-fifteen, the paintings had been rearranged to her satisfaction and, with the constant heavy lifting and endless climbing up and down of stairs, she was finding herself in need of food. At any other time, she would have checked the fridge or the bread bin but, having had no one else in the house over the weekend, she hadn't bothered to go shopping and knew the cupboards were bare. She picked up her phone and glanced at the screen. Eight missed calls, all from the same person. She chewed her lip. Holiday or no holiday, some clients couldn't be ignored. And this was one of them.

Octavia Lovett-Rose's wedding to hedge fund tycoon Charlie Rosenberg would be the society wedding of the year. And it had fallen into Fiona's lap, without her even trying.

'I want a different slant on things,' the It-girl-slash-radio-star had told her at their first meeting. 'Otherwise, all these events just end up looking the same, but bigger. Do you know what I mean? The same bouquets, only bigger; the same sort of cake, only bigger.'

'I know exactly what you mean. But you do realise I mainly organise corporate events now, don't you?'

'I do. I do. But Uncle Dom speaks so highly of you. And you did do weddings once, didn't you? I thought I found some of your things online…'

After a week of back and forth emails, and even a bunch of flowers from Dominic Tan, Fiona was officially back into wedding planning, or at least this one. And so far, so good. Although, judging from the myriad calls she'd missed, that might not be the case any more. Picking up her bag, she headed out of the door for one of London's newest and hippest bars. At least she wouldn't have to worry about food shopping.

'Fiona, I'm *so* sorry.' Octavia rose from the leather sofa as she approached. 'I rang your office eventually and your girl there said you were on holiday. I'd completely forgotten. I didn't mean for you to come in specially to see me.'

'It's not a problem. I was at home. If anything, you've given me an excuse to stop spring cleaning.'

'In September? I'm not sure that counts as a holiday.'

Chuckling politely, Fiona leaned in for the standard greeting.

Octavia was a triple-kiss person, she had discovered. Three were needed before you could sit down and get on with business. It was something she had to do with all her new clients, learn which of them were one, two, or three kissers and which were simple hand-shakers, or none of the above. Generally, she let them take the lead.

Light bounced off Octavia's engagement ring as they separated into their seats. It had been in all the magazines. The size, the cut, the colour – the *cost*. Without thinking, she glanced at the three rings on her own finger before turning her attention back to her client.

'You sounded worried,' she said. 'How can I help?'

Octavia waved a hand at the waiter who arrived promptly with menus.

'I'm being ridiculous, I know I am. I just need you to reassure me that I'm not going crazy.'

'Well I can't do that, but I can definitely help with the wedding.'

Octavia chortled. 'I don't know what's wrong. I mean, I was so happy with everything, and then I got talking to some friends and now, well, I just don't know.'

Fiona eyed the menu. There was no way she could order yet without seeming insensitive. It would have to be business first, food later. She nodded slowly and leaned across the table.

'Just tell me what's up and I'll see if I can put your mind at ease. Remember, we still have months. We can change things. Unless it's the venue?' she added hesitantly. 'You're still okay with the venue, aren't you?'

'The venue is about the only thing I'm certain of.' Octavia sighed with a watery smile.

'Well that's the only one that really matters,' she reassured her, heaving a massive internal sigh of relief that she didn't have to deal with that catastrophe. 'And remember: you pay me to do the worrying, so you don't have to. So, shoot. What seems to be the problem?'

Octavia's eyelids fluttered as she started the list.

'First off,' she began, 'it's the centrepieces.'

Fifty minutes and three pages of notes later, Fiona had managed to put Octavia's mind at rest about everything from the colour trim on the bridesmaid dresses, to the number of courses the wedding breakfast needed to include, to whether the favours should be edible or not. She'd not yet managed to order any food from the waiter, who was looking less and less impressed by the second, but they were reaching the end now. She was certain of it.

'The other thing is the children's room...' Octavia came to her final issue.

Knowing it was probably going to need at least one more page, Fiona turned the leaf in her notebook.

'Do you still want to go with the clown and the magician? I can try to talk the hotel round about the miniature zoo. They were pretty adamant it was a no but, given that you now have the magazine photo shoot, they may be a little more helpful...'

'The clown and magician are perfect,' Octavia assured her.
'But it's the decoration. I realised we hadn't even thought about
that. And I know the wedding is not really for the children, but I
want them to have a nice time, you understand?'

'I understand completely. Happy children mean happy
parents.'

'That's exactly what I thought.' She took a breath. 'So, I was
thinking that maybe we'd opt for some kind of rainbow balloon
arch. Do you know what I mean?'

'I'm following.' She wrote the words *rainbow balloon arch* on
her pad. 'That actually sounds great.'

'I thought it would brighten the whole room up and the
magician and the clown could do their acts under it.'

Fiona looked up from her notebook with a smile. 'When
you come up with ideas like this, it leaves me wondering why
you need me at all!'

'You know I need you.' Octavia grinned back. 'Anyway. You
think that would work? Balloons? I'm worried they might look
tacky.'

'Why?'

'Well they do sometimes, don't they? I mean, I know it's for
the children, but I don't want it to lower the tone of everything
else.'

'It won't.'

'You're sure?'

'I'm positive. Balloons can look brilliant. And all children
adore them. In fact, balloons were the very best part of my son's
sixth birthday party which, obviously, I planned myself. And,
not blowing my own trumpet or anything' – her eyes lit up at
the memory – 'it was amazing.'

She let her mind wander back more than a decade, to their
old living room. The house they'd lived in then was substan-

tially smaller than the one they now owned, but it had felt like a palace. And, compared to the poky little flats they'd shared at the beginning of their marriage, it had been. Initially, the party was only going to include a few children for Joseph and some of their old friends, like Holly. But then they had started to write the invitations, and more and more people Fiona simply *had* to ask had appeared on the list. And soon, all of Joseph's class were coming, too. Omnivents was just getting started and she was on the lookout for any new clients she could get. She knew that her son's birthday party was a marketing opportunity too good to miss.

'It was jungle themed,' she recalled, as the memory played in her mind. 'Well before all these specialised parties had become popular. And it took the whole of the night before to get it ready and turn our living room into that jungle. God, we had the works, including an animal-noises soundtrack playing in the background, green streamers hanging from the ceiling like vines, and cuddly snakes and monkeys. And the food! I can't take all the credit for that, but still. Anyway, to get to my point, we had balloons. Some incredible ones. And everyone loved them.'

'They did?'

'Of course they did. Who doesn't? They're fun. Children adore them. Think about it, honestly; when have you ever seen a child whose day wasn't made happier by a bright, colourful balloon?'

'You mean, apart from when it bursts?'

'Okay, yes,' she conceded. 'But apart from that. You haven't. They love them. And, like you said, happy children mean happy parents and happy parents mean a wonderful wedding.'

Octavia's eyes lifted ever so slightly in a smile. She had sold it, Fiona could tell, although her thoughts were still distracted by the memory of a wonderful day she had almost forgotten.

'You know, we had one particular balloon – people thought it was a parrot, but it was actually a parakeet.' She'd purchased it from her favourite little party shop on Cook Avenue. The same, sweet, old lady had run the place for years and, while her prices were quite high, she often stocked unique decorations that really made party settings pop. As far as Fiona knew, it was still there. 'I can't remember why I only bought one, now. I seem to recall it was the tail end of a limited-edition run, or something like that. Anyway, it was beautiful. Honestly, you could have forgotten everything else I did, because Joseph was obsessed with that balloon. Even after the party.'

'How sweet.'

'It's funny, I haven't thought about it in such a long time. You know, he wouldn't let me get rid of it? Not for weeks, even after it had gone flat.' She recalled her and Stephen's laughter, as six-year-old Joseph had run around trailing the deflated balloon behind him. He'd even scribbled his name on the back with a marker pen. Eventually, though, he had seemed to tire of it and they had slipped it into the bin while he was sleeping. It had taken more than a week for him to stop asking about it.

'Okay.' Octavia had visibly relaxed. 'So balloons it is. And you definitely don't think four-foot centrepieces are too high?'

'I definitely don't.'

Next came chatter about dress fittings, fitness regimes and whether Fiona had ever considered using Botox. Then, thankfully, they ordered food.

'Charlie and I have decided to give 10 per cent of the money from the *Hello!* exclusive to charity,' Octavia announced, once their salads had arrived and she was chewing on something green. 'We feel like we should. You know, we've been so lucky in our lives.'

'That's incredibly generous of you,' Fiona enthused, looking at her own plate and wishing they'd had something as dull as a plate of chips or a burger on the menu. 'Which one are you considering?'

'Oh, we're not sure. Charlie's thinking something for dogs or cats, you know. But I think maybe we need to look a little bigger. Like the environment. Definitely something animal related.'

'That's fantastic.'

'And Uncle Dom tells me you're helping him launch his new coaching platform next year.' Octavia changed the conversation effortlessly. It was no wonder the public had taken to her so easily. She had an earnestness about her when she listened, Fiona had noticed. As if every word she heard was important, no matter how much drivel was spoken.

'Well, hopefully. He's still got to hear my latest proposal.'

'Which he'll go for straight away. You know he will. He loves everything you do.'

Fiona smiled and tried to look modest, despite the fact they both knew it was true.

As the conversation slowed and the plates were cleared away, Fiona asked for the bill.

'I'll let you get on,' she said, rising to her feet. 'I know how busy you are.'

'Okay then.' Octavia started the kissing regimen again. 'And thank you so much for coming in on your holiday. I promise I'll try not to pester you too much if I have any more mini meltdowns.'

'Pester away,' Fiona assured her. 'Only, let me have the melt-downs, okay? Like I said, that's what you pay me for.'

With a final hug goodbye, she headed back outside, in search of the first fast food outlet she could find.

5

The impetus with which Fiona had started her house reorganisation had lessened somewhat by the time she arrived back home that evening. But, given that stopping would mean leaving the house in disarray, she ploughed on, shifting cobwebbed boxes and faded containers up and down the stairs, Marie Kondo-ing her wardrobe and clearing out drawers so crammed full, it took a spatula to prise them open. It was in one of those particularly jam-packed places – a unit in the living room where she stuffed all the birthday cards they received each year, with the promise of going in and sorting them out at some point – that she stumbled across the photos from Joseph's sixth birthday party.

In truth, she'd been on the lookout for them. Her reason behind the wardrobe clear-out had been that, perhaps, they'd been stored away in one of the shoeboxes at the back. And, had she not found what she was looking for downstairs, she'd planned to move on to her mother's old belongings in the spare room, in case they'd ended up in there. But she'd found them.

The paper envelope was creased and yellowed, but inside sat thirty-six photographs of that memorable day.

It had helped that his birthday had coincided with Stephen's photography phase, although it did mean that there were very few of Stephen himself among them. In fact, most of the pictures were of herself and Joseph. Or at least, parts of Joseph. He had been so excited, she remembered, he'd refused to stand still for even a minute, meaning over half the images were blurred, or of single limbs: an arm that was still in shot when the shutter clicked, a leg, twisting as he ran away.

Somehow though, they'd managed to grab him and pin him down long enough for someone to take one of the three of them together. Stephen was holding the cake – a two-tiered creation covered with fondant snakes and leaves and topped with an edible elephant and tiger – with the candles lit and Joseph was sitting on her lap. Eyes scrunched shut, she was ready to help him blow them out, while his hand was already reaching for the marzipan elephant. There, in the background, floated the parakeet balloon, just as she had described to Octavia. She was glad she'd been able to persuade her that the rainbow balloon arch was a good idea, even if she did wish she'd thought of it herself.

Shuffling them back together again, she placed the photographs in the envelope. All except the picture of the three of them. That one she wiped with her sleeve and placed on the mantelpiece. Tomorrow, she would look for a frame for it, she thought. After all, she was on holiday.

* * *

Shards of sunlight sneaked between the curtains as she rolled over onto the cold side of the bed, the sheet still perfectly flat and unrumpled. She'd slept in their bedroom. At least that was an improvement on the previous three nights although, from the way she was struggling to open her eyes, she probably could have done with going to bed a little earlier. What time had she finished tidying downstairs? She struggled to remember. Two? Maybe three?

Forcing herself to sit up, she checked the time, only to blink and do a double take. Ten thirty – that was practically midday! And no wonder her head was throbbing. The last time she'd gone that long without coffee must have been when she was pregnant. After checking that no emails or messages had come through while she'd slept, she swung her legs off the bed. Then, rubbing her temples, she made her way downstairs and straight to the coffee machine.

The television in the lounge was still on and tuned to a news channel. For some reason, the voices grated even more than ever today, and she went in to switch it off, when something caught her attention.

'Early-morning joggers first noticed the sperm whale this morning,' the presenter told her. 'The mature female, who has been nicknamed Martha, has been most obliging, swimming peacefully up and down the river. She looks perfectly happy, don't you think, Rick?' she posed the question to her fellow presenter.

'I do, Stephanie,' he replied. 'Now I've read here that sperm whales are the largest of the toothed whales, and females tend to stay in large pods for their entire life, so it is unclear at the moment how she came to be separated from her family.'

'Or how on earth she wasn't spotted before now.'

Fiona dropped down onto the sofa and stared at the screen. For such a large creature, it was surprisingly difficult to make out in the grey-brown water of the Thames. A minute of live footage showed nothing but passing boats and tourists on the bank, hoping to catch a glimpse of Martha. Her eyes were fixed on the television screen. She'd been whale watching herself, off the coast of New Zealand, and it had been an enjoyable trip but nothing amazing, like in the photos they showed you, where whales breach right in front of the boat. A vague dot on the horizon was the best they'd got. This is probably going to be the same, she thought. She was just about to give up and go and make her coffee, when out of the water came the head.

'Holy crap!' she exclaimed.

It was an aerial view, the sleek, grey body just breaking the surface, causing foaming ripples to fan out in its wake. She sat back in the sofa, her mouth wide open.

'We have with us today marine biologist Professor Ben Arkell.'

They were back in the studio. The image from the Thames had shrunk to a thumbnail in the corner of the screen.

'Professor Arkell, what can you tell us about sperm whales? I'm guessing that the Thames isn't their natural habitat?'

'No. It's certainly not.' The marine biologist looked concerned as he spoke. 'Sperm whales are usually found in much, much deeper water, although it has been the case that individuals, and sometimes pods, have beached themselves on UK shores before. But even so, this is highly unusual.'

The presenter nodded, attempting to appear knowledge-able. 'And so, can we expect to see more appearing? Whole pods, as you say? Or is this just a slight navigational error by one lone specimen?'

'I think we can agree it was definitely not a *slight* naviga-tional error here,' the biologist replied, his expression pinched. 'The question is how she became stranded and so far from her pod.'

'Pods are important to this type of whale, I take it?'

More cheek sucking and nodding from Professor Arkell. 'Sperm whale pods can reach up to sixty individuals, normally females and juveniles. A female of this age would almost certainly have calves and they're exceptionally family orientated. It's worrying to think what might have happened.'

The live picture expanded to fill the screen again and the cameraman zoomed out to show just how alone poor Martha was.

'So, do you have any idea what could have happened?' It was the female presenter now.

'I have several,' he told them, 'but all unsubstantiated. What is paramount is to find a way to get her back to the open sea.'

'And to her family,' Fiona whispered to herself.

She remained glued to the screen. Sixty whales, she kept thinking over and over. Sixty whales meant fifty-nine other family members. Fifty-nine who should be by this whale's side, but weren't. And here Fiona was, finding it odd in a house with only two fewer people. It must be awful for Martha. Then again, perhaps she liked the peace and quiet? Christmas Day with all the nieces and nephews was enough to put Fiona off family gatherings for another year, and there were only twelve of them all told. Maybe the Thames was Martha's equivalent of a spa break. Fiona took out her laptop and began a search of the general behaviour patterns of female sperm whales.

It seemed the expert on the subject was indeed correct in what he was telling them, but it still felt ridiculous. How could such a giant creature – or *Physeter macrocephalus*, as she now knew its correct name to be – possibly end up in the heart of London, without someone having noticed it before? It was the size of a bus.

Throughout the morning, more information and images arrived on her screen. Perhaps the whale has a son, she thought, watching Martha glide under Vauxhall Bridge. Perhaps she'd been looking out for him, doing what she thought was best for him, only to be blindsided and suddenly ending up on the wrong path, all on her own. Fiona's heart ached. How was this right? How could someone not have stopped the whale making this mistake, long before she even got this far? But there were rescuers with her now, at least. Surely they would get her safely back where she belonged.

The arrival of the eleven o'clock news headlines made her suddenly aware of the time. Looking down at her bare legs, she blinked as she realised that she'd not even showered yet, let along dressed nor, as evidenced by the dreadful taste in her mouth, had she cleaned her teeth. The thought of staying that way – undressed as opposed to unwashed – flitted through her mind. She was allowed to wallow, wasn't she? Isn't that what women do when their husbands walk out or their only child flies the nest? And she was faced with the double whammy. She could break with routine. A momentary pity party began to form in her mind, only to disappear at the sight of Martha passing a group of intrigued rowers. Placing her coffee cup down, she stood and faced the television.

'You're still going,' she told the whale, whose silhouette she could just make out under the water. 'If you can, then so can I.'

After cleaning her teeth, including an extra-long gargle of mouthwash, she showered and dressed, picking an outfit from the back of the wardrobe. The short, burgundy number was something she'd put off wearing, on the basis that it seemed a bit too glam for daywear. But today, glam was what she wanted. Glam and confident. Empty nest syndrome, that's all it was – for Stephen too. He would see it soon enough. Besides, however bad her day was, it wasn't anywhere near as bad as poor Martha's. And if that whale wouldn't give up, then nor would she. It had been a long time since she could remember having a role model in her life but, standing there, thinking about Martha, she was pretty sure she'd found one again. Or at least, a kindred spirit.

* * *

'Fiona?' Annabel leapt to her feet the moment she came through the door. 'What are you doing here? I thought you were in Brussels until Friday?'

'Yes, well...' She took off her coat in an elegant sweep and hung it on the rack. 'Stephen got called away unexpectedly. So, we decided to cancel.'

'Oh no!' Annabel looked genuinely devastated by this news. 'Is everything okay now? What do you need me to do? Your schedule's all clear.'

'It's fine. I'll just reply to some emails.'

'Coffee? Lunch?'

'If I need anything, I'll buzz through.' With a fixed smile, she stepped into her office.

The journey to work had taken less than fifteen minutes, yet her first course of action, after switching on her laptop, was to head straight to the television news channel to see if there were any updates on Martha. As it turned out, there were.

'...There was a sighting of a small pod just north of Aberdeen last week, and it's thought that Martha could have been a member of this, although it still remains a mystery how she became separated from them.' It was Professor Arkell on the screen again. 'In recent years, there have been cases of marine mammals' navigational abilities being disrupted by military sonar. Of course, let's not forget Benny the beluga whale who made head—'

'Can I get you any lunch?' Annabel's head appeared around the door. 'I know you said you were fine, but I was about to take a break and grab a sandwich. So I thought I'd check again.' Her eyes widened at the voices from the computer. 'Oh, you've been watching the news too? Sad, isn't it?'

'Her poor family.'

'I wonder what happened.'

Together, they stared at the screen. Martha was cruising gently through the water, her dark silhouette gliding beneath the surface. Another group of rowers – or possibly the same ones as before – had come up alongside her and were keeping a far closer proximity than Fiona would have thought was safe.

'The news said it could be something to do with the military using sonar,' Fiona said after two minutes of silent study. 'Anyway, they're talking about using boats to guide her back out through the Thames Estuary.'

'Would that work?'

'They think so.'

After another minute, Annabel made a more concerted effort to leave. 'Are you sure I can't get you anything? I'll be going past that New York sandwich deli you like?'

'Perhaps just a coffee,' she replied, mainly to get the conversation over with. 'But really, there's no need to rush. I'm fine.'

Annabel grinned, squinting and shifting her glasses half a centimetre up her nose.

'Well I'll see you in a bit then. Let me know if there is any more news.'

'I will,' she promised, although quite what Annabel expected, she wasn't sure.

It had always been the people aspect of her job which she enjoyed the most. That and the logistics. Working out how to operate five projectors in a room with only two plug sockets might have been a nightmare to many, but this was the sort of challenge that made her day. However, that afternoon, she was enjoying the simple monotony of filling plastic envelopes with papers and keeping up to date on Martha as she worked.

By quarter past four, however, the novelty of doing this menial task had well and truly worn off and, grabbing her coat from the stand, she bade farewell to Annabel and headed out.

Four-fifteen finishes were as unusual for Fiona as home-cooked meals, and the sudden freedom of time on her hands left her standing on the street outside the office, wondering which way to go. She'd texted Holly earlier in the day, just to mention she was out of the house, in case she'd planned to drop by, but hadn't yet had a reply, meaning her friend was either busy, or sleeping. Either way, she wouldn't be available. It wasn't a bad thing, necessarily. Another round of talking about when Stephen would be back and all the possible reasons for his departure didn't appeal to her. All she knew was that he wasn't ready to return home yet. What she needed was a distraction.

The overcast afternoon left the Thames the colour of sludge, grimy-grey waves rippling over the surface, occasionally breaking into weak, dirty-white froth. The air was thick with car fumes as she took a break from her stroll and rested her hands against the railing, looking out over the river. A blend of disappointment and sadness mingled inside her. In hindsight, it was ridiculous, thinking she would simply walk to the water's edge and stumble upon the giant creature floating in front of her but, somehow, she'd thought she would see something. A crowd perhaps. People with placards reading, *This way to Martha*. Maybe she was already gone, she thought optimistically. Perhaps a few hours' guided swimming was all it had taken to get her back to her family. That would be something. At least that would mean one of them had resolved her problem before the day was out. She cast her gaze up and down the Thames one last time before turning around and heading home.

* * *

'...There's no accurate estimate we can give on how long she can survive here. Currently, the most worrisome threat is that she will beach herself in one of the shallows.'

Any hope Fiona had of a happy-ever-after for Martha had been dashed the moment she'd turned on the television.

'But what about food?' the presenter asked. 'Will she be able to find something? I'm assuming there's not much krill in the Thames? Or is it plankton they eat?'

Professor Arkell was back on screen. He had lost the smart suit from the morning show and was now dressed more casually in a polo shirt. He looked exhausted.

'Actually,' he began, 'the sperm whale is a toothed whale. Unlike baleen whales – such as the blue whale and the humpback which do feed predominantly on krill – toothed whales feed on a range of marine life. In the sea, their diet would consist predominantly of squid.'

'And I'm assuming there aren't many of them in the river either.' The presenter offered a jovial chuckle, to which Professor Arkell remained utterly poker faced.

'No, but they can survive on fish. And there are fish there, including sturgeon, trout, and even catfish.'

'Catfish?'

'Yes, surprisingly they're a native species.'

Fiona twisted a mouthful of noodles onto her fork and waited for them to show more footage of Martha, hopefully heading the right way this time. By her plate was her third drink of the evening.

Despite both her own and Martha's current predicaments, she was feeling relatively optimistic about things. The meeting with Octavia had given her something to focus on and she'd arranged a midweek lunch date with Holly. There was still no news from Stephen, but she was taking that as a positive sign too. He was a man who liked control. Hopefully, her radio silence was giving him all the time he needed to work things out for himself. Two weeks, she thought. Two weeks tops. Then he would be back, she was certain.

6

Lunch get-togethers were a regular suggestion from Holly which, given that Fiona rarely said yes more than a handful of times a year, was a testament to their friendship. On Holly's side, anyway. They had special dates pencilled in, of course, birthdays mainly, but even some of those Fiona had cancelled at the last minute over the years, when either her own or Stephen's schedule had interrupted their plans. So, on Wednesday morning, after checking in on the situation with Martha, running the vacuum around the house and firing a couple of emails off to clients to let them know that she was now available should they need her, she headed to the rendezvous in Holly's message.

There was no need to rush. Generally, Holly arrived fifteen minutes late, even later in the evenings, when she'd already have been drinking. Bearing that in mind and factoring in the time it would take her to get there, Fiona left the house exactly two minutes before the arranged time.

Her friend had spent several years writing horoscopes for two well-known papers and acting as agony aunt for various other publications. Occasionally, she'd turn her hand to writing book reviews – despite the fact that the only time Fiona had ever seen her reading was when forced to at university. Food critiquing was now something she was trying to get into. So, when she arrived at the restaurant, which turned out to be only one stop away from her office, it needed a double take for her to decide she was in the right place. It didn't look at all like the type of establishment Holly would frequent.

'I think my friend has made a reservation,' she said, hesitantly, as she stepped inside to the reception desk.

'Name?'

'Holly. Holly Winter.' She looked around her with growing unease at the bare-concrete and plastic-drainpipe décor. Potted plants – some weed-like monstrosities – formed the table settings, while all along the windows were full-length planters, filled with a variety of more random foliage. Most bizarre of all, however, were the hanging baskets, which appeared to be growing tomatoes.

'This way.' She was escorted to the far corner where a large pebble, daubed with paint, announced that the table was reserved. Honestly, she thought, it looks like something Joseph would have brought back from primary school.

Offering a warm smile to the perversely sullen waitress, she took a seat. Already fifteen minutes later than she and Holly had arranged to meet, she was glad she hadn't set out any earlier and decided to check her phone while she waited. Finding two emails from the office, she began to reply.

'Excuse me.' The waitress, who had a nightmarish number of piercings, including a large ring through her top lip, loomed over her.

'Oh, I'm waiting for my friend,' she said, assuming she was expecting her to order.

'No phones,' the woman replied.

'Sorry?'

'No phones. We don't do phones here.' She pointed to the wall between two sections of drainpipe, where *Life is short. Talk to each other* had been painted. 'You need to put your phone away,' the waitress clarified.

Frowning, Fiona glanced back down at it. 'That's a very lovely sentiment and everything,' she said, 'but I don't actually have anyone to talk to yet. And it's not as if I'm annoying anyone, is it?'

'No phones,' the woman repeated. 'And you're annoying me.'

Fiona pursed her lips, affronted at being treated like an adolescent, at her age. The list of reasons why she would not be coming here again was growing. But was this a battle she wanted to get into right now? Probably not. She glared at the woman and dropped the phone back into her bag.

'Drinks are on the menu. Food is on the board,' the waitress announced, with a less-than-subtle smirk on her lips, before turning and leaving.

Fortunately, Fiona had barely had time to reach for the menu before Holly appeared.

'Sorry, I got held up. Have you been waiting long?'

'Five minutes?'

She pulled out a seat and dropped her bag to the floor beside it. 'I was worried you might have a problem finding the place. Great, right? And what is that? Can you smell it? Is that pizza?'

Fiona sniffed. Whatever Holly could smell was lost on her. The overriding aroma seemed to be one of soil and compost emanating from the random vegetation.

'What *is* this place?' she asked, turning over the corner of her hessian placemat and prodding the mismatched cutlery. 'When you said lunch, I thought you meant a proper lunch, you know, in a proper restaurant. With alcohol.'

'I think they do cocktails here.'

Fiona looked at the drinks menu.

'Kombucha cooler?' she made no effort to hide the disdain in her voice. 'Mint Mockjito? That's not what I had in mind.' She sniffed again. 'Honestly, can you not smell that? It's like they've got a compost heap out the back.'

'That's probably because they have.' Holly picked up her own drinks menu. 'It's one of those *farm-to-table* places. They grow loads of their produce on site here.' She plucked a leaf from the weed in the centre of the table and popped it into her mouth. 'See, spearmint,' she said after she'd finished chewing. 'This place has been going for a couple of years. It's well ahead of the game.'

'And yet you've decided that you want to try it now because...?'

'No reason.' She plucked another spearmint leaf.

'Holly.'

Just as sure as Fiona had been that Holly would arrive late, she knew exactly what the current evasion of eye contact signalled.

'Fine,' she relented with a sigh. 'I overheard some of the men at my new yoga class talking about it. I've got a date with one of them next week. I thought it could be something to have in common.'

While intrigued to know how eating at a place which didn't know if it was a greenhouse or a restaurant would achieve this, any opportunity to delve further into the bizarre workings of her friend's mind was cut short by the appearance of a man at their table.

The hair was the first thing she noticed about him. His wavy, blond mane was tied in a loose bun, which he wore near the top of his head. Paired with a full, dark beard and studded eyebrow, it was difficult to see how someone like him could work in an eatery without violating several food hygiene laws.

'How are you ladies doing today?' he asked.

'Great.' Holly smiled broadly enough for the two of them, which was fortunate as Fiona's face had set itself into a scowl. 'We're great.'

'Aces. Well. As I'm sure my staff explained to you, food is all on the blackboard, but take your time and feel free to ask any questions you might have about it. I see you've already found the drinks menu. Are you ready to order, or do you need a little more time?'

Suddenly realising that he was talking to her, Fiona hastily turned her attention to the list of cocktails in her hands. Turmeric iced tea? Watermelon and ginseng Fresca? It didn't take long for her to know there was nothing there she wanted.

'Do you do coffee?' she asked.

'We do.'

'Great.' A glimmer of hope flickered. Even a bad coffee was better than none at all. 'I'll have a cappuccino.'

'Awesome.' His eyes glinted as they remained fixed on her. 'What kind of milk would you like with that? We've got cashew, almond, oat—'

'I just want milk milk.'

'Milk milk? You mean dairy milk?'

'I do. Yes. Dairy milk. *Milk* milk. Milk from a cow.'

'Okay.' His lips pressed together in a half smirk. 'Great, one cappuccino with *milk* milk. Any preference on the bean?'

'The bean? I get to choose my bean?'

'The list is there on the drinks menu.'

Turning it over, she found herself staring at a selection even Stephen would have had a hard time turning his nose up at. Assuming they were brewed properly, of course.

'We've got Turkish, Colombian—'

'I'll have the Blue Mountain,' she said, finding her first choice near the bottom. His smile broadened.

'Of course you will,' he said, smiling at her in a way that made her feel uncomfortable and nervous, yet tingly at the same time. She wasn't entirely sure what it was about him that had caused any of those reactions.

'I'll have the same,' Holly said.

His eyes lingered on Fiona for a second longer and then, in a heartbeat, the connection was broken and the man was smiling at her friend. However, while his gaze might have gone, the tingling persisted a fraction longer.

'So,' Holly said, when the long-haired, inappropriately smirky hipster had gone to fetch their drinks. 'Has Stephen made contact at all?'

'Not yet. But no news is good news, right? I don't suppose you've heard anything have you? On your grapevine? About him? Or this woman?'

Holly shook her head. 'Sorry. I haven't been asking though, you know. I thought you wanted to keep the whole thing confidential.'

'You're right. Of course, you're right.' Her fingers found the stem of the herb in front of her. She tore off one of the leaves, slowly. Being discreet would be better for all of them in the long run, when she and Stephen had sorted things out. 'I just wish I had something to go on. A name. An age. Anything.'

'Would it help?'

'Probably not.'

The moment's contemplation was cut short.

'So, here you are. Two *milk* milk cappuccinos. Have you decided what you'd like to eat yet, or do you need a little more time?'

Ignoring the question, Fiona lifted the drink to her lips. A small sigh escaped as the coffee hit her throat. There was little in the world that didn't seem better with a nice, strong coffee.

'It's good,' she said to Holly.

'I know,' the man replied.

This time, she was smart enough not to look at him, in case he caught her with that arrogant, wide-eyed grin again.

'We're going to need a bit more time,' she said, deliberately looking down at the menu. 'I haven't had a chance to choose yet.'

'No, me neither. Can you give us five minutes?' Holly asked.

'Sure, no worries.' He turned back to Fiona. 'Although everything we've got food-wise is on the board over there. That's just the drinks menu, I'm afraid. You've already looked through that one.' From his tone, it was clear that he was trying to get a reaction out of her. What with the no-phones rule and now this, it certainly wasn't a place that majored on customer service.

'I'll be back in a couple of minutes,' he said.

Peeking over the top of the card, she watched as he sauntered away to the counter. Even from behind, she could tell he was smirking.

'I wouldn't say no to that,' Holly said, leaning over the table in a conspiratorial manner.

'What?'

'What do you mean *what*? He was flirting with you. And he's cute.'

'He was not flirting,' she spluttered. 'He was doing his job. And badly at that, I might add.'

'He is cute though.'

'Don't be ridiculous. He looks like a hipster. And he must be ten years younger than me and... besides, why are we even talking about this? I'm married.'

'Well, all I'm saying is, I wouldn't judge you.'

Fiona refused to dignify that remark with an answer. In her line of work, she was never short of attention. Men, away from home at a conference, were often looking for company in their lonely hotel suites. Over the years, she'd had one or two more permanent admirers too: clients who had developed a crush on her. But she knew it was nothing more than a bit of harmless flirting on their part. A bit of fun. Nothing to be taken too seriously. After twenty years of marriage, she wasn't sure she would know how to flirt any more. Not properly. And she certainly wouldn't know how to take it any further. God, she could barely remember any other position than missionary, legs behind her ears while Stephen pounded away, after two decades still unable to locate her clitoris.

'What are you thinking?'

'What?' she dropped the menu, her cheeks colouring rapidly. 'Er, nothing,' she stammered.

'About the food, I mean. It looks good.' Holly studied the blackboard as she spoke. 'You know, I miss growing my own.'

'When did you ever grow your own food?' She knew her friend better than anyone, but this was clearly a phase that she'd missed.

'You know, when I had that little courtyard in Woolwich. The one behind the railway.'

The memory took a while to locate.

'Didn't you just grow tomatoes and weed?'

'And mint for mojitos. Don't forget the mint.'

Laughing at her comical friend, she turned her attention to the menu in earnest.

'The Dumpster Dive,' she read from the top of the board. 'Why would anyone put that on a menu? That has to be the most off-putting thing ever.'

'Ahh, so you don't know much about us then? The Dumpster Dive: it's our name.' The owner was back again. 'We specialise in reclaimed food and zero waste. We've also got a small shop just over the road that's all zero waste too. We're looking for a place big enough to house the café and shop together, eventually.'

'Waste food?' Fiona fired a look across at Holly, trying to indicate how unimpressed she was with her friend's choice of lunch venue. If Holly wanted her to come on any more of these lunch dates, she was going the wrong way about it. And Fiona didn't like the way he'd diverted the conversation away from the food either. 'What does that mean? You sell leftovers?'

'In a way. We collect food from supermarkets and shops that's close to its sell-by date and therefore about to be thrown out. Then, each morning, we design a menu based around that produce. That's why it's on the blackboard, because it changes every day.'

'Is that safe? I mean, if it's near its sell-by date?'

'Do you know what the sell-by date was on the last piece of meat you ate in a restaurant? Of course you don't. What about the cheese or milk? Nope, you don't. Obviously, we'd never cook something that was going off. Trust me, nothing here is going to make you ill. We want people to come back and, as you can see,' he stepped back a little and gestured to the bustling tables around him, 'they do.'

She remained unconvinced, particularly since the comment came from a man who looked like he'd needed more hepatitis and tetanus jabs than your average stray dog catcher.

'And all the food is *dumpster-dived* as you say?'

He shook his head. 'Not yet. Most of it is, but there are still a couple of things we buy in, without packaging of course. Hopefully, after we've been going a bit longer and got a few more supermarkets involved, it'll all be waste produce. If you're interested in learning more, I'd love to sit down and chat with you about it.'

She looked back up at the menu board. A salmon burger was distinctly less appealing when there was an increased chance of it keeping you up all night. And the same could be said for the gorgonzola ravioli and goat's cheese tart. Every item brought visions of mould spores and bright-green fungus.

'Do you know what?' she asked, 'I think I'm good with just coffee.'

* * *

She was thankful when Holly had finished her meal. While it looked nice enough on the pretty grey slate with edible flower garnish, the thought of eating food that had been heading to landfill made her stomach turn.

'I'm not going to lie,' Holly said, using a slice of bread to mop up the remaining sauce. 'You missed out here. It was really good.'

'I think we'll see who missed out tomorrow morning when you're up at 3 a.m. with a dodgy tummy.'

'Oh ye of little faith,' Holly replied, before sliding her plate to one side. 'So, what are you going to do?' she asked, with her serious face on.

'About?'

'About everything. Stephen, life, work.'

'Well, work is fine,' Fiona replied. 'The wedding is shaping up to be quite the event.'

'I can't believe they've sold the photos.'

'I know. Crazy really.'

'Your wedding. In all those magazines. You know your business is going to explode, right?'

She wrinkled her nose. 'I don't know. I mean, I don't mind doing a wedding as a one off, but I couldn't go back to it. Too much emotion. You don't get that with a business event. Just facts and figures. Not worrying about choosing a flower that might upset your Aunty June because it reminds her of her mother's funeral.'

'You're not serious?'

'It's happened before. Anyway, work is going well. Annabel and I were talking last month about taking on someone new. Just to work with the smaller clients.'

'That's brilliant.'

'And the other stuff? Well, I guess I'll just keep myself busy until he comes around.'

'And you still think he will? Come around, that is.'

Pursing her lips, Fiona didn't spend long contemplating the question. 'He will. He has to. This is our whole life. And, like I said, I've got plenty to keep me busy at work until he does. It might even be good not to have any distractions for a bit.'

Holly's expression changed from concern to annoyance. 'Really. You're going to focus on work right now? What you need is some proper *you time*.'

'Work *is* me time.'

Holly wasn't convinced. 'At least come to yoga with me on Friday. You used to love it.'

'I used to be able to touch my toes without worrying about slipping a disc too,' she replied.

'All the more reason to come – strengthen your core.' Holly paused. 'Oh, come on. There'll be more hot men to flirt with.'

She nodded in the direction of the restaurant owner, who was showing someone to a seat.

Fiona shuddered. 'That's not the way to get me there.'

'Well then, come because I want you to. I hardly ever get to spend time with you doing things like that. It'll be fun.'

And then, because it was easier than inventing a plausible excuse, when she knew she didn't have one, Fiona said, 'Oh all right then.'

7

Friday marked a full week since Stephen's departure. It was also four days since Martha had first been sighted in the Thames.

'Come on, girl,' Fiona muttered, flicking through the television channels until she found a news item that was discussing the whale. From the angle of the camera, she looked almost stationary and, although Fiona didn't know if it was actually possible, paler.

'Do whales turn pale?' she asked herself. It definitely looked that way but, then again, perhaps it was just the change in the weather. The darker clouds turning the river a deep brown could well be emphasising the contrast with Martha's skin. Still, it was another question for the Internet which, she'd discovered, had the answer to every sperm-whale-related question she'd asked it so far.

A sperm whale's life expectancy? Over seventy years. That one shocked her to start with. Gestation period? Fifteen months. She didn't envy that. Do sperm whales mate for life? Thankfully, the answer to that one was no. It was tough enough thinking of Martha calling out her clicks – that was how whales communicated – to her pod and her children, let alone imagining a devoted, non-adulterous spouse desperately crying out for her. Every free moment Fiona had, she was on her computer, learning everything she could about Martha and her situation.

Not that she had that many free moments. At work, she was more on top of things than she could remember being in years. She'd spent the whole of Thursday sending out informal emails to all her clients, to see if there was anything more she could do for them. She also managed a full hour of staff appraisal for Annabel and booked her in for two professional development courses in January.

Friday morning, she'd decided to spend at home, working on reorganising the bookshelves and clearing out any remaining nooks and crannies that had escaped the blitz earlier in the week, all while checking in on Martha. Professor Arkell had been AWOL for a couple of days. It was a shame. She preferred him to the older, more-gentrified expert they had replaced him with. This guy was sombre and pessimistic. Not what she wanted to hear at all. At least Professor Arkell tried to put a positive spin on things.

At twenty-to-one, she got ready to leave for yoga. The class didn't start until three, allowing plenty of time to grab some lunch, then perhaps go for a stroll along the Thames. She'd seen on the news that small crowds had been gathering along the riverfront, watching preparations for a full-scale rescue operation that was being planned for Martha, if she didn't manage to get herself back on track by the end of the weekend. Given that the chances were the great whale would be moving on in the next few days, one way or another, Fiona didn't want to miss the opportunity to see her in the flesh.

Dusting down its case, she hooked her yoga mat under her

arm, checked her keys were in her bag, and went to leave. Her
fingers were barely on the handle when it turned and the front
door sprang inwards.

'Stephen!' Her voice caught in her throat. 'You're back.'

Dressed in his usual work attire, he had his phone pressed
to his ear.

'I'll call you back,' he said, and lowered it to his side. 'Fiona.'
Her name came out like a gust of wind. 'I didn't think you'd be
here. I thought... Brussels.'

It was as if all the tension she'd been under for the last week
had suddenly been released. He had come back, just like she
knew he would. A sigh of relief left her, as she fought the urge
to throw her arms around him. She wasn't an arms-throwing
type of woman and he wasn't the type of man who would like
that anyway, but the urge was there.

'I decided not to go away. Better to be here. Sort things. You
know.'

His eyes moved past her to the hallway.

'You've been making some changes.'

'I have. Come in. Come and see.' She stepped back, her
pulse rate climbing as he brushed against her. 'I think you'll like
what I've done. In the dining room particularly. Come in. Don't
just stand there.'

He walked in slowly, as if he were expecting an ambush. It
was nerves, she could tell. Most probably about the apology he
was going to have to make. He'd never been good at that. Not
that she was great either but, right now, that was hardly the
issue. It wouldn't be her who would be doing it. And she would
give him a little time to find the right words.

'You've moved the painting.' Having reached the dining
room, his eyes sought out the changes. 'It looks good there.'

'It really does. I don't know why we didn't put it there before.

There are other changes too. All over. And I thought we could get another. Another Tuan, I mean. I'd forgotten how beautiful it is.'

With her husband's gaze still on the picture, she sidled up beside him, just as she would have done, all those years ago, when they'd spent their free time trawling galleries together. It was such a long time ago. A lifetime. The fluttering in her chest started up again. It was ridiculous, she thought, feeling like this just because she was standing next to him. Ridiculous, but good. Thinking of the past, she moved to slip her hand into his.

'What's that?' she asked.

Her first assumption had been a bag of freebies from work that he'd come to put in the fridge but, on looking down, she discovered he was holding a large envelope, not a carrier bag.

Flushing, he pulled it to his chest.

'Stephen?'

'I thought you'd be away,' he repeated, quietly.

She shook her head in confusion. 'I don't understand.'

His cheeks darkened.

'Stephen, what's that in your hand? Was it in the post? Is it for me? You're being very odd.'

Something was off. His stoicism. His avoidance of her questions and her gaze. It was as if her brain was on delay. She couldn't seem to piece it all together. When she finally realised, it was as if someone had hit her in the stomach. She staggered back.

'You're serious? You're not serious. You can't be.'

'Fiona, listen.'

'No. No!' She snatched the envelope out of his hands. Tearing at it, she ripped the seal and pulled out the documents. The subject line shouted out at her. 'Divorce papers?' She shook her head and read them again, as if the words must be transmuting between the page and her eyes. 'How? You've only been gone a week!'

He stared at the carpet.

'Fiona, this has been coming for a long time.'

'No.' She pulled his head round, forcing his eyes to meet hers. 'No, it hasn't. What happened to working through our rough patches? Talking about things? We were supposed to be a team.'

His eyes narrowed, meeting hers. 'A team? Fiona, let's be honest, the only side you ever support is your own.'

'That's not true.'

'It is and I'm not saying that's a bad thing.' He retrieved the papers from her hand. 'Look, it worked well once. It did. We both got a lot from it.'

'Pardon?' Her jaw dropped. She couldn't be hearing him right. It sounded like he was discussing a bloody business deal, not a marriage.

'We've had a good few years. And Joseph, well, he's grown into a great young man. We did well. And I've done well. And so has your business. But you know it wouldn't be where it is without me.'

That was the final blow.

'Excuse me?' She edged backwards. 'I built that business from the ground up, Stephen.' Her voice quivered with rage as she spoke. 'Me. On my own.'

'With connections I gave you. And that's absolutely fine, it's how it's sup—'

'Are you kidding?' she cut him short. 'You're going to take credit for what I've achieved, because you made a couple of introductions to your golf club buddies?'

'Fiona, all I was trying to say is that the last—'

'Get. Out.' The enunciation couldn't have been clearer as she spat the words into his face.

'Fiona, look, if I said—'

'I said *get out* before I do something we'll both regret.'

He drew back his shoulders. 'Look, I'm sorry if I offended you. That wasn't the plan. And I don't want to rush you on this.' He placed the envelope down on the table. 'I guess it has come as more of a shock than I thought it would. But there's no point pretending. And the sooner we get this sorted, the sooner we can both start moving on with our lives.'

The modicum of self-restraint which she had so far managed to hold on to evaporated.

'Start moving on?'

'Fiona, I—'

'Isn't that what you started doing a year and a half ago? Isn't that what this is all about?'

'I shouldn't have said anything.'

'Oh yes, because lying about it is just so much better. Let me guess, she wants the money from the house?' She didn't wait for his answer. 'Well it's not happening, Stephen. My money went into this home. *My* money from *my* business. If you think that I'm going to stand back and let you take that from me, you've got another thing coming.'

His jaw clenched. She held her breath, anticipating his next move. He'd come back with his own counter, defend his position as alpha male. Well just let him try.

His eyes went down to the papers, then came back up.

'I'll leave these here and grab a few things. Take your time,' he said.

8

It was a testament to her liver that Fiona managed to get to the gym without any hiccups, other than physical ones, although she did arrive nearly ten minutes later than she'd said she would.

'It's fine,' Holly assured her as she apologised for the fourth time. 'We've still got another ten minutes.' Her forehead wrinkled as she looked at her friend. 'Are you okay?' she asked, 'you look funny.'

'Like all I had for lunch was half a bottle of wine and a double whisky funny?'

'Possibly.'

While the nutritional value was, without doubt, less than ideal, heading straight to the drinks cabinet had been the one thing that had stopped Fiona tearing the house apart, or going after Stephen and tearing him apart. The audacity! The outright arrogance! To think that he could stand there and claim responsibility for her success. It was outrageous. So what if he'd made a couple of introductions? That was years ago. Did he really think that people kept working with her because they played a couple of rounds of golf a year with him? Of course they didn't. They did it because she was good. Better than good. She was the best at what she did. And if Stephen didn't know that about her by now, then maybe it wasn't such a bad thing that he'd packed his bags after all. And that thing about Joseph. What was it he had called him? *A great young man?* Whoever he was sleeping with had to be slipping him something on the side.

Apparently oblivious to the ranting going on in her best friend's head, Holly pushed open the door.

'You're going to love this place,' she said, stepping inside. 'I bet you. One class here and you'll be dropping all your others.' She paused. 'Well, you would if you did any other classes.'

The floors were polished hardwood and large prints of seascapes and forests lined the walls. It looked more like a spa than a gym.

'My nephew, Ed, told me about it. Apparently, it's where all the cool kids hang out.'

'Are we cool kids?'

'No, we're the rich tossers; that's the other category that come here too.'

The neutral palette of colours continued down the corridor and into the studio, where a huge window took up the entire length of one wall. Even with the vertical blinds – which obscured the view of the car park below – the space was flooded with light, yellow and warming. Combined with the seven units of alcohol Fiona had recently ingested, it felt like an appealing spot to take a nap.

'No, we need to go to the back,' she said, as Holly began to unroll her mat just a few feet from the front of the room. 'I haven't done this in ages, remember.'

Holly chewed her lip, glancing at the half dozen men who

were filing in, all toned and tanned and looking like they'd just stepped out of a Hugo Boss commercial.

'All righty. The view from the back's pretty good too,' she conceded.

Fiona pouted. 'Still married,' she said, although the words caused a wave of nausea to flood through her, quickly replaced by anger. Talk about rich tossers; Stephen was the biggest tosser of them all. Well, screw him. He could see how much she needed him. She was done with it. Done with whatever midlife crisis he was going through. It was going to take more than a few fancy dinners and some jewellery to get him out of this when he came to his senses. Then, noticing how everyone was now sitting on their mats and looking to the front, she decided to focus on the class.

Yoga was something she always felt she should enjoy, but never really did. 90 per cent of the time she spent frustrated. For some reason, her limbs just wouldn't move the way others did. Then there was the breathing. All those people who could manage to inhale for thirty seconds then exhale for a minute-and-a-half without getting dizzy and falling over clearly had some form of genetic pre-disposition. Today was bound to be a disaster, she knew, but at least it meant Holly would never invite her again. That would be a bonus.

At 3 p.m. on the dot, the instructor came into the room.

'We've got the good one today.' Holly grinned.

Broad shouldered and slightly taller than average height, he was darker skinned than Stephen: a deep olive, as opposed to Stephen's pale pinky-white that she was used to. His tousled hair looked like he'd just climbed out of bed, but then into freshly ironed sportswear, while his almond eyes were creased in a smile, one side ever so slightly more than the other. Fiona's alcohol-filled stomach fluttered.

'*Namaste*,' he addressed them, moving over to a small table and lighting two incense sticks, which quickly filled the room with a heady aroma.

'*Namaste*,' Fiona replied with more enthusiasm than she'd felt all week.

The problem with all her previous yoga experiences, she reflected, as she moved from a relatively stable Mountain Pose, to a slightly more-shaky eagle, had been that she'd never done it drunk before.

'Inhale and release.'

She puffed out for what must have been a full minute with minimal dizziness. *Take that*, she glowered at the man in front of her, who'd twisted around just to stare at her for some reason. Yoga breathing was meant to be loud. And she was going to be the loudest.

Alcohol, it turned out, wasn't just the secret to the breathing. It was the secret to following all the moves too. She wasn't *drunk* drunk – clearly, they would have asked to leave if she'd been that – yet it was surprising how limber those drinks had made her.

'Inhale.'

She watched the muscles under the instructor's T-shirt flex.

'And exhale to *Urdhva Hastasana*: Upwards Salute.'

She continued staring. The fabric of his top clung to him in all the right places. Stephen had never had a body like that. Not that he'd had a bad figure. All the years of rugby and cricket had kept him moderately toned. But it had never, ever looked like that. *Chiselled*. That was the word, chiselled. Her hand moved forward, just imagining what it would be like to touch something that solid and well formed.

'And exhale.' Again?

The instructor's eyes moved to hers, glinting with a hint of amusement. Only then did she realise she was still standing in the same upwards salute, while the rest of the class had moved into a Downward-Facing Dog. Hurriedly, she lowered herself to the ground. *It could have been worse*, she told herself, eyes now on the mat. At least she hadn't farted. She'd been in classes where people had done that. That was definitely worse.

Still, for the rest of the lesson, she tried desperately to keep her eyes firmly away from the instructor's abdominals, although it wasn't easy. Every forward lunge would result in a different set of muscles rippling, more than once causing her to topple slightly towards her friend.

'What are you doing?' Holly hissed.

'My mat is all slippery,' Fiona whispered back. 'I must have spilled something on it.'

When she moved her eyes back to the instructor, he was staring at her with a pinched expression, denoting either deep annoyance or great amusement. Either way, she didn't care; if he'd wanted people to concentrate, he shouldn't have worn such a tight-fitting top.

When the lesson ended, Holly rolled up her mat.

'So, what did you think? Enjoy it?'

'It was... good,' Fiona replied, for want of a better word.

'I know. And that view, right? Good call going to the back.' She tucked her mat under her arm as she spoke. 'Are you okay for a minute? I just want to go talk to Jim there. Get him to agree to a date next week.'

'I thought you said you'd already arranged one.'

'Well, I will do, if you give me a minute.'

With no option but to agree, Fiona bent down to roll up her own mat, only to be struck by a sudden bout of light-headedness that resulted in her best Downward Dog of the day.

'So, how was your first time?'

In an action that was part attempt to stand up and part to pick up her mat, she sprang from the ground, inadvertently swinging it through the air and catching the strap in her hair.

'Oh, umm. Sorry?' With one hand on her hip and the other trying to yank the Velcro free, she glanced up past the overly tight T-shirt.

'Here, let me.' The instructor reached forward and gently pulled her hair free. Static prickled across her skin.

'Your first time?' he asked again.

'Sorry?'

'You've not been here before, have you? At least, not to one of my classes.'

'Well...'

'Believe me, I would have remembered you.'

'Well.' Swallowing repeatedly, she searched desperately for somewhere safe to look. His almond eyes were a vivid blue, with an almost ethereal luminance. And his smell! Good God, how was it even possible to smell like that? As if he'd just been for a two-hour spa scrub and then dressed in clothes that had been washed by woodland sprites.

'I should probably get going. My friend and I... we need to head back.'

'She looks like she's pretty occupied.'

Turning her head, she located Holly leaning against a wall, chatting to a man who she assumed was Jim, who was standing with his head thrown back mid laugh. Of course there would be a date next week. Knowing Holly, she'd made the reservation before she'd even asked.

'So, did you like it?'

'Sorry?' She had momentarily forgotten that she'd been in conversation.

'The class? Did we impress you? Are you thinking about coming back?'

She rubbed her temples, the effects of the alcohol leaving her system now kicking in. 'To be honest, I'm not much of a yoga person.'

'You could have fooled me. I mean, maybe your focus needs a little work, but your flexibility... I feel we could work on that together.'

Starting to feel embarrassed, she racked her brain for a suitable excuse to leave. A loud chime cut through her thoughts.

'Sorry,' he apologised, pulling his phone out of his pocket. His jaw tightened as he frowned and deep lines furrowed what had previously been a perfectly pristine forehead. 'Shit,' he said, reading whatever was on the screen.

'Is everything all right?' she asked, feeling it was a rather personal question but that it would have been rude not to comment.

'It's Martha,' he said. 'You know? The sperm whale who—'

'I know,' she interrupted, not needing the rest. 'What is it? Is she okay?'

He shook his head. 'Apparently, she just collided with a barge. That's got to be a bad sign. Sperm whales shouldn't do that.'

Her heart sank. She had quite forgotten about poor Martha because of Stephen and his stupid divorce papers.

'Maybe it's the river traffic, disturbing her signals. Perhaps echolocation isn't possible there, the way it is in the sea.'

His eyes widened. 'You're following her too?'

'Everything I can get my hands on.'

He smiled. 'I don't suppose you want to go down and see if there's anything we can do to help, do you?' he suggested.

For the first time since leaving the house, all thoughts of

Stephen slipped entirely from her mind. A spontaneous grin stretched across her face.

'That's the best thing anyone's said to me all week,' she replied.

* * *

'So, what is it you do?'

They'd been walking for a few minutes, talking entirely about Martha and sperm whales and the thousand facts about them that she had learnt over the previous few days, but a lull in the conversation had caused her unexpected whale-watching date to move the conversation to a more personal level.

She hesitated. 'I'm an events planner,' she said, deciding that there was no reason not to tell the truth.

'Really? Wow, like business launch parties, that type of thing?'

'That's fairly spot on.'

'Wow, that's great.' There was a youthful enthusiasm about him. A kind of effervescent energy that just seemed to bubble up. 'I've got these friends with a start-up. Some big tech thing. Massive. Just landed the backing they needed. Going to blow a whole lotta companies out of the water when they go live. Maybe I could pass on your number? I know they'll be looking to do something pretty damn hot when they launch.'

'Oh,' she replied, trying to sound intrigued by this. Nearly every other person she met had some friend or relative who was about to hit it big with their new start-up. But she followed the standard reply procedure. 'I'm fairly full at the minute,' she said, pulling out a business card and handing it to him. 'But you can always get them to give me a ring.'

'Thank you,' he said, glancing down at it before slipping it into his pocket. 'I will.'

Talk turned back to Martha and whale watching and how she'd been whale watching years ago in New Zealand.

Before long, they hit a barrier.

'What are we supposed to do now?' she asked.

'Sorry, but you can't go any further. They've got the Coastguard down there. And a bunch of specialists.' The police officer guarding the railing was apologetic, yet weary. It was obvious, from all the crowds gathered at the riverfront, that she and her newly acquired yoga teacher were not the first people he'd had to explain the situation to that afternoon.

'But what are they doing?' she asked. 'They said they might have to try towing her back to sea after the weekend. Is that what they're up to now?' The nervous excitement she'd had at the thought of finally getting a glimpse of Martha in the flesh was giving way to a burgeoning anxiety. If the would-be rescuers had moved their schedule forwards by two days, that didn't bode well.

'If there's something that can be done, then I'm sure they'll do it. They've got the best people down here.' The police officer moved on to repeat the exact same information to another group who'd just arrived.

It was a strange crowd that had gathered in the unseasonably sticky heat. Clusters of men, women and children peered over the police barricade, trying to get a closer look at the animal in her distress. Many children perched on their parents' shoulders for a better view although, even with the extra height, Fiona doubted they could see anything between the orange lifeguard boats and various blue and white patrol vessels that were swarming around. A heaviness settled on her as she watched.

Hadn't the poor thing gone through enough stress already? Surely there was a better way to do this.

'Are you okay?' While the yoga teacher's eyes still sparkled, they also showed concern, as he placed a hand on her shoulder. 'You don't look so good.'

Swallowing the lump in her throat, she nodded mutely. The effects of the alcohol had definitely waned. Now all that remained was a feeling of overwhelming bleakness.

'It's just... I just have...' Her words dried up. 'She's a mother, you know. Why didn't someone notice she was in trouble earlier? Why did she have to get this far in?'

He leant over and took her hand. 'You never know. There's still time. They still might get her back to sea.'

She wasn't going to cry. She didn't cry. Yet her whale-watching partner was clearly unaware of this as he reached up and brushed her cheek with his thumb. Her eyes closed at this tender gesture. One simple touch, yet it contained more warmth, more connection, than she could remember feeling in years. Her chest pounded and she felt her body moving towards the warmth of the man in front of her.

'This is not a good idea,' she muttered, his lips now just inches away from hers.

'I don't know,' he replied. 'It feels pretty good to me.'

9

It could have been the plot from some cheesy rom com: the type she refused to watch. Standing there kissing, with crowds and policemen and feral children running around them. Then hailing a black cab, tumbling inside, and kissing again the moment the door slammed shut. With her pulse pummelling away, she barely heard what was said as they separated just long enough for him to give the driver an address, before the kissing recommenced. As she pressed against his chest, she discovered that it actually was chiselled. And not only his chest. His arms, his shoulders, his back, all of it taut and toned in a way that demanded her touch.

When the cab pulled up, she threw the driver two twenty-pound notes. Then it was in through the front door, up the stairs, ripping each other's clothes off before they'd even reached the landing.

'I don't normally do this kind of thing,' she gasped, in a break from kissing.

'Me neither,' he said, his lips moving down her neck before

grabbing her T-shirt and pulling it up over her head in one swift motion.

'I mean it.'

'I know you do.' With surprising ease, he successfully unclipped her bra and lowered her onto the bed.

'God, you're gorgeous,' he said.

She tensed.

'What is it? Is everything okay?' His hands moved up to her face.

She nodded mutely. 'Only, it's been a while...'

He smiled, then returned his attention to the top of her neck. 'I guess you better let me do all the work then.'

* * *

The last thing she had planned to do was fall asleep afterwards. In fairness, the last thing she'd expected to do was jump into bed with the first yoga teacher she met, the same day her husband told her he was filing for divorce, but sleeping had definitely not been on the agenda either.

Whatever the reason – either the effect of midday drinking or the most exertion she'd experienced in a bedroom in over a decade – she had slept, and was more than a little surprised to find herself blinking her way back to consciousness. Moaning a little, she moved to stretch, only to find herself pinned by a very muscly arm.

'Hey, sleepyhead,' he said. 'How are you feeling?'

'Good,' she sighed. 'You shouldn't have let me sleep, though.'

'Why not? You looked like you needed it.'

Her brain was still processing his words when his lips were back on hers. There was less urgency than before, more tenderness. If anything, it was more indulgent. Slower, deeper. His touch sent shivers along her skin.

'Are you good to go again?'

No, Fiona! The voice in her head yelled. *You're not. You're not thinking straight, you need to head home – now!*

'Because I would love to go again.'

Do something, Fiona, you need to stop this!

'I think there's a lot more fun we can have.'

Don't let his hands go there again, Fiona. You need to call a halt. You need to stop them—

'Oh!' Her eyes pinged open with a sudden gasp. Now completely unable to regulate her breathing, she let her gaze drift across the room.

'You have a lot of books,' she observed, momentarily distracted from what she was feeling.

'Uh-huh,' he mumbled, mouth otherwise occupied.

'They look like, proper *book* books.'

'Uh-huh. I have to do a lot of reading at the minute.' He was still distracted. 'Not for long though,' he added.

'Until what?'

'Until I graduate.'

Her eyes closed as the feeling intensified. A second later, they flew back open again.

'Until you *graduate*?'

She pushed herself up to a sitting position and stared at him. 'You haven't graduated yet?'

'I'm doing my Masters,' he said, attempting to pull her back down.

'But you mean part time, right? Like, alongside your job. Like, a mature student, right?' She looked at him. There was no denying it now; it was a baby face. Cute and fresh and oh so adorable.

'Yes, I work. I met you at my job, remember? I work at the yoga studio.'

Relieved, she relaxed back down onto the bed, only to spring back up again.

'Sorry,' she said, biting down on her lip and now unable to take her eyes off his perfectly clear complexion. 'I'm sure you mentioned this earlier, but exactly how old are you?'

He cocked his head to the side, combing his fingers through her hair.

'I'm twenty-five, why?'

'Twenty-five!' she almost choked. 'You're twenty-five?'

'Yeah,' his eyes narrowed. 'I took a gap year.'

In her entire life, she had never once suffered the experience known as *The Walk of Shame*. She'd lost her virginity to her sixth-form-college boyfriend, after three months of dating and while she had a few notches on her bedpost, they all were all from what she would have considered relationships of one form or another, as opposed to one-night stands. This was very definitely, a one-night, or one-afternoon, stand.

Shaking and frozen stiff as she stood on the pavement, it seemed impossible to hail a cab. Students milled about. Young students. Each one a reminder of the reprehensible – and at the same time mind-bogglingly heart-pounding – acts which she'd carried out at the hands of a twenty-five-year-old. Twenty-five! He'd have barely started school when Stephen proposed to her. Good God... Stephen. What was he going to say when he found out? No, he didn't have to know. She would keep this to herself – a momentary lapse in sanity, for which she was most certainly not culpable. Clutching a nearby railing, she pressed her hand against her chest and forced herself to calm her breathing.

In the end, she gave up on the taxi and headed for the nearest Tube station.

The train arrived and the doors hissed apart. She hopped into the nearest carriage.

'You have to be kidding me,' she said out loud. Every seat, every handrail, every spot in the entire place, was taken up by a habit-wearing nun.

'Do you need to sit down, my dear?' one of them offered, as Fiona struggled to find a hand hold between all the wimples and veils. 'You look quite pale.'

'I... I... I'm getting off at the next stop,' she replied, not actually having any idea of how many stops there were before home and wondering if the incense at the yoga studio was, in fact, a form of hallucinogenic. It wasn't as if she was religious or even superstitious, but a whole carriage full of nuns the very afternoon she'd broken her marriage vows? What were the odds?

By the time she reached her house, the air was thick with the promise of a thunderstorm and sweat had soaked the underarms and back of her shirt. What she desperately needed was a shower although, from all the missed calls on her phone, that would have to wait a while.

'Where the hell have you been?' Formal greetings were abandoned when Holly picked up on the first ring.

'I can't explain.'

'Well can you try? I was worried.'

X-rated images flashed through her mind. There was no way she was sharing any of those.

'I need you to come over,' she said as she slumped down onto the sofa.

'Why, what happened?' Holly's voice grew even more concerned. 'I sent you a dozen messages. Is everything okay?'

Her mouth turned dry as a thousand-and-one feelings of guilt overtook her. She wasn't going to tell Stephen. She couldn't. But Holly? She needed someone to talk to about it. She would go mad otherwise. But this couldn't be discussed over the phone. It would be spoken of just once and it would happen in person, as soon as possible.

'I'll explain when you get here. If I'm in the shower, just let yourself in. I'll leave the door open.'

'I'll be there as soon as I can. Do you need me to bring anything?'

'Vodka, bring lots of vodka.'

With every part of her scrubbed with her most expensive L'Occitane shower gel and her hair wrapped in a towel, she tried to work out exactly how she was going to explain the situation to her friend when she arrived. Stress eating was well underway. In a moment of inspiration, she had dug out two Easter eggs that Joseph had forgotten in the lounge cupboard. She wasn't entirely sure they were even from that year; the milk chocolate was now speckled with white flecks. But it didn't matter. They went perfectly well with the bottle of gin and can of coke she'd found in the drinks cabinet.

* * *

'If I tell you what happened, you have to promise you're not going to judge me.' Fiona downed the rest of her drink, the towel still firmly around her head.

'Of course I'm not going to.'

'You say that now...'

'I mean it. You know I do.'

Placing her glass on the table, she flexed her fingers as she worked out where to begin.

'You know, this is actually all your fault...' she started.

Five minutes later and Holly's lips were twisting painfully as she failed miserably to conceal her amusement.

'I don't see how I'm to blame,' she protested. 'I just asked you to come to yoga. I didn't say you had to sleep with the instructor.'

'But you were the one who left me on my own.'

'Really? That's why it's my fault? Oh, Fi.' Unable to hold it in any longer, she collapsed in a fit of laughter. 'The yoga teacher?'

'This is not funny.' Fiona yanked the towel from her head and flung it at her friend. 'This is serious.'

'No. This is funny. This is so, so funny!' Tears ran down Holly's face.

'I did not invite you here to laugh at me.'

'No, then why did you invite me?'

Fiona pressed her lips together. She knew Holly well enough to have known what her reaction would be.

'Look.' Holly wiped her eyes. 'It's done. You had fun. Don't beat yourself up about it.'

'But I'm married!'

Holly planted her drink down with a thud.

'Don't you dare tell me you feel guilty about this! You're not serious?'

'Of course I am. I'm married.'

'And so is Stephen. He has also been married for the last eighteen months, remember? And that didn't stop him screwing around.'

Fiona shifted her gaze to the bottom of her glass. This, she knew, was why she'd asked Holly to come over: to say the words she couldn't say to herself.

'You can't tell anyone about this. Ever. You understand?' she asked, feeling only marginally better about the situation, despite her friend's support.

'But it's amazing. Twenty-two! You should be proud. Haven't I always said you look amazing for your age?'

'Twenty-five. Not twenty-two.'

'Still, it's such a compliment. He obviously didn't think you were old enough to be his mother. Or maybe he did! Kinky...'

Fiona tightened her grip on her glass. 'I swear, I'll cut you dead if you say a word about this.'

'Even to you?'

'Especially to me.'

'Okay,' Holly eventually agreed, with the first almost-serious look she'd managed since Fiona had confessed all. 'I will not say another word. But you have to help me out with something.'

'Really?'

'Really.'

Relieved that the conversation had turned from her infidelity, Fiona retrieved the towel and folded it over the back of a chair.

'I will if I can.'

'The thing is, I've been going to that gym for three months now and I still have absolutely no idea what the instructor's name is. He's told me twice but, after that, I had to stop asking. Is it Drew, or Seth? Or Angus? I'm sure it's something like that.'

A moment's silence was all it took for Holly to cotton on.

'Oh, you are priceless,' she said, her grin now stretching from ear to ear. 'Absolutely priceless.'

10

After more drinks, and more details of Fiona's humiliating fumble with the student-slash-yoga teacher, Holly agreed to stay the night. The storm that had been threatening all afternoon had settled in and, while it wasn't as bad as some of the ones that had been in the news reports that week, it wasn't the sort of weather you wanted to walk home in. Besides, it felt like old times.

Perhaps, if Stephen was as serious about the divorce as he was claiming to be, she could get a lodger, Fiona thought, strangely comforted by the sound of running water and gargling that came from the bathroom next door. It would be a bit of company and help cover the cost of the mortgage. After all, once she'd bought him out of his share of the house, money was going to be tight for a while. Then her thoughts flipped again; obviously, it wasn't going to come to that. It was still a test. Rightly or wrongly, he was testing her. It wasn't the end. He hadn't even signed the papers he'd left.

Holly poked her head around the door. 'Night night, sleep tight, don't let the bed bugs bite.'

'Night,' Fiona replied.

'And seriously, don't stress about today. This is a good thing. It's reminded you who you are.'

'A middle-aged train wreck who can't handle lunchtime drinking?'

'There are worse things to be in the world,' Holly countered. 'I'm going to have to go first thing,' she added, yawning. 'I won't wake you if you're not up.'

'I'll probably be up.'

'No worries if you're not. Sleep well.'

The moment Holly closed the door, Fiona's mind was back in overdrive, listing the myriad possible futures over which she had no control. Perhaps Stephen and this new woman would get married, she thought. Have children, even. Would she lose all the friendships they'd made as a couple? Not that there were loads, just a few, like people they'd met when they'd first moved to the area and when Joseph had started school. They were bound to go with Stephen. They weren't good-enough friends to be loyal to her; he was the one who worked for the billion-dollar company, after all. That's how it would be. On her own in a one-bed flat with a pull-out sofa and ageing cats. She would have to introduce herself as a *divorcee*, whenever the occasion arose.

Outside, the rain pelted down. Her thoughts skipped back to Martha. Would the rescuers be able to work in this? she wondered. Hopefully. Maybe a bit of rain would be exactly what she needed. Could sperm whales survive long in fresh water? she wondered. Realising she'd stumbled across yet another possible problem, she picked up her laptop and continued where her last whale fact-finding search had left off. Two hours later, she went downstairs and grabbed a sleeping pill.

When she finally awoke, Holly was long gone. She rolled

over and instinctively reached for the television remote. It was a stark change from seven days ago, she mused, easing a crick in her neck and pointing the device at the television she'd brought in from Joseph's room.

A week ago, she would have considered anyone who watched television in bed a layabout. She would also have deemed someone who slept with a younger man, whose name she didn't even know, and just five hours after receiving divorce papers, clearly unstable. However, at that precise moment, there was nothing more pressing to do and she felt remarkably calm, all things considered. In fact, nothing mattered more than hearing that the rescue had worked and Martha was on her way back out to sea – not her job, nor her apparently pending divorce. That would make everything seem better.

While a crawler about some oil spillage off the coast of South America traversed the bottom of the screen, she waited impatiently for news from the Thames. Then, suddenly, it rolled into view. The remote dropped from her hand with a clatter.

Martha the whale has died.

If Stephen handing her the divorce papers had resulted in numbness then the effect of seeing those words was full-body paralysis.

'You can't have. She can't have died. Oh no.'

But the pictures on the screen were all the confirmation she needed. Martha, her grey-blue skin pitted and scarred, floated lifelessly on the surface of the river, while half a dozen boats and a news helicopter buzzed around her like flies with a piece of meat.

'The body will be removed this afternoon,' the news reporter announced. 'After which we can expect a necropsy, which will hopefully reveal not only how she died, but how she ended up so far from home in the first place.'

Fiona continued to stare. Even after the programme had moved on, she sat there, duvet over her knees, the image of the gigantic whale's inert form on replay in her mind.

* * *

It wasn't that Holly wouldn't have come back if she asked her, but how could she? Fiona had barely mentioned Martha in relation to the misadventure with the yoga teacher, let alone even hinted at the extent of her obsession with the creature. Besides, her friend had only just gone. Knowing Holly, she would probably dismiss Fiona's reaction as a subconscious response to Stephen and Joseph's departures. But it wasn't. It was more than that. She'd invested something in Martha, something she'd been lacking. Hope. And now it was gone. There were no other friends she could call either, not without looking like a complete nut job. At last, her mind went to the one voice she wanted to hear more than anyone else's.

'Mum?' Joseph picked up the phone after three rings. 'Everything okay?'

'Yes, yes.' She forced her face into a smile, despite the fact he wasn't there to see it. 'I just thought I'd call up and see how your first week went. Only if you've got time to talk, that is? I don't want to make you late if you're going out for breakfast or anything.'

'Actually, now's good,' he replied. 'Just finished a bowl of Shreddies and I'm going out to meet some guys from the rowing club at eleven.'

'Cereal? What happened to the cooking?'

'I can't afford to cook all the time, Mum. Besides, it's just breakfast and I needed something quick so I'm not late meeting everyone.'

'Rowing. That's new.'

'Figured I could give it a go,' he said with a nonchalance that she knew would be accompanied by a shoulder shrug, but deep down meant he desperately wanted to do well. He took after both his parents and being less than excellent at anything he did simply wasn't an option.

'Well what else have you tried? Tell me everything you've done.'

'You don't need to go to any events or anything?'

'It's Saturday. I've got nothing booked. Your dad and I were meant to be coming back from Brussels today, remember?'

'Oh yes, sorry,' he replied.

'No, I didn't mean anything by it, other than I've got time to talk. So, tell me, what have you been up to?'

Without question, she received a highly edited version of his Fresher's Week experience, but she didn't mind. Just hearing her son's voice was more therapeutic than any session of yoga could ever be. Limiting her interjections to simple prompting or reassuring noises, she curled her legs under herself and relaxed back to listen.

When Joseph was at primary school, he had wanted to tell her about every last detail of his day. Or, more often than not, the same detail on a loop. Not to mention the questions that she struggled to answer, like did she know which type of dinosaur would win in a fight? Or who would last longer on the moon, Batman or Spiderman? No, she didn't. And to be honest, she wasn't that bothered back then. But, eventually, these discussions had stopped. Truth be told, she hadn't minded all that much. She'd never been particularly good at kiddie talk. Besides, he'd become his own person and she'd hated it when her parents had tried to pry into whatever was going on in her life as a youngster. Only now did she realise how much she missed these conversations.

'And lectures, what about them?' she asked, anxious to prolong the call.

'Start properly on Monday,' he replied, 'now that we've got our timetables and everything. I've already met one person on the same course as me, although he seems a little odd.'

'Well, ring me after you finish your first one; I want to know how it's all going, okay? And what about money, have you got enough? I can transfer more if you need it.'

'Mum?' His voice hesitated. 'Are you sure you're all right? You sound different.'

'What? Asking about my only son's health and wellbeing is unusual?'

'Pretty much, yes.'

She laughed. 'I want you to understand that, whatever happens between your father and me, you're still the most important thing in the world. To both of us. You know that, don't you?'

'I know—'

'And I realise I work a lot. And maybe I should've been around a bit more, but—'

'Mum, I know.'

The line went quiet. She massaged her fingers against her temple. 'Well, I should let you get back to your friends. Good luck with the rugby this afternoon.'

'Rowing,' he corrected her. 'It's rowing.'

'Of course.' Her eyes started to sting. 'Well, you should go. But ring me, okay? Ring me if you need anything.'

'Of course.'

'And...' She hesitated.

'Mum?'

'And if you speak to your dad... Tell him I love him.'

Another pause. 'I will.'

She hung up the phone. 'Shit!' she said to herself, pummelling a cushion with her fist. 'Shit, shit, shit!' What a ridiculous thing to say. And where had it come from? That certainly hadn't been the plan when she'd phoned him. And now he would pass it on to Stephen and she would end up looking like some crazy, manipulative nut job, using her son as a go-between. With the intention of calling him back, she picked up the phone again and flicked back to his number, only to change her mind. She would send a message instead. It would stop any more unpredictable nonsense escaping from her mouth.

> Please ignore last comment. I'm fine. I love you.

She hit send. Who knew what Joseph would do, though? He would probably feel it was his duty to inform his father that she was cracking up. Only she wasn't. Stephen was the one doing that, thinking of ending his marriage for some cheap hussy.

Deciding that a strong coffee was called for, she fixed herself a large mug, before settling back down in front of the television. Once again, the image of the dead whale appeared on the screen.

'Fears are that, if we don't move it soon, the carcass may end up washing onto shore or getting itself wedged somewhere. Either of those could pose a major health risk to the area. Though one thing is certain: however they move the whale, it is not going to be an easy operation,' the outside broadcaster reported.

Fiona glared at the television. The whale. The carcass. *It.*

'She has a name!' she shouted. 'What's happened to Martha?'

Only twenty-four hours ago, all they had been talking about was the type of mother she would have been, how she was an integral part of a community. Now she was nothing more than a carcass. A sodding health risk. Fiona fumed at the callousness of it all. There was no way she could spend all day at home listening to this. She needed to get out. Go somewhere, do something.

Good old Professor Arkell appeared on the screen, his head hung in sadness. At last someone was showing the respect Martha deserved. Fiona continued to watch for a moment, but his words faded into the background of her thoughts.

Dressing quickly, she grabbed her bag and keys and raced out of the house. She needed air. And something to distract her.

11

Had she reflected on it, Fiona would have probably considered it a sad state of affairs that, on autopilot, she headed directly and without hesitation to the office. At least within those four walls, she could exert some control over events.

She opened a window. Last night's rain had dispelled the humidity and added a crispness to the air. After a double shot espresso and an aimless rifle through her cupboards, she opened up her computer and stared at the screen. Thirty minutes later and she was still staring.

This level of unproductivity was unheard of. Admittedly it was the weekend, but she'd just had a full week off. There was the VertX presentation for Dominic on Monday, ahead of the conference in two weeks' time. She could check that, of course, but she didn't feel focused enough to deal with something so important. And, as good a friend as Dominic had become over the years, she needed this presentation to be top-notch.

Sighing, she flicked on the Internet. An image of Octavia Lovett-Rose popped up. Fiona often set alerts for news of her clients. That way, she didn't miss anything important going on

In their lives. For Octavia that week, it was a guest spot on breakfast television and 'stepping out' at a gala, in an almost-identical dress to the Princess of Wales, followed by an online poll of 'Who wore it best?'

Shaking her head at the absurdity of what was considered news, she switched to a more serious site. A short video clip captured her attention.

'The mammoth exercise, involving three tug boats, has begun to drag the ten-metre sperm-whale carcass closer to a bank of the Thames, where it can be loaded onto a trailer and transported to the Institute of Marine Life and Conservation in Plymouth. Volunteers have been working around the clock to ensure this is dealt with as quickly as possible.'

Aerial footage showed various netting and buoyancy devices being placed around Martha's body. One of the boats rammed into her side. Fiona gagged. They backed up, only to ram into Martha again. *Enough.* Fiona clicked off the screen and staggered across the room to pull a bottle of water from the mini fridge. Finishing it off, she felt the room getting hotter and hotter. She had to get outside again. Almost unable to focus, she fumbled for her bag and keys.

As much as she'd hoped it might, the cool air did little to stem the tightening that was spreading across her chest. *That was it*, her mind raced as she walked blindly along the pavement. Martha was gone. There was no coming back from this. And what about her family? This thought caused the pain in Fiona's chest to increase. What would happen to them? Would they know? How could they? It wasn't like they were going to watch it on the nine o'clock news. Fiona had read so much about sperm whales in the past week. The bonds between mother and calf, the hundreds of miles their clicks could travel to let them keep in contact with one another. Would they carry on calling for Martha? And for how long? What would her children think? That their mother had simply decided to stop answering them now?

Trying to steady the trembling that was overtaking her, Fiona crossed a road, oblivious to the route she was now taking.

Orange leaves tumbled to the ground around her. Autumn, then winter, then Christmas, she thought. At least she would have family with her then. At least she would have Joseph back home for Christmas. Or would she?

This thought knocked the air from her lungs. If Stephen went through with this, would Joseph even come home to her for Christmas? There was no guarantee. It was the time of year when she and Stephen usually went to town: two trees, endless presents, and enough food to keep them in leftovers for a month. But it was Joseph and Stephen who did the cooking together. It always had been. Of course, it helped that Alton Foods gave him a huge, seasonal hamper. Their cupboards were always full of jars and tubs of delicious things and the fridge would be loaded with everything from cheeses to goose fat and double cream. Christmas was when Joseph had learned to roast his first potatoes and stuff a turkey. How many times had he said that cooking was his favourite part of Christmas Day?

Mind whirring, she stumbled on, bumping into Saturday shoppers and families trying to make the most of the last warm days. She felt herself dragged along with the tide. Her direction changed once, then a second time. Then she was standing at traffic lights, ready to cross a road she barely recognised. Not that it mattered. What did it matter where she ended up? Not when Joseph was going to abandon her too. As if he would come to hers for a frozen turkey crown and a jacket potato, if he was lucky.

Her breathing grew shallower still. She was going to faint,

she thought, a new wave of light-headedness engulfing her. Her body was spiralling. The pavement seemed to have become spongey.

'Hey, are you okay?'

'I... I...' she stuttered. The ground was slipping away, rolling in waves beneath her feet.

'Come on. You need to sit down. Let me help you. Let's go inside.'

A hand grasped her elbow. Another was placed in the small of her back.

'I'm... I'm...' *I'm okay*, was what she was trying to say. She was okay. But the words refused to leave her mouth.

Slowly, she felt her body change position, as the hand shifted from her back and guided her down onto a chair.

'Just sit there and breathe slowly, okay? I'll go and fetch you some water. Don't move. I won't be a second.'

Holding her face in her hands, she waited for the dizziness to subside. She'd only fainted twice before in her life: once when she'd been at a Take That concert, desperate to get to the front – which she managed – only to pass out three minutes before the band came on stage; and a second time when she was with Holly, who was getting a tattoo. Neither time had it felt like this though.

'There you go, drink this.'

With her eyes still blurry, she took hold of the proffered glass and lifted it to her lips.

'Thank you,' she managed, following the first sip, then taking a second and a third, which turned into frantic gulps until she'd finished the whole thing. A minute later, her head had cleared enough to notice her surroundings, including a large cup of coffee on the table in front of her.

'I made it with *milk* milk.'

She frowned. 'What...?'

Her head was still fuzzy and the smallest movement resulted in the whole room spinning again. She tried focusing again.

'You!'

She didn't remember her pulse racing so much when she'd felt faint before. Nor her skin becoming so clammy. She just needed a moment to regroup.

Had she been in her right state of mind, or even close to it, she would no doubt have leapt to her feet again as the Dumpster Dive owner pulled out a chair to sit down opposite her. Even if he had stopped her collapsing in the street. Unfortunately, her brain was still working at a third of its normal pace.

'Do you want me to call someone for you?'

A miniscule shake of the head.

'Are you sure? I think you gave yourself a bit of a fright.'

She looked up and scanned the room. The lip-ringed girl behind the counter was clattering crockery, while a large group of customers had just come in, all laughing loudly at something. The coffee smelt appealing but she needed to get away from her Good Samaritan.

'Thank you.' She pushed herself up to standing, not really sure if she was ready to achieve this or not. 'For the coffee and the water. Thank you.'

He rose quickly too, blocking the way between her and the door.

'Are you sure you're good to go? You looked like you were having some pretty harsh panic attack out there.'

'Panic attack?' She snorted with a laugh. 'I just haven't eaten recently. A bit light-headed, that's all.'

'Well, if it's food you need, I've got a whole restaurant's

worth you can choose from. On the house. And you haven't touched your coffee.'

She smiled as politely as she could. Leaving a Blue Mountain to go cold was a sin on any level, but at that precise moment, it was all too much. He was too much. Too helpful. The place was too noisy, too bright. Besides, one glance at the blackboard reminded her why she'd refused to eat here in the first place, and it would take a lot more than a bit of light-headedness to persuade her to ingest something from landfill. Thanking him once again and trying not to bang into any of the genuine customers, she lurched out of the door. She needed to get home.

When she finally stumbled through her front door, she didn't even bother looking at the time, before popping a sleeping pill out of its packet and washing it down with half a glass of wine.

She awoke the following morning with a bitter taste in her mouth. However, a coffee, a shower, a rinse with mouthwash, and another coffee and she was feeling ready to tackle the world. She had to be. She had a presentation to work on.

VertX. She read the single word heading, before changing the font size by one point. Something like that could make all the difference. And perhaps it needed to be just a fraction off centre? She used her cursor to nudge it slightly to the left. Yes, she thought, moving her head back to get a better view of the screen. That was much better.

She continued to go through each slide with the same attention to detail. Fonts changed; margins were realigned. She was back to her old self again. This was where she excelled. Only when her stomach began to growl, around midday, did yesterday's little episode creep back into her thoughts. Panic attack, indeed! Why on earth would he have thought that? Forty-six years old and she had never been even close to one. Panic yes, but panic attack: definitely not. They were for people who didn't organise their lives properly. People who let stress control them, rather than taking control of situations themselves. Yes, she'd possibly endured slightly more than normal that week but, still, disorders like that didn't come on overnight and she'd never taken on more than she could chew. It was a lack of food. That was all.

With the thought of food causing her stomach to growl even louder, she pushed her computer to the side. There was no way she could stomach takeaway again and the fridge was in need of a refill.

Her aim was to be in and out of the shop as quickly as possible. Unfortunately, it appeared that was also the aim of half her neighbourhood. People blocked the way to the frozen-food cabinets, picking things up to read labels only to put them down again. *You're choosing dinner, not a partner for life, for crying out loud,* she wanted to scream.

Shuddering at both the cold of the chillers and shopping in general, she squeezed between two dithering old ladies and grabbed three ready meals and a few smoothie bottles. The latter would hopefully replace whatever her body was currently craving: antioxidants or macrobiotics or whatever the latest jargon was. She headed to the checkout. With two plastic bags loaded, she marched back home for a final run through of the VertX presentation.

She would have an early night, she told herself, as she pressed save on the computer for the final time. Tomorrow was a big day.

* * *

As was generally the way during the working week, she woke a full five minutes before her alarm rang. It was a bizarre adaption of her body, she often thought. After all, if she'd wanted to get up five minutes earlier, then she would have set her alarm for that time. Still, it was a relief to feel that part of her routine was at last returning to normal, even if half the bedsheets still remained flat and unrumpled.

After switching off the alarm and taking a gulp of water from her bedside glass, her eyes moved instinctively towards the television.

'What's the point?' she said out loud. 'You know what's happened to her.'

She moved towards the en suite, only to stop. That wasn't entirely true. She didn't know exactly what had happened. And they'd said on the news that they would be performing an autopsy – or whatever – that weekend, meaning they might now have actual evidence as to why a thirty-year-old sperm whale had made her way all the way up the Thames to London. She reached for the remote.

'What we need is government intervention,' someone was saying. 'The fact that this can happen in this day and age is simply preposterous.'

From the images of sand dunes and tanks, it was clear they weren't talking about Martha. With a shrug of disappointment, she crossed the room. This was another reason she'd always refused to have the television on in the house first thing. Disturbing perfectly pleasant morning thoughts with politics or world affairs before even having a coffee. Surely that never put anyone in the right frame of mind to start the day.

She was almost through the door, when she heard the story change.

'For those of you who are just joining us: the Institute of Marine Life and Conservation has just released photos of the contents of the whale's stomach, which was said to have contained over sixty pounds of plastic.'

She stopped and twisted her head back to the television.

'Everything from plastic cups, bags and bottle tops to synthetic clothing and even novelty decorations were found there.'

They cut to the other presenter. 'We wish to warn you now that some viewers may find this disturbing.'

They doubtlessly carried on talking over the pictures, in the annoying way they always did, to keep your attention as you washed up or packed lunchboxes or whatever but, from the moment the images appeared on the screen, Fiona heard nothing but the drumming of her own pulse.

Sixty pounds of plastic was a lot. That was for sure. Especially when you saw it displayed on a table, the way they had. It was the type of table she used for company seminars – long and fold-away but light enough to need only two people to carry. Normally, she would have been wondering what make it was but, at that moment, her eyes were focused only on what was on show. A hand shot to her mouth as she stifled a gasp. There was a stench that accompanied the shot. She couldn't smell it, of course, but she could sense it. A smell of rotting flesh, of sickness and decay. Of poisons, thick and viscous. Even when the urge to gag had passed, her hand stayed covering her mouth.

Most of the items were stained red: the one hundred plastic cups; the countless plastic bags. She could even read the label on one of the plastic bottles. But none of that mattered as something else grabbed her attention.

Despite being stretched out as flat as it would go, it was still crumpled and raggedy. Age and a trip in a giant mammal's intestinal tract had caused the once-iridescent surface to dull into the ferrous tones of the dead whale's insides. She leaned towards the screen, her heart pounding harder and harder. It was impossible. It couldn't be. The remote clattered to the floor, spilling its batteries.

'And what is that?' one of the presenters asked. 'Is that some kind of plastic bag?'

'Actually,' her partner replied, squinting at their monitor. 'I think it's an old foil balloon. It looks like a parrot.'

'No,' Fiona whispered, barely able to speak. 'It's a parakeet.'

12

Fiona stood transfixed, staring in horror. The shot changed back to the presenters.

'No, come back! I need to see that! Come back. Come back!' she shouted, dropping her remote, but the story had already moved on. 'I need to see that again!'

Scrabbling across the floor, she desperately tried to fit the pieces of the remote back together. When the second battery clicked into place, she began flicking frantically through the channels. 'Please. Please let me see.' Politicians, politicians, knife crime, politicians. There!

She lunged towards the television, her nose almost on the screen but, a second later, the picture had once more disappeared.

'We'll have more on this after the break,' the newsreader intoned, shuffling the papers on her desk.

With her heart still hammering against her ribs, Fiona inched back towards the bed. 'You're being ridiculous,' she muttered to herself. 'You're being utterly ridiculous. You need to get ready. You've got to get to work.' She said the words out loud in the hope that she would convince herself. But she didn't. She couldn't think of anything else. Not until she'd seen it again. Not until she was certain.

She rested her hands on the duvet and tried to carry out the yogic breathing that had been so easy in the class. Now she was finding it a miracle that she was breathing at all.

After another sip of water, she placed the back of her hand against her forehead and felt the flush of heat. Maybe this was all part of the menopause, she thought. It would make sense. And hormones did all sorts of funny things. Perhaps they were causing her to see things. To make personal connections where there weren't any. That would explain yesterday's turn too. She was retrieving her robe when the photograph popped back onto the screen. All hope faded when the picture zoomed in on the exact piece of detritus she was dreading seeing again.

'No, it can't be. It can't be!'

Hands trembling, she lifted her hand towards the screen. Could it really be? It was definitely a bird, there was no denying. But the wings looked more brown than green like hers had been. Maybe she was wrong. Maybe it wasn't the same one at all. She needed her photograph. She needed to compare. She dashed down the stairs. There was one way to put her mind at rest.

By the time she'd grabbed the photo of Joseph's birthday party from the mantelpiece and switched on the lounge TV, the news story had, of course, changed again. This time, instead of trawling through the channels, she turned to her phone. The pictures would already be online, that was for sure. Her fingers fumbled on the keypad as she typed in the search bar.

'It can't be,' she kept telling herself again and again. How could it possibly be her balloon that had ended up in this whale's stomach? It couldn't have, surely. The idea was preposterous. And yet it had looked so similar. Maybe it was a trick of the light. Besides, the news reporter had been sure it was a parrot, and he'd had the chance to study it for longer. It was a complete travesty, of course, for anything like that to end up in the belly of an innocent creature, but it wouldn't be Fiona's fault. It wouldn't be her doing. It couldn't be. A few seconds later, the picture appeared on her phone and she drew her fingers across the screen to zoom in. Sitting down rapidly, she held the two images side by side.

'No,' she whispered.

* * *

The hall clock chimed the hour. Which hour seemed irrelevant. It was as if she had stepped outside the normal flow of time and was no longer bound by its rules. She could have been sitting there for minutes or days. She didn't know and no longer cared.

She'd discovered more information, scouring the Internet.

The necropsy took place at the Institute of Marine Life and Conservation, one report told her, *after the whale was driven to Plymouth over the weekend.*

Although once a relatively rare occurrence, this is the eighteenth whale to have died on the coast of the UK in the past year. Last month, three sperm washed up on the shores of Norfolk and, earlier this month, two minke whales beached themselves just north of Skegness.

'It can't be possible,' she kept repeating, looking down at her photo again. 'It just can't be.'

Her self-defence mechanism refused to give up, no matter how much was evident from what lay before her in black and white. Or rather in colour and sepia tones. The wings were the most striking thing. A couple of tiny red feathers right at the top of one. On both birds. Both balloons. They were the same.

Only when the clock chimed again did she look at it. Eight o'clock. She blinked in surprise and checked again. Standing up, her eyes fell on her reflection in the mirror above the fireplace. Her stomach plummeted. She pinched her cheeks and turned her head from side to side. Her face was gaunt. Her skin seemed to droop and her eyes were blotchy and threaded with tiny, red blood vessels. The VertX meeting was only an hour away. There was still enough time to get there. With her thumbs on her temples and fingers pressing against her forehead, she tried to remember the key points of her presentation.

'VertX Wellbeing Assistance...' She'd barely got past her opening sentence when the image of Martha's final dinner jumped into her mind. Another wave of nausea hit her. She bolted to the toilet. With her stomach empty, it was nothing but dry retching and stinging eyes. She wasn't fit to go anywhere. Not now. Not like this.

'Annabel.' She didn't bother waiting for her assistant to respond when the call went through. 'I'm not going to make it in this morning.'

'You're not?' The note of surprise was unmistakable. 'Is everything okay?'

Fiona turned to the television. It was back to politics again, but it didn't make any difference. All she could see was the whale and the contents of her stomach spread out on the long display table.

'I'm not feeling too good. A stomach bug or something. I need you to push everything back until this afternoon.' She paused and changed her mind. 'No, tomorrow. It had better be tomorrow.'

'Push back?'

'Yes.'

'You know that it's the VertX meeting this morning?'

A spasm went through her already aching head. 'I know.' She stopped to reconsider her decision. Down the line came the nervous tapping of Annabel's pen. VertX, Octavia Lovett-Rose, did it matter who she was supposed to be meeting? It should. It definitely should.

'I'll be in tomorrow,' she decided, and hung up the phone.

She picked up the envelope of birthday photos and made her way back upstairs. In the twelve years since they had been developed, never had she studied them quite so intently. Mid-morning light diffused into the room, giving the illusion of summer sun, as she spread out the collection on her duvet. Never before had she noticed how the person standing behind her and Joseph in the cake photograph had their face angled down, brow furrowed, as if telling someone off. Never had she spotted the half-eaten sandwich dumped on the sideboard, without even so much as a plate. Joseph was probably to blame for that. It was something he would do. She was scowling in some of the images, she discovered, her eyes looking almost furtive. She was probably worrying about what people were thinking of the party, how she was being judged, or how many were going to ask for her to help in planning their next event.

But there were several more where she'd been oblivious to Stephen and his camera, and she seemed more relaxed. In some, her eyes had been scrunched up in laughter, her hands thrown haphazardly into the air. Those didn't even look like her. And she certainly hadn't remembered ever feeling that way: carefree and at ease.

She was still lying there, sifting through the photographs and her memories, when the clock chimed to signal the passing of another hour. She rolled over. Her head was pounding from lack of coffee and her limbs felt like they'd tripled in weight. *You're being ridiculous. You should get up. Do something*, she told herself. But she didn't.

Another hour went by and news bulletins were replaced by a documentary that she didn't care about. Wars in countries she couldn't have even located on a map were nothing to do with her. It was all very sad and everything, but what could she do about them? Nothing they were showing had anything to do with her. Except Martha. Martha did.

It was a balloon, for crying out loud. Fiona tried to instil some reason into her thinking. One balloon. Hundreds of balloons were sold every day. Thousands, more likely. Everybody used balloons at some point in their lives. It didn't mean anything. Then again, how many people had bought one that looked identical to that parakeet?

It was as if a spark had fired somewhere in her head and connected two previously unrelated parts of her brain. No, she didn't know how many of those balloons had been sold. Not a clue. But she knew someone who might. Galvanised by this sudden hope, she jumped off the bed and into the shower. There was somewhere she needed to go.

The fact that Frolics and Fancies was still in business was a minor miracle in the current climate for small, independent businesses and only went to show how damn good the place was. Not that she'd been there in a long time. Nostalgia swept through her as she moved down the narrow streets towards the red and yellow awning.

A pair of young girls were laughing as they walked out of a nearby clothes shop, arms laden with bags. It could have been her and Holly from a different time, she thought, staring at the way they giggled together. How would the twenty-year-old Fiona view herself now? she wondered. She'd certainly applaud the professional success she'd achieved, which she'd always dreamt of, but the rest of it was debatable. Can a marriage which ends in adultery ever be classed successful? At least there was Joseph, the one ray of sunshine in the whole sorry story.

Her sense of optimism had increased on the trip over. While the Internet hadn't managed to give her the exact information she was after, a quick search had informed her that California alone sold over forty million balloons a year. Forty million in one American state. The UK was nearly double the size in terms of population, so even sixty million would be a conservative estimate. Per annum. Of course, that was all types of balloons – helium, water, rubber, party – not just novelty parakeet ones, with extremely distinctive feather patterns but, still, the chance of her being responsible for the one that appeared in Martha's stomach was looking slimmer and slimmer by the minute.

A small bell tinkled above her head as she passed through the doorway and into the shop.

'Welcome to Frolics and Fancies. How can I help you?'

While it was still another month away, Halloween displays were already up. Life-sized witches with crooked noses and flowing black capes, sitting on broomsticks, hung from the ceiling, and plastic pumpkins and paper-chain bats decorated the counter.

Picking her way past the fancy-dress outfits, Fiona steeled herself as she wondered how exactly she would start the conversation.

'Hello,' she smiled and observed the woman in front of her. Unless they had a time machine in the back, there was no chance that this was the same person, although she did have remarkably similar frizzy hair. 'I'm hoping you could help me with something?'

'I'm sure we can. What is it you're looking for?'

'Well,' she placed her hands on the counter. 'I made a purchase here a little while ago.'

'Do you have a receipt?'

She cleared her throat. 'No, not any more.'

'Well, if you want to return anything, you'll need the receipt, I'm afraid,' the woman said brusquely.

'No, no, it's nothing like that.' She tried again. 'I bought a specific item, a while back now, and I just wanted to find out how many more like it were sold.'

'You want to know how many sales were made of a specific item?'

'Yes, exactly.'

The woman stared at her but a glint of curiosity registered in her eyes.

'Well I can try. Let me have a look.' She turned to the computer on the countertop. 'What was it precisely?'

'A balloon, a helium balloon.'

'A balloon?' The woman sighed and raised an eyebrow. 'Do you have any idea how many balloons we sell?'

'Well a lot, I expect, but I wouldn't ask if it wasn't important. Could you just have a quick look for me?' She offered her most endearing smile.

With a huff, the woman turned back to the computer. 'When was the purchase made?' she asked.

'Just over twelve years ago.'

'So that would be two thousand and – sorry, did you say *twelve* years ago?'

'Yes.'

A small vein pulsed in the woman's forehead. 'Is this some kind of joke? You want details of a balloon that we sold you twelve years ago?'

'Yes,' she replied.

The woman was not a happy bunny. 'I don't think I'm going to be able to help you, madam,' she intoned and then, to further indicate the conversation was over, added, 'Thank you for shopping at Frolics and Fancies.'

Fiona's stomach churned. Clearly the woman's patience had been pushed to its limit. With no alternative than leaving empty handed, she opted for all-out begging.

'Please,' she stretched her hands out across the counter. 'Is there anyone else I could ask? There was an older lady here back then.'

'Look, I don't—'

'It's ridiculous. I know I sound crazy. I think I might be going crazy.'

'I'm sorry—'

'But, believe me, if you knew what was going on in my head right now, you would know how desperate I am.'

'I think that maybe—'

'The old lady.' She tried a last-ditch attempt. 'Do you remember her? Might you have her number? If I could speak to her, she'd understand. Please, I just need a few words. Is there any way I could contact her? A number she left when she went?'

Tilting her head, the frizzy-haired woman scratched her eyebrow.

'An older lady, you say?'

'She must have had the place before you. She'd owned it for years.'

Pressing her lips together, the woman gave a small, barely discernible nod. 'Just give me a moment.'

13

Fiona paced the shop as the woman disappeared into a backroom, returning a short while later.

'She's coming in now,' she said. 'She should be about five minutes. Are you okay to wait?'

'You rang her? The previous owner? You know her?'

'She's my mother. I took over from her seven years ago. And just so you know, I spend half my time trying to keep her out of here.'

'Thank you. Thank you so much.' Fiona grasped the woman's hands, only to drop them again quickly. Judging from her expression, she was not someone who liked to be grabbed.

The old lady, however, turned out to be exceptionally fond of physical contact, shaking hands and kissing cheeks. Hovering around her late seventies, possibly pushing eighty, her frizzy hair was now a mass of silver curls, although her cheeks retained a glow of colour that lit up her face as she spoke.

'I remember you,' she enthused. 'You used to organise parties, or maybe weddings, I think.'

'I did.' Fiona was a little taken aback. 'That was a while ago though. I mainly do corporate events now.'

'Oh.' The woman sounded distinctly disappointed by this. 'What does that entail?'

'You know, conferences, seminars. I've done a couple of trade shows too.'

The woman's smile widened uncomfortably, implying she actually had no idea what Fiona was on about.

Deciding that enough time had already been lost, Fiona tried to move the conversation along as quickly as she could. 'Thank you so much for coming in to see me like this. It must sound ridiculous and I know it's a long shot, but I wanted to ask you about something I bought a few years back.'

'How many years?'

'Quite a few.' She took a steadying breath. She didn't know why she was so nervous. 'There was a particular helium balloon you sold me. It was a silvery material, in the shape of a bird—'

'The parakeet.' The old lady's eyes widened. She leaned in and squinted at her. 'Of course. It was you. You've obviously seen it too, then. Oh, it made me sick to my stomach when I saw that today. Sick to my stomach.'

Fiona's mouth went dry.

'That's why I came in. I was wondering if you knew how many of those you'd sold?'

'How many?' The older woman's face crinkled up. 'That was it, dear. Do you not remember?'

'Remember what?' She shook her head. 'I remember you'd almost sold out when I bought it. That was why I couldn't have any more.'

It was the old woman's turn to shake her head.

'I never had any more. It was just the one.'

Turning around, the old woman crossed the shop to a stool.

Lowering herself down onto it, she took a deep breath as she started the tale.

'I remember it because it was that horrible winter we were having. Sleet, snow, rain. Every day. It was like the weather couldn't make up its mind what it wanted to do. That was why it was so funny that he came in with them that day.'

'Who came in with what?' The daughter had abandoned her post at the counter to join them.

'Some sales rep. Can't remember his name. He appeared in the afternoon with all these different balloons: boats, suns, flamingos. Summer things.'

'Parakeets,' Fiona added, smiling sadly.

'Well I remember thinking what a ridiculous time it was to come in with them. In the middle of winter. Anyway, I listened to his spiel, and he gave me a few freebies, you know how it is. And, lo and behold, half an hour later, in you came and bought one of them. That bird. You were proud as punch when I told you it was the only one I had.'

Fiona pinched the bridge of her nose. A vague memory fluttered somewhere in the recesses of her mind. It would make sense. That was why she'd been so pleased to get hold of it. No one else had one. It was unique.

'But after that,' she asked, trying another angle. 'You ordered more? You got more in?'

'Never got a chance. Wanted to, mind. The others sold as well: the flamingo, the dolphin. All of them.'

'So why didn't you order any more?'

The old woman rubbed her thumb across her chin. 'Company went bust, I think, or maybe they were taken over. Can't quite remember now. To be honest, I hadn't given it a second thought before this morning.'

Fiona nodded. The numbness that had engulfed her that

morning returned, catching her off balance. Grasping a display of wigs, she steadied herself.

'Hey.' The old woman was back on her feet, looking her squarely in the eye. 'Now don't you do that. Don't you go blaming yourself. You've no way of knowing if that was yours. They probably sold a thousand of those things before they went bust. They might have made ten thousand and dumped them because they didn't sell.'

'But, but...' Fiona could feel herself starting to stammer.

'No, you listen here. You need to forget about it. It could be anybody's.'

'But it—'

'No. It could be anybody's. It's not like it's got your name on it.'

'What did you say?' she asked, straightening up.

'I said, it isn't like your name was on it. It could be anyone's damn thing. You need to stop—'

Fiona leapt forward and kissed the old woman on the cheek. 'Of course, of course!' She grasped both the previous and current owners' hands and shook them enthusiastically, whether they wanted her to or not. Why hadn't she thought of it before? she asked herself as she made a dash for the door. That would have been a much better use of time than coming down here to listen to an old lady rabbit on about weather conditions she freakishly remembered. This way, she would know for sure. She could be absolutely certain she wasn't to blame. And all she needed was to get to Plymouth.

* * *

The midday train from London Paddington was scantily occupied. Four minutes before departure, Fiona found herself a seat in the optimistically named first-class section. She'd quickly grabbed herself some food at the station, which included an extra-large coffee, a small pack of sushi and a random chocolate bar that was on offer at the checkout. A mixture of nerves and excitement bubbled through her.

'Plymouth,' she said, handing over her credit card to the conductor as she approached.

The woman took the card and inserted it into her machine.

'How long will it take?' Fiona asked, typing her pin into the proffered keypad.

'Plymouth?' The woman frowned. 'Just over three hours.'

Three hours. Shit.

She studied her phone, starting to realise that she was thoroughly underprepared. Had she thought about it, she would have brought her laptop with her, so she could get on with some work. And a power bank in case the battery died. As it was, she was going to have to spend most of the train journey sitting doing nothing.

Empty fields sped past the window as she sipped her coffee. At least it would put her mind to rest, she told herself again as her destination approached. One day out of her schedule for a lifetime's peace of mind. It had to be worth it.

As luck would have it, the train was on schedule although, after walking for thirty minutes from Plymouth station to the Institute of Marine Life and Conservation – she had ensured she'd saved enough battery on her phone to view the map – it was already gone four o'clock. Standing at the foot of the steps, she looked up at the glass entrance. Nerves fluttered. It was a ridiculous idea. Ridiculous. But what other option was there? She could go back home and forget about the whole damn thing. That was an option. But she had to do something about the images that were haunting her. This was her chance to lay them to rest. All she needed was a little bit of courage. She straightened her clothes and, before she could change her mind, took the steps two at a time.

If the outside was anything to go by, the news programmes hadn't been lying when they said that the Institute was state-of-the-art. The modern architecture used simple curves to transform what would otherwise have been a plain box into something elegant and imposing.

Realising that she'd been holding her breath, Fiona pushed open the glass door and stepped inside. Minimalism had found a sanctuary. Sanded wood and hammered copper had been used to good effect and in the centre of the large foyer stood a small wooden table, with white computer. Behind the lone attendant, turnstiles lead through to the Institute beyond. That was where Fiona needed to go but she allowed herself a moment to indulge in her surroundings.

Turning in a circle, she gazed in awe. The stone flooring glittered under the spotlights and huge images adorned the walls. Seals basking in the sun, lying belly up on lichen-covered rocks. Puffins, their vibrant beaks loaded with dangling fish. But most of the pictures and, to her mind, the more striking ones, were of whales. Whales breaching, whales in family pods. She drifted from one to the next. Fins by the score, splintering out from beneath the water. And so many colours: greys, blues, whites. She'd seen a lot of pictures of them over the last week, but these were amazing. Magnificent and breath-taking.

'I'm afraid the last tour left at four,' said the man at the desk, startling Fiona from her trance. 'The next one's tomorrow at nine.'

'Tour?' she asked.

'Were you not looking to go on one of the tours today?'

'Oh yes,' she said, her mind in a fog. A second later, it cleared. 'Actually, no.'

Regaining the air of authority she adopted in situations involving people like this, she strode over to him.

'Actually, that isn't why I've come. I'm here to see Professor Arkell. Professor Ben Arkell.'

'Oh.' The receptionist moved his hands to the keyboard, ready to type. 'Does he know you're coming?'

She smiled her most toothy smile. It was fine. She knew it was going to take a couple of white lies to get through this.

'I was told my people would ring ahead.'

'Okay. And your name is?'

'Fiona,' she replied, realising a fraction of a second too late that it would have probably been better to have given an alias. She struggled for a surname, with disastrous results. 'Fiona Balloon.'

'Balloon?'

'No, sorry... Malloon,' she attempted to rectify the blunder. 'Malloon, it's French.' She prayed he wasn't French or didn't have a grasp of the language.

He frowned. 'I don't have anyone of that name down to meet Professor Arkell today. Where did you say you've come from?'

'From London.'

'I mean which organisation. Are you from the university?'

'Ahh, yes,' she hesitated, attempting to backtrack again. 'Yes. I meant I've just returned from London. To Plymouth. To the university, to my faculty.'

'Which is?'

'Which is what?'

'Your faculty. Which faculty do you belong to? Is everything all right?' He leaned forward with an expression of genuine concern.

She closed her eyes and allowed herself a second to regather her thoughts.

'Sorry,' she said. 'It's been a long day. A very long day. Look, I just need to know if it's possible to see Professor Arkell.'

'About?' He was viewing her with more and more suspicion and concern.

'About the whale. I need to see him about Martha.'

With a resigned sigh, he moved his hands away from the keyboard and sat back in his chair. His face had hardened, any trace of sympathy gone. 'What is it now? Some kind of conspiracy theory? You're going to tell me it wasn't real or that it's a Russian spy whale sent to keep tabs on us?'

'No—'

'Or are you just one of those sickos who wants the blubber for some home-made beauty cream?'

'No!' she grimaced. 'No, of course not. People do that? That's disgusting.'

'Well.' He stopped his tirade, although the scowling continued. 'It doesn't matter. You're still not coming through.'

Fiona pressed the heel of a palm to her forehead. If only she could rewind. She needed him on side.

While she was no longer a slave to her emotions, liable to burst into tears at the drop of a hat, this didn't mean she'd be averse to producing them if the situation demanded. It wasn't something she was proud of but she'd been known to coerce a little water from her tear ducts now and again, such as the time a few months back when she was pulled over for a broken headlight that she'd been well aware of but had been too busy to replace. She'd been let off with a strong warning to drive carefully and get it fixed the next day which, in her defence, she did. Of course, this didn't work on all men. Fortunately, this receptionist looked exactly like the type of man who would respond.

'I know it sounds insane,' she whispered in a voice from her childhood. 'But I just *have* to ask him about her. It's crazy, I know it is, but you see, I read all these things, about how she was a mother – and whales are such wonderful mothers, you know? They don't leave their calves for years.' She felt the tears forming in her eyes; she was getting there. But she didn't look up at him. Not just yet. 'And I'm a mother too, you see. And my little boy, well, he... well he...'

A second later and he was out of his seat and at her side holding a box of tissues.

'Sit down,' he said, guiding her towards a bench beneath the puffin picture. 'It's all right now, you sit down there.'

'I'm fine, I'm fine.' She gulped in a wobbly breath which dislodged a couple more tears. 'I think I just need a glass of water.' She looked up at him, sad and tearful.

All suspicion was gone now. Just oodles and oodles of sympathy.

'Hold on, I'll just be a minute,' he said and dashed out of reception.

It had been a bold play to risk, but she'd weighed up the options and thought it worth a punt. From her observations on arrival, it was obvious that there was no place in the immediate vicinity where he could get water. He would have to either go through the door to his left or head past the turnstile and out the back. Either way, he would have to leave her, for a few moments at least, in an entirely unguarded foyer.

The second he disappeared through the door, she grabbed her chance.

14

Fiona was generally a stickler for rules and regulations, but now was not the time for recriminations as she raced for the turnstile and hoisted a leg over the top. It was a far from flattering pose; she'd never appreciated how efficient the design was at stopping unauthorized entry until this moment. In hindsight, going under might have been a better choice but, with one leg already hooked over the top bar, she was now committed. Bracing herself against the sides, she toppled forwards onto the floor on the other side. She was through! The first hurdle had, quite literally, been overcome. Less than six feet in front of her were the elevators.

'Come on, come on.' She jabbed at the call button frantically, whilst keeping an eye on the door the receptionist had gone through. 'Hurry up!'

Above her head, the numbers counted down. Four. The lift lingered there. Three, two – it was on the move – only to stop again. *Come on!* This was her only chance. If the lift didn't arrive, she would be out in the open, exposed. One. *Ding!*

'Yes!' The doors sprang open and she leapt through, straight into a group of people on their way out.

'Sorry, sorry,' she muttered, slipping between them and ignoring their grumbles and glares.

Finally, she was alone. Leaning against the cold, metal wall, a sigh of relief burst from her lungs as the doors closed.

'Okay. Now you just have to work out where you're going.'

While the signage helpfully identified some of the key points of the building – Floor 2: Education Centre; Floor 3: Visitor Centre and Observation Deck – nowhere was it labelled *Lab where you would take a bloody great whale for dissection*, leaving her no option but to hazard a guess. The visitors' floor was definitely out, as, in her opinion, was the second floor. It seemed unlikely that they would have an elevator large enough to get Martha in – or that anyone would even consider travelling in one with a decomposing sperm whale. So that meant the most obvious floors were either the one she was on or the basement. Given that there was a fair chance of stepping back out and finding herself confronted with an angry receptionist, she hit B and waited to descend.

After a few moments, the elevator pinged open onto a dimly lit corridor with strip lighting reminiscent of a hospital wing, she thought. Not that that was a bad sign. Hospitals, animal mortuaries, there had to be a similarity in there somewhere. If anything, it meant she was on the right track. Tentatively, she headed forward.

The smell of the sea, mingled with the pong of disinfectant grew stronger the further along she walked.

Taking her time, she scrutinised the name on each door she passed.

Professor Holland, Marine Microbiology, the first one read, followed by *Dr Genis and Dr Krishnam-Jones, Cellular Biology*. Her footsteps reverberated on the stone floor. Next time she attempted something like this, she would wear trainers, she told herself. She was damn lucky she hadn't broken her ankle jumping-slash-falling over the turnstile. If that was her only way out, she would probably abandon her shoes. Especially if she had to run. They were replaceable.

Less than two doors from the end of the corridor, she stopped and a new sense of panic rolled through her. Her hands suddenly became slick with sweat as she read the metal sign.

Professor Ben Arkell. Environmental Toxicology

It took more than one steadying breath this time. What she needed was a strong drink, but that wasn't possible. Nor was dithering. If the receptionist had any sense at all, he would have already rung security to tell them where she was heading.

'It's now or never,' she told herself. With a trembling hand, she knocked. The sound echoed accusingly up and down the corridor. She stepped back, waiting for a response. Silence. She tried again. This time, when nothing happened, her eyes went to the door handle.

It'll probably be locked, she thought. It was a long handle, the type that can be pushed down with an elbow when the person entering has their arms full of heavy books or whale parts, rather than the round type you see in American films, when people are about to break in somewhere. It wasn't as if she was breaking in though, Fiona tried to convince herself. After all, she'd asked to see him. And it wasn't like she was going to take anything. All she wanted to do was look. Maybe find a large, brown box labelled *Balloons from Martha's Stomach* and make a closer inspection.

Knowing she'd reached the point of no return, she pressed down on the handle, pushed the door open, and stepped inside.

Like the foyer, the room was flooded with light although, rather than the clinical laboratory setting she'd been expecting, she found herself in a small but airy office. Surprisingly for a basement, there was a large window with a spectacular view looking out to sea. The Institute must have been built on a slope, dipping down at the back. A desk, which faced inwards rather than towards the wonderful vista, took up the majority of the space. The Feng shui seemed a mistake on the owner's part, although she conceded it was probably more productive that way round.

Time was of the essence but she had failed to focus on anything other than the view. She brought herself back to the moment. According to the clock on the wall, it was twenty to five, meaning that there was a chance Professor Arkell had already left for the day, if he'd even been in. She didn't know what sort of hours a marine biologist kept, but she guessed they wouldn't be a normal nine-to-five, not when they could be called upon at any time of the day to go on national television, or organise the dissection of the rotting remains of a giant mammal. She should wait five minutes though, she thought, taking a seat on one of the chairs facing the view. If he wasn't back by then, she would go.

The desk was far tidier than she thought a boffin would keep it. Although, on closer inspection, it was somewhat reminiscent of a school lab table. She was busy admiring the aesthetics of the chairs and pen pot, too, when her eyes fell on a pile of flat, brown folders. *Physeter Macrocephalus*, the top one was labelled.

A week ago, that would have meant nothing to her. It could have stood for a tree or an earwig or even a saucepan for all the

Latin she knew. But now... Her eyes went quickly from the files to the door and back again. They were in there, she could tell. The facts she needed about Martha were right in front of her.

Pulling a pen from the pot, she tapped the folder. Pages shimmied out into the open. She tapped again. Her heart leapt. Photos!

Trying to stop herself from trembling, she strained to hear if anyone was approaching. Her own shoes had sounded like a jackhammer, she reminded herself, so she should get plenty of warning. Besides, she only needed a glance.

Holding her breath, she slipped the pen under the cover of the folder and flipped the whole thing open.

'Oh God,' she gasped.

Somewhere, in the back of her mind, she'd hoped that perhaps, today, she would get to see Martha herself. That, by some miracle, she might be allowed to stand next to the mother who had spent her last week so close to Fiona's home. Maybe get to place her hands on her scarred, grey skin and offer a silent apology for the way the world had treated her, to let her know how much her plight had meant to Fiona – the bond she had felt. She realised now it had been a naïve pipedream.

Her hand went to her mouth, as she moved from the top image through to the second and then the third. Some of the photos had been taken as workers were hoisting the whale out of the water; others later, on the lorry, a tarpaulin inadequately covering her, as her tail lolled off the back. Even that was bearable, compared to the ones that came later, of Martha in the lab. It could have been a scene from a sci-fi movie – no, more like a horror film: flesh ripped open, coils of intestines flowing out.

'What the hell are you doing here?'

She snapped the folder shut, jumping from her seat.

'Professor Arkell,' she faltered, reeling from what she'd just seen. 'I'm sorry. I just—'

'That's private information. Bloody press! This is how you spend your time, really? Like you didn't get enough shots earlier. This is breaking and entering. Who do you work for?'

'I, I'm... I'm not press.'

'Then who are you?'

She swallowed, a whale-sized lump blocking her throat.

'My name is Fiona Reeves. I just wanted to speak to you about Martha. I'm just an ordinary person. I'm not a journalist or anything. I wanted to ask you some questions.'

His angry, red face was a far cry from the gentle one she'd watched when he'd been talking so passionately on the television. His jaw jutted forward as he held the door open. 'If you don't leave now, I'm going to call security.'

'Please, please.' She lifted her hands in supplication. 'I'm going. I really am. I just need to know if there was anything on the back of the balloon. Any writing.'

'The balloon?'

'The balloon you pulled out of Martha. The one that... one of the things that...' *The one that killed her*, was what she wanted to say. She stopped herself. Even now, there was no way she could manage to get those words out. 'I need to know if there was anything drawn on the parakeet balloon you found.'

His brow loosened slightly, switching from anger to confusion. 'The press called it a parrot.'

'I've told you, I'm not with the press. And it wasn't a parrot, was it? It was a parakeet.'

'Well, I'm no ornithologist...' he replied. The rest of his sentence was left hanging. They were at a tipping point. She could feel it. He was only an arm's length away from the telephone. Lifting the receiver was all that it would take to get her removed.

'Why does this matter to you?' he asked.

'Why do you think?'

From outside there came the lapping of waves on the shore. Seagulls squawked, dipping and diving at the white caps that broke on the pebbles and were sucked out again.

He bit down on his lip. 'When we pulled out the balloon, it was scrunched up in a ball,' he told her. 'Most probably due to the way it was swallowed. When it went into her digestive tract, it remained crumpled.'

She didn't understand what he was saying but knew he was trying to explain *something*, so she waited.

'One side of the balloon remained protected. That's why all the colours are still visible. The other got the brunt of the stomach acid.'

'Meaning?'

'Meaning even if there had been something drawn on that side, it's gone now. All the ink, all the colour was eaten away – nothing left to see.'

'Meaning I'll never know.'

The floor began to shift beneath her feet. Somehow, in the silence, the importance of her quest registered with him. He didn't need to enquire further. When he did finally speak, it was to apologise.

'I'm sorry. I really am. I don't know what to say.'

She forced her lips into a smile, although how she had no idea.

'"Innocent until proven guilty", isn't that what they say? I guess that means I'm off the hook.'

'Ms Reeves?'

She moved towards the door, barely aware of him any more. "'Innocent until proven guilty",' she repeated. Only it didn't feel like that. It didn't feel like that at all. It felt as if she had just taken her first steps towards the gallows.

She moved outside the room, barely aware of the receptionist speaking until posture and... she tensed. Only in bed, on her side, that position, such this was at all. It felt as if she had just risen her first steps toward the pillow.

15

It was ironic that the tears she'd faked to gain entry were now flowing freely, and more genuinely, than they had in decades.

It had started in the professor's office, the pain behind her eyeballs, sharper and sharper with each breath she took. Then the tears began and there was no way to stop them, Fiona realised, as the air quivered in her lungs. It was ironic. She'd not cried when her mother died, after years of watching her deteriorate in a home. Nor had she cried at any of Joseph's milestones: birthdays, graduation, whatever. Even Stephen cheating on her and then abandoning her had left her dry eyed. But the tears were falling now and there was no way she could stop them.

'I'm, I'm... Thank you.' She stumbled from the professor's office, sniffing and snivelling and barely able to see where she was going. It was easy to forget how unattractive crying was. Or at least how unattractive she was when she cried. There was none of that lightly dabbing a single tear with a frilly hanky, just ugly, gulping breaths and a streaming nose.

On arriving at the elevator, she went to press the button, only to have the doors fly open in front of her. The receptionist stepped forward, accompanied by a hefty, orange-clad colleague.

'That's her.'

The guard reached out to take hold of her as she flinched back.

'No, wait! Wait!'

Had it been Fiona shouting the word *wait* at the top of her lungs, she had no doubt that it would have been ignored. When she turned around to the source of the voice, she was surprised to see Professor Arkell running towards them.

'It's fine. She's with me. She's with me,' he panted.

'I thought you said she'd broken in?' The disgruntled security guard directed his lack of amusement at the receptionist.

'She... She...' He looked both confused and concerned. Fiona was still unsure as to which way this was going to go, when Professor Arkell once more came to the rescue.

'My mistake, gentlemen, I'm sorry. I forgot to put her on the visitors' list for today. Ms Reeves, wasn't it?'

She took a second to realise he was talking to her.

'Oh, me? Yes. Mrs actually, Mrs Reeves.'

'Sorry, Mrs Reeves. I realise there are a couple more images I hadn't shown you. If you would like to come back through and take a look?'

Fiona's eyes widened. Professor Arkell blinked, in a manner even less subtle than a wink.

'Oh, oh yes. Thank you. Of course.'

Leaving a confused receptionist and a frustrated security guard behind her, and feeling totally bemused by what had just occurred, she turned on her heel and hurried down the corridor after the professor.

Back in the office, fresh from his heroics, he seemed to have forgotten she was there and stood staring out of the window.

After waiting for what she felt was a reasonable length of time, she decided to take a seat. Still nothing.

'Are those the photos?' she asked, innocently, implying that she hadn't already been looking at them five minutes earlier.

'Ahh yes,' he sounded relieved at the conversation starter. 'The photos. Would you like to see them?'

She wasn't entirely sure she would. The one or two she'd cast her eyes over previously were already seared into her memory. But she was here now and, given that the good professor could have easily left her to the tender mercies of the security guard, it seemed only polite to show an interest.

'What caused all these marks on her?' she asked, noting the lattice of white lines crisscrossing the animal's head. 'They're scars, aren't they?'

'They are. Most probably from attacks: orcas, sharks, that kind of thing. Quite often boats are involved too.'

'But there are so many of them.'

'She's not a young girl.'

It wasn't hard to imagine how much she would have suffered, to end up like that. 'How old was she?' she asked.

His reply came with a slight wavering of the head. 'We can't be exact, I'm afraid. Probably somewhere between thirty and forty.'

'So, she was a mother?'

'Probably a grandmother as well, by that age.'

She swallowed, her eyes moving onto the next image, this one taken from the side, with the mouth open a fraction.

There was one other question that she had to ask, if for no other reason than to put to rest, one way or the other, the naïve hope to which she had been clinging. Perhaps the press had been exaggerating when they'd reported on the cause of death. Preferred to sensationalise. Or hadn't listened to the experts properly. After all, they kept on about the balloon being a parrot when it was a parakeet.

'Was it definitely...' she started, only to stop again. 'I mean, do you know for certain, you know, that there wasn't any other cause? That the plastic was definitely what...' The words caught in her throat again. 'That there wasn't anything else wrong with her? That she wasn't sick too?'

Pity shone in his eyes. 'She starved to death,' he said. 'A whale, of her length and size, should have been around fifteen tonnes. She was barely eleven. There was finally no way for her to digest her food.'

Fiona nodded mutely. Her throat burned and tears were threatening again.

'Is this... is this common?' she sniffed.

He tapped the pile of brown folders on his desk.

'These are just what we've had in the last three months.'

'May I?'

He slid the pile over. With trembling hands, she flipped open the first file. After a few sheets, she found herself staring at a photo of a beautiful pebble beach. Beautiful if you excluded the three dead whales washed up on it.

'This was near Skegness around March time,' he told her.

Two large carcasses and one baby. It could have almost been Martha's family.

'I thought sperm whales travelled in bigger pods than this. Why are there just the three of them?' she asked.

'Likelihood is they went a little further afield than the rest of their pod. Got themselves beached. When that happens, there's not that much they can do to save themselves.'

'So, this one wasn't us? It wasn't rubbish that killed them?'

'It hadn't done yet,' he replied, scratching his temple. 'But, judging by the contents of their stomachs, it wouldn't have been long. This one...' he dug down into the pile until he found what he was looking for, 'had over 20 kg of plastic in her. Including two separate flip-flops. Can you imagine that? Flip-flops.'

She could, she realised, wondering exactly how many pairs she'd gone through in the last few years. She wasn't a particular fan of that type of shoe. More often than not, they caused her blisters or, at the very least, ungainly strap marks across her feet. But, still, she bought a new pair every now and again, usually at the airport. She would often leave them in the hotel when she left. They weren't even worth the effort of packing and were cheap enough to pick more up if she felt like another pair.

'This one makes me want to cry.' He'd selected another folder. 'You'd think I'd have grown hardened to it by now, the number of these I've come across, but sometimes, well, it's not an easy job. Pen lids, for crying out loud. This seagull swallowed a felt-tip pen lid, completely blocking its intestinal tract.'

Nothing was left to the imagination in this photograph. The bird had been dissected, with its head and tail left intact, while revealing everything in between with startling clarity.

'Crazy, right?' he asked. 'We think our actions don't make any difference in the world. But they do. Governments need to ban this stuff. I know they're making noises, and that's all well and good, but they need to do more. They really do. People on their own can't be trusted to make the right choices. What has it come to when the economics and convenience of a disposable plastic pen become a bigger priority than the wellbeing of every other living thing on Earth? I mean, if you take a look at—'

'No,' she raised her hands to stop him opening another file. 'I mean, thank you and everything, but I don't need to see any more. I don't. I can't.'

She rose to her feet and stretched her hand across to him, a gesture met with obvious disappointment.

'I know,' she said, reading his expression. 'I should look at all these, but I can't right now. I can't. Martha... she was...'

He looked frustrated. Then, with a sense of urgency, he flipped to the back of the first folder and pulled out one of the photos.

'Here,' he said. 'Take this.'

Bile rose in her throat. It was so much clearer than the television image. It was as if she had in her hand an original crime-scene photo.

'I don't want this,' she said.

'Neither does anyone here,' he replied. 'But maybe it'll help you. Maybe you can use it somehow.'

'How?'

'I don't know.'

They stood in silence, both pairs of eyes on the reddish-brown image that she held in her hand.

Outside, seabirds called shrilly to one another and the burgeoning waves continued to buffet the shore.

As with her lunch on the way up, Fiona bought her dinner at the station. Once she'd sat down in the busy carriage, she started wishing she'd refused the unwanted gift more vehemently. The large, A4 photograph poked out of her bag and she could barely go a minute without her eyes being drawn to it. And every time her hand slipped inside for something and met its smooth surface, she would recoil.

So that was it, she thought. She would never know if it had been her balloon. And the owners of the flip-flops would never know where the missing partner of their pair had ended up, nor would all the thousands of people, who carelessly discarded small plastic items, find out their final resting place. They could all be her, she realised with a sudden wave of shock. It was hardly likely, but it wasn't beyond the realms of possibility.

She flicked back the lid of her coffee and gulped down half the cup.

You're being ridiculous, she told herself. Still, it was a tough thought to shake. She'd certainly owned enough pairs of flip-flops through the years to make it possible. And pens. How many of those had she discarded at school, college, university? It was only now that Annabel ordered her decent-quality ones that she didn't go through them at a speed of knots.

Her mind was momentarily pulled back to thoughts of the office and the box of mislabelled plastic puzzle cubes. Would whales eat those? Possibly. If not, then something else probably would. Her heart pounded. Maybe if she sent them back, the manufacturers would be able to take off the stickers and reuse them? Although what would happen to them eventually?

She bent down to her bag to pull out the photo. As she did so, her eyes landed on the tray table in front of her. The coffee lid and stirring stick were sitting next to the takeaway bowl her salad had come in. The plastic fork, which had been cracked before she'd even started to use it, was now broken in the bottom and, underneath it all, was a thin plastic shopping bag.

'Shit,' she said.

16

'I got your messages, but I wanted to double-check with you in person before I did anything,' Annabel said the moment Fiona arrived at the office. 'Are you sure you want me to cancel all these orders?'

'Don't worry about it. I've already done it. Have you completely cleared my schedule?'

'Everyone, apart from Octavia. Is she coming here?' she asked, part trepidation, part excitement in her voice. It was difficult for Fiona to remember that her client had a rather large fan base among the younger generation, although that was what she was now counting on.

'Yes,' she nodded, pulling out one of her coffee pods, only to look at it and let out a groan of frustration. She dropped it back into the packet. 'She's coming here at ten. And I'll explain everything when we've got a little time to ourselves. But first I need you to do a job for me.'

'Of course, what is it? What do you need?'

Fiona pressed her lips together and studied her coffee machine. How many early mornings had it got her through?

Too many to mention. And was it really that bad, a couple of little coffee pods now and again? With a resolve she knew she couldn't allow to waver, she turned and, with a renewed determination, said to Annabel, 'I need you to go buy me a cafetière.'

While Annabel was scouring the shops for a decent coffee-making device and ground beans, Fiona went through her notes. It had been years since she'd had to resort to little aide memoires. But there was a lot to remember today.

It was after eleven by the time she'd reached London the previous night. At home, she'd immediately gone to her laptop, to her contacts list. It had been far too late to speak to anyone then, even Annabel. But she'd started on the research and emails.

There had been so much to read up on. She had skimmed through every last paper and article she could find. Not to mention all the orders that had to be cancelled. Maybe that could have waited until the morning, but some of the suppliers worked in different time zones. Better to deal with them straight away. When she'd finally packed up for the night, she had been through each and every single one of the documents that she'd created for the Lovett-Rose–Rosenberg wedding. She was prepared. Or as prepared as she could be. It was all very Jerry Maguire-esque.

Ordinarily, she would have felt exhausted on so little sleep, but there was too much adrenaline in her system. In fact, she couldn't remember when she'd ever felt more invigorated than this. Pacing around her office, she read and re-read the cards, trying to commit as much as she could to memory.

'Do you want me to get anything else?' Annabel asked when she arrived back, with the coffee maker swathed in bubble wrap. *Oh my God, I can't escape it,* she groaned to herself, balking at the sight. She shook her head. She would find a use for it.

'Maybe I should go get some Champagne?' Annabel offered, unpacking the device and placing it next to the demoted coffee machine. 'Ooh, I saw on her Instagram that she loves elder-flower wine. Perhaps some of that?'

'Maybe.' Fiona pondered whether her client might be more receptive to new ideas if plied with alcohol. She shook her head. If nothing else, she needed a clear head right now and, if Octavia had a glass, Fiona would be obliged to join her. 'No. On second thoughts, I don't think that's a good idea.'

'What about croissants or pastries? I could pop down to the bakery and get a few things.'

'That sounds better,' she agreed. 'Yes. Yes, see if you can get something nice.'

Annabel made a motion as if to leave, only to hesitate and stop.

'Are you sure you don't want to tell me what's going on?' she asked.

A swarm of butterflies flapped excitedly around Fiona's stomach.

'I will. After I've spoken to Octavia. Then I'll tell you exactly. It's going to be good. Trust me, it's going to be really good.'

With another hour to go, she tested out her new cafetière to make sure the adrenaline didn't drop off before Octavia arrived. It didn't seem likely, although there was no need to be nervous. Her clients trusted her. Particularly Dominic. She'd asked them all to take risks with her in the past and they'd all been glad they had. They would trust her on this too. But, right now, the wedding was the biggest issue. The wedding was *the* issue.

'You need to believe in yourself,' she said aloud, as she closed her eyes and took a few deep, meditative breaths. Octavia was a reasonable woman. Wasn't that why they got on so well? And when she came on side, the rest would follow.

Her eyes fell on her bag and the photo. 'Don't worry, Martha. I'm going to sort this out. I'm going to make it right.'

Ten minutes after the appointed time, Octavia Lovett-Rose burst into her office.

'I'm *so* sorry I'm late,' she said, kissing twice on each cheek this time. Four kisses in all. It was a good job the wedding was only three months away. Any more of this and Fiona wouldn't be sure what level of intimacy a simple greeting would entail.

'Don't be silly.' She ushered her towards the comfy seats in the alcove. 'It's entirely on me. I'm so sorry I had to call you in.'

'It sounded urgent.' Octavia hovered, still not taking a seat. 'It's not the venue is it? Please don't tell me it's the venue.'

'It's not the venue,' she replied, raising her hand and gesturing to a seat. 'The venue is fine.'

A wave of relief washed visibly over Octavia, as she dropped down into the chair. She pressed her hands against her chest. 'Thank goodness. Well,' she sighed, 'as long as it's not that, I can pretty much deal with anything.'

Fiona smiled discreetly to herself. That was just what she needed to hear. 'All right.' She dropped her smile and took a deep breath. 'The first issue as I see it—'

'The first issue?' Octavia's jaw dropped in alarm. 'You mean there's more than one?'

Fiona shook her head, attempting to start over. 'Let me explain.' Another deep breath. 'The first issue is with the balloon rainbow arch you wanted.'

'Can they not do it?' Octavia was clearly in a fight-or-flight mode. 'Will they not allow it? I thought you said that wouldn't be a problem. I've seen things like that before, online.'

'Well...' She paused, ensuring she was picking the right words. 'It's not so much that they wouldn't, but whether they shouldn't.'

Octavia's eyebrows creased. 'What do you mean, whether they shouldn't?'

A lump had formed in Fiona's throat. Rising from her seat, she poured two glasses of water, handing one to Octavia.

'I was thinking about all the conversations we've had, you know, about doing our bit. And obviously you're giving a large portion of the photo shoot money to charity—'

'A hospice for arthritic dogs,' Octavia interrupted. 'That's the charity Charlie and I have decided on.'

Fiona smiled. 'That sounds wonderful. So, I guess what I'm asking is whether, from an environmental point of view, a balloon arch is the type of thing you want associated with your wedding?'

Octavia looked even more puzzled. 'From an environmental point of view?' she asked, slowly.

'You see,' Fiona leaned forward, flexing her fingers as she fought to arrange the stream of words racing through her mind. 'Think about it,' she said. 'What will happen after the wedding? Maybe some of the children take a couple of balloons home. Some of the staff at the hotel too. But what we're talking about here are standard balloons. Within a week, they'll all have burst or deflated and be nothing more than scraps of waste plastic destined for landfill. Or worse. Did you know that balloons are responsible for more sea bird deaths than anything else?'

'That's terrible.' A line formed on Octavia's brow. 'So, you mean go for something with a bit more longevity? Like, maybe those helium ones?' She shrugged. 'That could look great too.'

'No, no.' Fiona shook her head and gulped down more water. 'That's not what I mean. I mean you should scrap them. Get rid of them altogether.'

'Scrap them?'

'Yes, all the balloons.'

'But I thought we agreed the room was too bare?'

'We did. I was thinking maybe you decorate it with plants instead.'

'Plants?'

'Like giant sunflowers. Children love sunflowers. And they'll go so well with the clown theme too.'

Holding her breath, she watched as Octavia's jaw moved from side to side. Contemplative, but not yet dismissive. 'Not to mention the flower wall in the spring room. It would be like a children's extension of that.'

The jaw rolling changed to a slow nod.

'So, you like the idea?'

'I do.' Octavia smiled. 'I really do.'

'Great.' Fiona allowed herself a second's respite to enjoy the first victory. 'Okay, the next thing is the candle holders on the tables. I was thinking you could change them for vintage ones.'

This time, Octavia's nose wrinkled. 'We were looking for something fresh, unique.'

'Exactly. If you buy new, you're going to be copied and you will lose the unique look you are hoping for. It's annoying, but true. As soon as people see what you've done, you know they're going to go out and buy the exact same thing. It's flattering, but I'm sure it's not what you want. This day has to be different. Just about *you*. If we go vintage on it, there's no way that can happen. And, trust me, I will find you the freshest, most summery-looking centrepieces in history.

'And on that front, the confetti cannons when you come down the aisle? I think they should fire real petals. I know you won't get the sparkly effect you were thinking of but, let's be honest, real petals would look *so* much classier. And,' she added with a wink, 'be far better for the environment too.'

Octavia grinned. As did Fiona. It was all going to plan.

Exactly as she'd hoped. There was just one more issue to tackle. A big one, but with Octavia so on board with the rest of it, she didn't feel there was any need to hold back now.

'The winter forest and snowflakes in your winter wonderland room...'

'Is everything okay there?'

Fiona inhaled deeply. This one was going to take some doing.

'I need to be honest with you,' she said. 'I cancelled the trees.'

Octavia's jaw dropped. 'You did what? The trees were the key feature of the whole day! The four seasons. You can't have four seasons without the winter wonderland.'

'I know, I know, I completely understand that.' Fiona nodded supportively. 'But do you *need* them? There are other ways to do this. I was searching online and look.' She turned her laptop around to show the image on the screen. 'You could have these. Branches. They're cut from real trees and I think they look just as good as, if not better than the white ones we'd chosen. And for the snowflakes, I've found some amazing paper ones.'

'You mean like the sort you cut out when you're at nursery school?'

'Exactly!' she gesticulated energetically. It had taken less time to explain this part of the vision than she'd anticipated.

'You want painted twigs and paper snowflakes. You want my wedding to look like it was decorated by a bunch of toddlers?' The tone in Octavia's voice came as a surprise, given her previously accepting manner. 'We were going for crystals, remember? Fairy lights and crystals.'

'I do, I do. But you can get some amazing things created

more sustainably now. Artists are doing phenomenal things with paper.'

'I think you're losing me here.'

Fiona lowered her hands and sat back into her chair. 'I get it. I do.' She waited a second, giving Octavia time to digest what she'd said. She wasn't deterred. New ideas always met resistance, and she still had her ace up her sleeve.

'Look,' she said, when she felt she'd given Octavia enough time to ruminate. 'When we first met, you told me how you wanted your wedding to be different. How you wanted it to stand out. That's why you hired me.'

'I know. And you've done a great job.'

'Have I?' she asked. 'What's different about it though? What's new? Nothing. Not really. It's in a great venue, you've got fun ideas with the different sections of the room but, honestly, is it that special? You and Charlie could start a trend. A green wedding. An ethical wedding.'

'I happen to like the wedding we'd planned.'

'Really? You like pandering to the whims of the high-society fashionistas? And spending a grotesque amount of money on things you don't even need? You said to me you want to be different,' she repeated.

'It *is* different.'

'No.' Fiona could hear her voice rising, but she needed to get her point across. It was too late to stop now. 'It isn't different. It's extravagant—'

'Extravagance stands out.'

'Yes, in all the wrong ways. Why the hell do you need to pay three thousand pounds for a kid's clown, for crying out loud? It's absurd. And twenty-five grand on flowers? Do you have any idea how much that would be worth to the average person? And you're just going to throw them away at the end of the day.'

'Actually, we were looking at donating them to charity,' Octavia growled.

'Great.' Fiona's enthusiasm was at its peak now. 'That's a good thing. A great thing! Now look at all the other things you could do. Look at what you could achieve. You influence people. You have power over today's youth. If you have this wedding as we'd planned it, what does that tell them? That excess is the thing they should aspire to? That you're not successful unless you can afford a cake layered with real gold?'

'That's the autumn theme,' Octavia spat.

'It's obscenely over the top. You're an intelligent and reasonable woman. Surely you realise that all of this is just to satisfy some entitled part of your own ego? Don't you want something different? Don't you actually want to do something worthwhile for a change?'

Only when she saw that Octavia's cheeks had taken on a distinctly purplish hue did Fiona realise that she may have taken it a step too far.

17

'Sorry?' Octavia blinked repeatedly. 'Could you just repeat that? You feel my wedding is a grotesque extravagance for the sake of satisfying my own ego?'

Fiona's palms started to sweat.

'It doesn't have to be,' she said hurriedly, sensing that perhaps she'd laid it on a little too thick, a little too soon. 'It doesn't. It's just the way it is now—'

'The way it is now is the way I want it. It's the way I've spent the last nine months looking forward to it being.'

'But surely you can see it's not necessary. Not all of it. One hundred white Christmas trees? For one day? Do you really need them?'

'It's not a case of what I need. It's my wedding day. It's the only one I'm planning on having. And I'll have them because they're what I want.'

'For crying out loud, could you sound more like a brat?'

That was when she knew she'd blown it.

'Octavia,' she reached out to take her client's hands, only to have her jump up, snatching them away. 'Look, I'm sorry. Please, please sit down. Let me explain to you where I'm coming from.'

'I think you've explained enough.'

'Honestly, there's a reason.'

'Other than calling me in here to tell me I'm a grotesque, selfish socialite?'

'That's not what I said.'

'Not in so many words.'

Octavia span around and plucked her handbag from the floor. Fiona's eyes moved desperately from one side of the room to the other, searching for inspiration. They fell on the corner of the photograph, sticking out of her bag. She wasn't wrong. Not about this. Martha needed her to be strong.

'You have a choice here, Octavia. You could do something great. You could make a difference. You talk about wanting to help the anaemic dogs—'

'Arthritic dogs.'

'What does it matter? It's all bullshit.'

'Pardon?' Octavia's mouth hung open.

'Seriously. I mean it. You go to charity galas and have your friends over to discuss what tiny fraction of your money you should donate to people who have had their legs blown off in war-torn countries, or to the orangutans because their rain-forest homes are being decimated, but you still keep millions squirrelled away in your bank accounts. Oh yes, I know you care. You just don't care enough to give up your way of life. To give up some of your little luxuries. I mean, when it comes down to it, when it comes down to doing something that would actually make a difference, you won't. And why? Because I'm right. You don't care. You care about the image that caring about these things portrays.'

She was going for broke. There was no way back now. She might as well tell it like it was, through to the bitter end.

'And do you know what? Sod whatever I said before. You had it right. You're just an egotistical, selfish socialite. Enjoy your wedding. I sure as hell won't be having anything to do with it.'

A second later, the door slammed.

'What happened?' Annabel appeared, bouncing as if she was standing on hot coals.

'She's gone, I take it?'

'Practically ran out the door! She looked devastated.'

'Good.'

'What on earth did you say to her?'

* * *

Later, on reflection, Fiona felt sure that Annabel had asked this question in nowhere near the tone that she'd imagined at the time. And, given that she had never been anything other than the most loyal and helpful assistant anyone could have ever wished for, it would seem most likely that that was the case. But, right then, the words struck her eardrums like a spray of bullets.

'What did I say?' Fiona's forehead compressed and reddened simultaneously. 'What I said was absolutely none of your business. When precisely did you think you could just waltz in here, questioning my judgement? It's my name on the door, remember!'

Annabel inched backwards, shoulders hunching.

'I didn't mean anything—'

'No, no. Only that it had to be something *I* had done.'

'I just—'

'Screw this.'

Fiona grabbed her bag, swung it over her shoulder and marched out of the door. So much for trying to do the right thing. To hell with them all.

She was in the right, she reminded herself, as she marched furiously out of the building. She was trying to make a difference. Trying to make people see sense.

'Argh!' She pulled at her hair as she pushed past yet another person. How the hell did it end up like that? She was trying to help.

She carried on walking, barely checking if the road was clear before crossing. *When did people lose the ability to think rationally?* she asked herself. *Beyond their own narrow agenda?* Someone appeared out of the ether ready to block her path, clipboard at the ready, but she wasn't in the mood. Practically growling, she barged through, causing the person to jump aside. *They should be mad about what's happening*, she thought as she continued her rampage. *Everyone on the whole damn planet should be hopping mad.*

Only when the streets became quieter and her pace slowed just a fraction, did the whirring in her head also begin to die down.

Maybe she had gone a little overboard, she thought, starting to take stock of her surroundings. Perhaps she hadn't worded things very diplomatically. But it wasn't as if it wasn't true. People like Octavia had the power to influence others, to really ignite change in a community. If Octavia wasn't going to stick her neck out and do something, then who would? One hundred white plastic Christmas trees, for crying out loud. How had she even said yes to that in the first place? she wondered. She sighed, attracting the attention of a man in a biker jacket, walking beside her. Catching her eye, he nodded. No words exchanged. What she needed, she realised in that second, was someone on her side.

She'd try the restaurant first. Standing outside the door, she watched as people stared up at the blackboard, while tattooed staff took orders and brought drinks. Was there anyone left without a tattoo in this city? They used to be just for skinheads and ex-cons. Now it felt like every wannabe hipster had them.

After five minutes and with no sign of him, she remembered something he'd said to her on her first trip there, about the shop. *Just over the road.*

It didn't take long to find the place. With its slate facade and minimalist window display, it certainly stood out among the sleek chain stores that surrounded it. She hovered, still contemplating whether or not she should head in, when the door opened from the inside.

'We should really stop meeting like this.'

Given how intently she had been staring at the building she was surprised to be caught off guard.

'Were you planning on coming in, or simply casing the joint? I'm gonna be honest, there's a jewellers down the street you'd probably have much more success with. Unless you have a thing for artichokes. We've got a lot of artichokes in at the minute.'

Today, his sheepish grin was accessorised with a faded T-shirt and ripped jeans. The hair, so thick and wavy, any woman would be envious of it, was currently in a ponytail.

'You seem to be pretty focused there,' he said, realising that his quip was going to pass without so much as a smile. 'Is there something I can help you with?'

Behind them came the beeping of pedestrian lights. She turned towards them, and watched a woman cross, holding her child's hand.

'Actually,' she twisted her shoulders back to face him, 'I think there is.'

Given the myriad thoughts that had crossed her mind in the fifteen minutes it had taken her to walk there, she was surprised to find that, once she was sitting down with a coffee in her hand, she was struggling to find a single word to say.

'Sorry it's not as good as the restaurant,' he said. 'I only have a kettle here.'

She looked around the room, at the various jars, tins and bottles that filled the shelves.

'And you own this place too?'

'I do. This came first, actually. A long time ago now: nearly eight years.'

'I've never noticed it.'

'I don't expect you were looking for it before.'

They lapsed into a comfortable silence. She blew at the steam coming from her drink. It felt bizarrely natural, the two of them sitting on the little tub seats in the corner of the shop. Almost like a shoe shop. But with no shoes, just a cup of coffee that was too hot to drink.

'Was there something—?'

'How many customers do you get here?' she interrupted before he'd had a chance to finish his question. 'The shop I mean. How many people actually buy into this whole thing? Is it enough to make a difference?'

A smile flickered at the corners of his mouth. 'I guess it depends on what you mean by making a difference?'

'I don't know. Just a difference.'

'How about I give you some statistics,' he offered after a minute. 'You seem to me to be more of a quantitative than qualitative type of person.'

'Quantitative works well for me.'

His smile flickered again as he adjusted his position to settle in for a chat.

'Okay, in numbers. We're talking about waste, right?'

'I guess. Plastic rubbish?'

'Okay, good… Just so we're clear, that's what you want me to tell you about.'

'Uh-huh.' She felt like a child again, sitting in class, waiting for the teacher to explain something impossibly hard, that she didn't really want to know about but, according to the curriculum, she needed to know.

'All right. We'll deal with the UK, because that's where we are. Are you okay with that?'

She nodded.

'Right. So, the average British person produces around half a metric tonne of waste per year. That's five hundred kilograms.'

'I'm aware what a metric tonne is,' she interjected.

He suppressed a smirk.

'I apologise. Lots of people don't know that. Anyway, five hundred kilograms of waste a year. Now, say that an average bag of household rubbish weighs about five kilograms.'

'Okay, but what about recycling? I recycle at least half of my rubbish.'

It was tough to tell if the look her gave her was pitying or patronising.

'Yeah, I'm gonna be honest. You might want to look into recycling. It's a bit of a wormhole.'

'It is?' She had already encountered more than enough wormholes for one week. Banishing that thought to the back of her mind, she prompted him to continue. 'Okay, so around five kilos a bag,' she repeated.

'Right, five hundred kilos a year, means one hundred bags a

year. One hundred rubbish bags going into landfill, where they will do nothing but pollute the planet.

'Now, let's say I can help people to reduce that by a quarter. No scrap that, say by just a fifth. Suppose I can manage to help people reduce their waste by a fifth. That's twenty bags of rubbish per person that I've stopped going into landfill. Per person, remember. Twenty per year per person. Now I'm not exactly supermarket size here, so let's say I have fifty loyal customers. Fifty people that will cut their waste by one-fifth. Then that's one thousand bags that I've saved every year. Five tonnes that aren't going to clog up the ecosystem. Can you imagine that? Five tonnes of rubbish that my little shop has prevented all on its own.'

'That's crazy.' She really was surprised.

'So,' he said, taking a sip of his coffee, ignoring the cloud of swirling steam. 'In answer to your original question. I would say, yes. Yes, it most definitely makes a difference.'

Taking a moment, Fiona tried to recap the numbers in her head. It certainly sounded impressive. There was no doubt about that. But then it could have just been the way that he said it. There was something alluring about the way he spoke. The way he drew her eyes to every part of his face.

'And do you?' she asked.

'Do I...?'

'Have fifty loyal customers? Fifty people who've managed to cut back a fifth of their waste?'

'We didn't at first.' He had a refreshing honesty. 'But now, we're probably on our way to double that. I mean, this place is never going to make me millions, but stopping eight hundred buses' worth of rubbish going into a tip each year... I'm happy with that. And that's just the shop part, remember. The restaurant runs zero waste too. Honestly, the amount some of these big chains – well, most places actually – produce would make your eyes water. Don't get me started on that. You'll never get home.' He paused to take another sip of his drink.

The door opened and a family – parents, children, and grandchildren – ambled in.

'Can I just quickly ask you one more thing?' she asked, realising the shoppers would need his attention sooner or later.

'Go ahead, shoot.'

'Do you ever get tired of it?'

'Of what, this lifestyle?'

'Of the struggle. Of the endless battle.'

'With whom? With the government, you mean? Of course. I'm constantly infuriated with the lot of them. At least half the plastics used in packaging should have been banned years ago, and stricter regulations on restaurants brought in. And, honestly, I told you, don't even get me started on commercial food waste.'

'So how do you keep going? How do you keep yourself motivated? Wouldn't it just be easier to give in? To live normally. Like everyone else does.'

'How?' He looked at her, bemused. 'What other option do I have? Go back to throwing my rubbish away without a second thought and pray I don't one day see my crisp packet turn up in the stomach of a whale that's been washed up on a beach somewhere?'

Fiona gulped at her coffee, scalding the roof of her mouth.

'Why would you say that?'

'Say what?'

'About the whale?' She heard the hitch in her voice. 'Why would you mention that?'

He frowned again. 'You must have seen it on the news? You

couldn't have missed it. The whale in the Thames? Surely you saw how it died.'

'But why did you need to bring it up? About seeing something in its stomach?'

His eyes narrowed. 'You were the one who was asking the questions. I was just giving you some context, that was all.'

Her pulse was racing and her legs began to tremble. Fighting the feeling, she stood up and handed him the mug.

'Are you okay?' he asked.

'I'm fine. I'm fine, I just need some air.'

She turned to see if there was a clear route through the family who had somehow managed to occupy every aisle in the shop. Realising that it was going to be a case of barging rudely past and upsetting them or staying put and experiencing what she was now almost willing to admit might be some form of an anxiety attack, she marched towards the door.

'Hey, do you—'

'Air,' she repeated. 'I need air.'

18

Simply being outside in the cool wasn't enough to stop the hammering in her chest. But it did help a bit. The cold air opened up her lungs a little, but it was the proximity to the shop that kept the adrenaline pumping. He would come out and check on her, she was sure. She didn't know much about the man, but she knew he was that sort of person. The sort who would race out to help a stranger, despite the fact he had a shop full of customers needing help.

With no other option but to get as far away from the place as possible, she raced forwards. Two sets of traffic lights, four random right turns and two left later, she finally veered off into a small alleyway and slumped against the wall. Her eyes closed with a sigh. Time passed as she propped herself there, mind in overdrive.

When she finally decided to acquaint herself with her surroundings and opened her eyes, it was the busyness of the street that alerted her to the fact that it must be around lunchtime. After a few moments rummaging in her bag, it dawned on her that she had left her phone in the office.

'Shit,' she said, and then, realising that heading back there meant substantially more than simply *heading back there*, she repeated the word. 'Shit.'

In the nearly five years that Annabel had worked for her, they'd managed the last four years and eleven months without any yelling, or even exchanging an uncivil word. It wasn't a testament to Fiona as a boss. She'd had employees in the past who she did nothing but yell at, or so it seemed. Sometimes it worked, sometimes it didn't. But with Annabel, it had only taken four weeks for her to reach the conclusion that she was a person you shouldn't, couldn't shout at. Annabel's natural good nature went far beyond simple manners. She would only verbalise appropriate thoughts in any given situation and Fiona had no doubt that her inner thoughts were just as pristine as those that she shared. Annabel never did anything unless she genuinely believed it was the right thing to do. People like that were a rare find. The scene that morning had, therefore, been a grave mistake on Fiona's part. And while she was certain Annabel would try not to hold it against her, she was mortified.

Her pulse rate rose steadily as she climbed the stairs back to the office. It was a struggle too, given that her arms were heavily laden and she was almost about to lose her grip. When the shopkeeper had offered her a plastic bag, the answer had been immediate.

'Don't you have any paper ones?' she'd snapped at the poor woman.

'We do, but they're too small for all you've got there. You're going to need a bigger one.'

'Can I just have three paper ones?'

'They'll probably just break. You're better off getting one of the plastic ones. That would be better.'

'Forget it, I'll manage without,' she had replied and loaded herself up. This was why people hated doing things to save the planet. It was too damn inconvenient.

Crossing the small distance between the top of the stairs and Annabel's desk felt more like a Walk of Shame than she'd experienced earlier in the week. When she reached it, her assistant lifted her face and smiled meekly, meeting her gaze with red-rimmed eyes.

'I'm ever so—'

'Don't you dare.' Fiona caught her before she started. 'It was on me. That was all me. I'm sorry.'

'I shouldn't have questioned—'

'You were perfectly within your rights. You were.'

'No, I shouldn't have.'

Fiona's face hardened. 'You need to stop apologising now,' she said. 'Or you will actually make me lose it again.'

A small smile flickered on Annabel's lips, before she looked towards the objects in Fiona's arms, at which point, her eyes almost popped.

'Are they...?'

'Harry Potter? Yes. Limited edition. All seven books.'

'They're, they're...' Annabel could barely string two words together.

'They're for you. By way of an apology.'

From the lack of reaction, Fiona started to wonder if she'd been off base with the gift, until Annabel suddenly leapt at her and grabbed her in her arms.

'Seriously?' The excited girl stepped back, shaking her head. 'No, I can't. You can't. This is too much.'

'No, it's exactly right.' Fiona put the books down on the desk and gave her arm muscles a good stretch. Carrying seven of any book would be hard work, but some of those volumes were huge. 'One book for each year you've worked with me. That's the perfect calculation by my count.'

'But I've only been here five years.'

'Think of them as books in lieu, then. Besides, you may end up needing to sell them, at this rate. I'm not too sure there's going to be as much in the end-of-year bonus this year as we hoped.'

'Why?' Annabel's expression changed. 'What's happened?'

'Well. Let's just say Octavia wasn't too happy with my proposals. And, as much as I like to think she won't, there's a fair chance she'll go running to her uncle about it. In which case, we might find ourselves in a spot of trouble.'

A shift in Annabel's gaze told her what she'd been fearing.

'He's rung, hasn't he?'

'Quite a few times.'

'Crap.'

'And I think he called your mobile too. I heard it ringing in your office.'

Fiona rubbed her hands against the tops of her thighs.

'Okay.' She sucked in a lungful of air. 'I'll deal with this. I'll sort it. Dominic and I have worked together long enough. I just need to talk to him.'

She was about to go to her office when she noticed how Annabel was staring at her, chewing on the inside of her mouth, as if she had a question she wanted to ask, but was now too worried to mention.

'What is it?' she asked. 'Has he already said something to you?'

'No,' she shook her head. 'Well, yes, he said he was mad, but no, it wasn't that.'

'Then what is it?'

She still looked worried.

'Honestly, you can tell me.'

'It's probably none of my business. I don't want to interfere.'

'Annabel,' Fiona growled.

The younger woman took a deep breath. 'It's only that, yesterday, when you were away...' She hesitated again.

'Annabel!'

'Well, I went to get my lunch from that little burrito place. You know the one. I really like it. But when I got there, I saw that he was there too. Stephen, I mean. And, well, it looked like he was—'

'He was with another woman,' Fiona said, finishing the sentence and saving Annabel the embarrassment of having to go on.

She nodded.

Fiona was silent. She hadn't even contemplated telling anyone besides Holly what was going on with Stephen. But if he was going public with this woman... Trust him not to make things easy.

'And then I thought about the fact that you didn't go to Brussels,' Annabel continued. 'And it was meant to be for your anniversary and everything and I just wondered if... Well, if...'

'If Stephen had left me? Yes. Yes, he has. He went straight after Joseph went to university. Said he'd met someone else. He's already given me the divorce papers to sign.'

'What?'

Fiona tilted her head in a half shrug.

'So, this thing with Octavia Lovett-Rose—'

'Has nothing to do with it. Or, at least, I don't think it has. It's quite separate.' She nodded slowly. Actually, it was true. Stephen hadn't entered her mind once during her meeting with Octavia. Not like Martha. Martha had been in her thoughts the entire time.

Annabel's smile returned. It was still a little feeble, unsure around the eyes, but it was getting there.

'Well, I know you'll be able to put it right. You're a Superwoman.'

'I hope so,' she said. 'It should be fine. It was all just a misunderstanding. After all, Dominic's a businessman. He knows that sometimes, things can get a bit messy.'

She left Annabel excitedly stroking the covers on her new Harry Potter collection. Retrieving her phone, she discovered fourteen missed calls. All from Dominic. It didn't feel good, not good at all.

* * *

Shouting and swearing would have been substantially easier to deal with; it would have given her something to feed off, to push back against. But she should have known that men who were as successful and shrewd as Dominic didn't get that way by losing control. Instead, she was subjected to long pauses, interspersed with tuts, which reverberated down the line. At least it wasn't in person, she thought during another of the long silences. At least she didn't have to try to maintain eye contact with him. Not today at least. That would come later.

'There are business relationships and personal relationships, Fiona, but I always liked to think that what we had was a mixture of both.'

'I know. I think that too,' she agreed.

'And on every level where Octavia is concerned – she's my niece, my baby girl – that's as personal as it gets for me.'

'I understand. I do.'

'But your relationship with her is business. Strictly business. Some of the things she told me...' He sighed, causing her to shrink a little in her seat. It was as if she was back at primary school, being told off for stealing someone's milk. 'She is your client, Fiona. Or at least she was. Now, I don't know if what she told me was exaggerated in any way—'

'I suspect not,' she admitted, not wanting to hear any more, but knowing she didn't have a choice. 'I was 100 per cent out of line. I went about things in completely the wrong way. But I need you to know that my intentions were always in the right place.'

'Telling my niece that she's an entitled brat came from the right place?'

'*That* was not what I meant. Please, if you could give me time to explain in person. If I could show you why I was so passionate. I know passion is absolutely no excuse for the way I spoke to her but, please, if you could spare the time to hear me out, I feel it would go some way to explaining my actions. It might even turn out to be beneficial. For all of us.'

More silence.

'I'm not sure what my diary looks like,' he said, finally.

'How about tomorrow?' she offered, knowing she needed a little time to prepare. 'Any time you choose.'

'Fine,' he finally agreed. 'But I don't know when I'll be able to make it.'

'As I said, *any* time. I'll clear my schedule. I promise you won't regret it.'

'I'd better not, Fiona. I'd better not.'

A second later, the line went dead.

Fiona decided she had to go with the truth. It was the only option she had that would be anywhere near powerful enough to explain her faux pas.

As requested, Annabel got to work, once more clearing her schedule for the following day, while she worked on a presentation for Dominic. It was going to take some smooth talking to come back from this.

Unfortunately, researching how to set up environmentally friendly seminars and conference workshops proved somewhat of a rabbit hole. Every click of her mouse took her from one page full of data and information to another, all of which she devoured with a ferocity she couldn't remember since university days. Some of the facts, she discovered, were truly horrifying. A thousand dead dolphins off the coast of France in six months, caused by fishing boats. So many dead grey whales washed up that landfills were no longer accepting them, and landowners were being forced to leave them to rot on their shores.

Pushing the plunger on the cafetière, she reloaded the PowerPoint and started again from scratch. She'd wallowed in self-pity for long enough. Now, she was going to be the person who made a difference.

As she curled up under the blankets that evening, she was convinced that there was no way Dominic could ignore what she was trying to do. Not if he was half the man she hoped he was.

Being well aware that her biggest client was an early-morning person, she was in the office at six thirty, coffee brewed, ready and waiting.

At nine, there was still no sign of him. At eleven-fifteen, still nothing and she had to stop herself drinking a fourth cup of coffee. This was the problem with the new cafetière, she decided. When you used it, you felt obliged to drink it all.

'Do you want me to ring through to his office?' Annabel asked. 'They can at least tell me if he's still in the building.'

'No, it's fine. You managed to clear everything I had on, didn't you?'

'Yes, but—'

'Then it's fine. It's fine. We wait. He'll come at some point. He'll be here eventually.' She went back into her office and paced from one end to the other before returning.

'I need to go out,' she announced. 'I need some air.'

'But what if he comes when you're not here?'

'I'm only going downstairs. I'll see him.'

As it happens, she didn't even get that far. She was halfway down the staircase when, dressed in a deep-green suit, he appeared through the front door.

'Dominic.' She raced down to greet him, only realising a moment later that, in doing so, she had him pinned in the tiny entrance. She hopped backwards, making room for the door to close. The polite, handshake-slash-air-kiss that followed was awkward, bordering on cringe-worthy.

'I assume now is a good time?' he asked, an eyebrow raised. 'You weren't going out, were you?'

'No, no. Now is perfect,' she enthused, gliding back up the stairs, trying not to trip. 'Absolutely perfect.'

They must have made the ten-metre walk from the top of the stairs to her office together nearly a hundred times. And, on those occasions, they'd be chatting, usually about something work related: what events they each had coming up, how the previous event had gone. But, sometimes, it would be about something more personal: Stephen or Joseph's birthdays perhaps, or how Octavia was getting on at university, all those years ago when she'd just started. Not to mention holidays. That was a favourite topic. This time, however, they walked in silence. Only when they arrived at the door and she leaned forward to push it open for him did he speak.

'I'm assuming this won't take all afternoon,' he said. 'I have an appointment at three.'

'No, no,' she said, ushering him through, while trying to stifle the feeling of nausea that was currently engulfing her. 'Not at all.'

'Good luck,' Annabel mouthed, giving her a nervous thumbs up, as she closed the door behind them. This was it.

After opening both windows – the room had become inexplicably warm since her return with Dominic – she proceeded to take his coat and hang it up.

'Can I get you a coffee?' she asked. 'I've got some of that Jamaican blend you like so much. Although I'm using a cafetière now, as opposed to the machine.'

He didn't even honour the question with a shake of the head.

'I don't understand what happened, Fiona. You and I have

always had such a great relationship. And Octavia was over the moon about working with you.'

'I know. I know. I can only apologise and hope you'll let me explain.'

His eyes suggested some uncertainty, his tongue drawing a line across his lips. 'I don't know how to say this, I really don't.' The worry lines deepened. 'Are you okay?' he paused, before adding, 'Personally?'

'Oh. Have you heard about Stephen?'

There followed the look that she'd experienced the previous day from Annabel. It brimmed with concern and sympathy but this time also implied that, because her husband had left her for another woman, she was no longer capable of making rational decisions.

'I'll admit,' she said with an ironic smile. 'I didn't see it coming. How did you find out? The golf club?'

He gave a nod. She sighed wearily.

'And I guess they've known there for months, haven't they? Everyone having a good laugh at my expense.'

'I don't know about the others. I only found out last week. I imagine people were trying to stay schtum around me, because of how closely we work together.'

'How decent of them. Well, it's done now. He's made his bed. Which probably contains someone substantially younger than me.'

He scrutinised her. 'For what it's worth, no one is laughing at you. If anything, it's him and the damn workplace cliché they're laughing at.'

'So, it's the secretary then?'

He blushed ever so slightly at the slip.

'Don't worry,' she said. 'I had guessed as much.'

A moment passed as she reflected on his words. It was a

cliché, he was right; the whole thing was. But that wasn't what this was about.

'Look, about Octavia—'

'Yes.' His demeanour altered, as if he had suddenly remembered the reason he was there. 'About that—'

'If you would give me a chance, please. I went about everything the wrong way, I really did. And maybe, just maybe, there was perhaps the slightest bitterness towards Stephen and weddings and whatnot playing some sort of mischief in there. But, honestly, I think if you'll listen to what I'm about to tell you, you'll understand why I suggested to Octavia that she make changes to her wedding. And why, perhaps, you'll consider making some similar changes to your own business too.'

He frowned. 'Okay, I'm listening,' he said.

Until that moment, the only person she'd divulged her secret link with Martha the whale to had been Professor Arkell, and that had only come about to avoid being arrested. But whether she wanted to or not, she had to share it now. Clenching and unclenching a fist, she brought the first image up on the screen.

'This is a picture of my son's sixth birthday party...' she started.

From there, she went through the whole sorry tale. Keeping the television on in the house when she was on her own to fill the void of Stephen and Joseph's absence. Learning about Martha, a mother, separated from her family and alone in the Thames. Researching more about whales. She talked about going down to the waterfront, when she'd first heard Martha was in distress – although, for obvious reasons, she skipped the part about ending up in bed with a twenty-five-year-old yoga teacher. Then it got to the bit about the death. About the stomach contents. About her role in it.

'It had never crossed my mind that I could be even part way responsible for something like that. We buy all these disposable items,' she said. 'Pens, plastic bags, plastic bottles. And in a hundred years, you'll be long gone but your water bottle is still going to be around. Maybe it will be recycled into another bottle and another, before it ends up as a plastic bag in the bottom of a massive landfill or washed out into the ocean, but it will still be here. At some point, somewhere along the line, something you have owned could end up being responsible for the death of an animal, and the only person to blame will be you.

'Sitting there, in that professor's office, I knew I didn't want to be part of it any more. I wanted to opt out. And I wanted to do everything I could to help other people opt out of it too. And if that meant telling Octavia that having two hundred rainbow-coloured balloons at her wedding was a bad idea, then what else could I do? I had to say something. I hope you understand.'

Despite her fears, she'd managed to hold back the tears during the presentation. It was only now that she'd finished, did she feel the familiar prickling sensation behind the eyes.

'I can't imagine,' he said, shaking his head in disbelief. 'I really can't imagine what you've been through.'

'You and me both.'

'I heard about the whale, obviously, but I would never have thought...'

'But that's the whole point, isn't it? We don't. We can't. We're all so detached from the process, it makes it impossible to believe that we could have any part to play in what happens a thousand miles from here. But the fact of the matter is, any of us could. That could have been any one of our plastic bags in there.'

A low hiss blew from his lips. 'I don't know what to say. I'll speak to Octavia. I don't know if she'll be willing to listen to you. If I'm honest, she's not exactly a forgive-and-forget type of girl, but I'll tell her. If you're all right with that.'

'There's no point in hiding it now,' she said.

He nodded. 'And, as for us.' His expression changed with a sigh as he made to leave. 'I don't know. I just don't know where we stand, to be frank. I would like to think we could continue working together. I really would. But that level of unprofession-alism, Fiona—'

'If you could just hold on for one more minute.' She stopped him with a hand. 'The thing is, there are a few more things I would like you to consider, too.'

20

She'd done the sob story part, got her voice heard, hopefully made her meltdown understandable. Now it was time for the business pitch.

'While governments aren't doing their jobs properly, it's up to companies like yours and mine to lead the way.' She brought up the next slide. 'This is the time to stand up and be counted as leaders, not only in in our field of work but on the impact it has on the environment too. You can buy trainers made from recycled sea plastic now. Sunglasses as well. We can be up there with these pioneers. We can be leading the way, showing how a green company should operate. I'm not talking about meat-free Mondays, or charging five pence for a plastic bag. I mean strip it back. Strip everything right back.' She paused. 'Take your event next month. How many of the delegates will have tablets, iPads, smartphones or some such?'

'Well, all of them I expect.'

'Yes, so do I. So why are Annabel and I filling goodie bags with paper pamphlets and plastic wallets with the day's schedule?' She didn't wait for an answer. 'How many of them own a pen?'

'Now you're being ridiculous.'

'Precisely!' She was starting to react like Annabel now, her body bouncing with excitement. 'It is ridiculous. What's the point of giving them something they already have, they don't need, and that's using precious resources to create, whilst damaging the planet when they dump it? I say we scrap it all. We scrap every piece of plastic, other than the chairs they're sitting on – for the moment, anyway!'

'You're not serious?'

'I am. We could send a notice out now, telling people that this is going to be the most environmentally friendly conference they've ever been to. We're not even going to provide them with plastic water bottles; they can bring their own refillable ones.'

Dominic's face pinched. 'I know what you're saying, I get it, but it won't work.'

'Why not?'

'Because,' he said, 'people have come to expect these things, you know they have. We have a certain standard to uphold. Do you know how much people talk about the quality of service we provide? And they're not just talking about the sessions and the personalised feedback. It's the whole package, including the goodies they pick up when they sign in. We offer a wellbeing service that's the height of luxury and we're the company that's setting the standard. That's the whole point of these conferences, isn't it?'

'But what if that wasn't the point? You trust your process, don't you?'

'You know I do,' he replied, brusquely.

'Then hear me out. How many companies have given you a branded pen or gadget over the years?'

'How many? I've no idea. Most of them, probably.'

'But which ones? That's what I want to know.'

'Well, probably every conference I've ever been to. All the hotels do, for a start.'

'Okay, which hotels?'

'*Which* hotels? All of them.'

'And you can remember each item? What it looked like? How it wrote, if it was a pen? Anything at all?'

Dominic steepled his fingers and rested his chin on them. Then recovered. 'That's not the point.'

'That's *exactly* the point! You don't remember who gave you what, when. Because you don't *care* about any of it. It had no personal, enduring significance. Just another piece of tat you discarded at some point, probably the next day.'

'I wouldn't say—'

'It's your *company* that sells itself. This amazing business you've built up from scratch. The online reviews. Word of mouth. They're what sell you. Your branding is your company and what you help people achieve. It's not some tacky plastic pen. That way of thinking is obsolete. Don't you see? That's why it's so important I have you to lead the way with me on this. You're better than that and you don't need it any more. That's why I'm asking you to jump on board with me here. I want to do it with you.'

That was it. She was done. Sitting back in her seat, she felt totally spent. Whatever the outcome, at least she knew she'd done her best. She'd given it her all, presented every useful fact she could come up with. Now it was up to him. It was on Dominic, a man who prided himself on his principles and putting his money where his mouth was.

'Maybe it's something we can start to look at next year,' he said eventually.

She frowned. 'Next year? No, it has to be this year. Next month. Your very next seminar. It's now or never.'

'People won't be expecting a change. This is something we need to prepare them for. We could consider launching it, maybe touching upon it at the next conference.'

She rubbed her eyes, as if clearing her vision would somehow make the things she was hearing make more sense.

'But I don't understand. Nothing has been finalised yet. All the orders can be cancelled.'

'I'm aware of that—'

'Then why? What's the point of sticking with it?'

'Because it's what people expect.'

She stared at the man in front of her.

'Then teach them to expect something different!'

'Fiona, it's not that simple.'

'It is. It really is. Look, if you give me the go ahead on this, you won't be disappointed. The next seminar will be a trailblazer.'

'I just don't feel we're ready.'

'But you will be after giving out a busload of rubbish?'

'Pardon?'

Her mouth was drying.

'I just don't understand you. I don't. I thought your whole line was *we give you the skills*? Not *we give you the rubbish*.'

'I can tell you're upset by my decision here, Fiona. But it's my final answer. We've got too many new themes we're bringing to the next meeting to throw in another one, on a whim.'

'On a whim. You think this is a whim?'

'Look, if you're still convinced about this at the end of the year, then maybe we could start discussing it more seriously then.'

'No.' The certainty in her voice came as a surprise even to

herself but, as soon as she had said it, she realised it was exactly what she had to say. And, as such, she said it again. 'No.'

'What do you mean, no?'

'I mean no.' She rose to her feet. 'I won't be doing next year, or even this year. I won't do any of it. The workshops, training days, Christmas parties. The lot. If I don't get to make this change and do it *now*, then I'm out.'

'Fiona.' Dominic's laugh was half threatening, half nervous. 'You can't be serious. We're your biggest client. I must provide half your revenue. You're honestly willing to throw all that away because you're having a crisis of conscience?'

With fists clenched, the consequences of her words flashed before her. She hadn't realised she was going to make the threat until it actually came out of her mouth. She hadn't thought that he would actually say no to her, after all the evidence she'd presented to him.

'Fiona,' his voice softened, 'I think you need to take a break. What with everything that's going on with Stephen. Why don't you give me a ring at the start of next month? When you've had a little time—'

'I don't need time,' she interrupted, her voice low but firm. 'And this is not about Stephen. I need people like you standing up. People like you pulling their heads out of their soft, money-stuffed arses so that we can achieve something together. That's what I need. And you're right. You're at least half my revenue. You leave and there's a good chance the company will fold. And that's going to hurt like hell. But I can live with that. The other option, I can't.'

The two of them were locked in stalemate and her mind roiled, yet seemed frozen at the same time. Her thoughts went to Annabel. There was no way she could keep her on full-time if

Dominic walked. But that was the fate of one person and, on the other hand, there was a whole planet that needed saving.

'I'm sorry, Fiona.' He levered himself out of his chair and reached a hand across to her. 'You really were a wonderful person to work with.'

21

Fiona poured herself a large scotch. It wasn't her drink of choice, but a couple of her clients had grown to expect it at meetings so she always kept a bottle or two on hand. Half the glass was gone when Annabel appeared at the door.

'What happened?' she asked. 'How did it go?'

She took another mouthful and let the warmth hit the back of her throat.

'Well, I thought it was going okay, but...' She had difficulty finishing the sentence.

'So what went wrong?' Annabel stepped inside the room. 'He didn't drop you? He couldn't possibly have dropped you?'

Her nod was infinitesimal, almost undetectable, even to herself.

'He said we could still do the seminar next month,' she added. Annabel dropped down into a chair.

'And after that?'

She filled another glass and handed it to her receptionist.

'I told him he could shove it.'

'You did what?'

'Uh-huh.' Having finished her drink, she moved to pour herself another, but stopped. She fetched another glass from the cabinet and opted for water instead. 'I told him I wouldn't – I couldn't – do what he wanted. So, he could shove it all.'

'So, what now? Where does that leave us?'

With a heavy heart, she looked at her assistant. The weight of the world seemed on her shoulders as she sank down in the chair opposite.

'I'm sorry,' Fiona said. 'I don't know what else to tell you. I considered backing down, but I couldn't. I just couldn't.'

A trembling started on Annabel's lips, which she quickly tried to hide. 'It's fine,' she said. 'You'll be fine. It was one company. That was all. You'll bounce back.'

Fiona glanced around at the room, the office, the little empire she'd built.

'You're going to be all right,' she said at last, in the most positive voice she could muster. 'You will. You're amazing and I'll give you an incredible reference and I've got contacts. I've still got plenty of friends. I'll find you something, don't worry. I'll start making calls tomorrow.'

Annabel paled. 'You're going to call it a day so soon? We've got other clients. Other events coming up.'

The sting of bile replaced the taste of whisky at the back of Fiona's throat.

'That's not the way it works,' she replied, only just starting to understand the full weight of her actions. 'Half our allure was that we work with VertX.'

'You don't believe that, surely?'

'Don't I? It's true. As soon as people hear Dominic's gone, they'll want to know why.'

'That doesn't mean they'll go too.'

'I wish I had your optimism.'

Annabel stood up from her chair and placed her hands on her hips.

'People want to work with you because you're *you*. Because you're amazing at what you do. So what if we're not in some fancy office for a few months? What does that matter? We can use your house as an office. Sod it, we could use my flat. It costs enough to rent the damn thing. And there's plenty of room, if you don't mind sharing with Hedwig.'

'Hedwig?'

'My cat.'

Fiona smiled sadly.

'That's so sweet of you to offer,' she said, nearly in tears. 'You should go home. Honestly, take the afternoon off. No one's coming in now; we cleared the diary. And there's nothing for you to do here, except watch me mope.'

'I've got some filing I ca—'

'Please,' she took her hands. 'Please go home.'

Annabel nodded.

* * *

First silence in the house, now in the office. Fiona had always thought herself a person who liked her own space, who enjoyed the luxury that came with having no guests to entertain or others to consider but now that she found herself seemingly all at sea on a solo journey, it felt even lonelier than before.

Twice she tried calling Holly. Twice it went to voicemail. She waited half an hour and tried again. Success.

'Fi? Is everything all right?' Holly had the now-familiar tone of panic in her voice. 'What's happened?'

Fiona considered the possible ways of answering truthfully and discarded them all. 'I was just wondering what you were up to, that's all. Whether you wanted to catch a film together or something?'

A throat clearing was followed by a slight pause.

'I would, I mean I can, of course, if you need me. It's just, I'm on that date. With Jim, from yoga. Remember?'

'That's today?'

'Well actually, it was last night. But it's been going remarkably well.'

Fiona responded with a sad half-laugh. 'Sorry, I'll let you get back to him.'

'Not if it's important. Honestly, he's great. He'd completely understand. He probably needs a break, actually.'

'No,' she said, with added certainty in her voice. 'If he's that great, then you absolutely have to stay. Honestly, I'm fine. Better than fine. I was just ringing to catch up, that's all.'

Another pause indicated uncertainty.

'You're sure?'

'I'm positive. Go, enjoy yourself. And make sure you fill me in later with all the details, okay? I want to know everything. Maybe we could do lunch some time.'

'Lunch sounds good. I love you, sweetie.'

'I love you too.'

She hung up. A simple silence had been replaced by a humongous, impenetrable vacuum. This was it. This was her life now. A business on the brink. A family disintegrating. Just her and her lonely existence.

She reached again for her phone and flicked to Joseph's name. She needed to hear his voice. Just hearing him call her 'Mum' would put everything right again. Her finger hovered over the dial button. She dropped the phone. This wasn't her.

She wasn't going to be the sad person who relied on their child for emotional support. This was her mess, after all. Even Stephen's affair she should have seen coming, if she'd kept her eyes open. It certainly shouldn't have blindsided her like it had. It all came down to her. And she wasn't going to inflict herself on anyone else. It would have just been nice if she could have had someone to talk to about it.

* * *

A little bell tinkled above her head, as she stepped through the café doorway.

'Sorry, we closed at six.' He didn't turn around from the table he was wiping down.

'But the door was unlocked.'

'I was just doing a bit of tidying. We're open tomorrow at— oh.' He stopped mid-turn, eyes wide with surprise. 'This is unexpected.'

'Well, I realised I've gone off without paying for two coffees now. I didn't want you to think I'm a serial cadger.'

'The second one was just instant, not a proper coffee.'

'True, all right then, so just one.'

A smile curled up at the corners of his mouth.

'I guess that's pretty honest of you. But the till's already cashed up, so you'll have to come back another day to pay your debts.'

'I guess that means the coffee's off too?'

'In here it is.' He grinned. 'Just give me a second.'

While he finished something behind the counter, she took the time to observe her surroundings. Perhaps she'd been a little harsh about the aesthetics when she was last here. There was a certain allure to the place. The ambience was gentle and understated, even if it did smell of wheatgrass.

'Right,' he said, wiping his hands on what looked like a hessian sack. 'That's me done. Just need to head back to the shop.'

She had a sudden attack of nerves. When she'd left her office, with the sun starting its descent, this had felt like the perfect place to head to. The only place she could think of, in fact. Now she was here, it very much looked like she was about to impose on someone who was a virtual stranger.

'Do you know what? I'll just leave you the money. It's fine. I shouldn't be disturbing you.'

'You're not.'

'But you're busy.'

'Says who?'

'Well you look busy.'

'Do I?' He shrugged. 'I'm not. In fact, I was trying to make a concerted effort not to be busy. That's why I closed early. You hungry?'

'I... well...' Her attempt to escape had been scuppered.

'Great. Like I said, we just need to pop to the shop.'

He opened the front door, causing the little bell to jingle again.

'My name's Rory, by the way. I thought I should tell you, given that I've just invited you to my flat, which is not something I tend to do with people until I learn their first name.'

'Your flat?'

'Is that a problem?'

She took a moment to study him. There had been a time when she'd considered herself a good judge of character. Sure, Stephen was never perfect, but there had been a lot of good in there. Generally, she hit the nail on the head when it came to clients too. And while she wasn't – recent evidence notwithstanding – in the habit of following young men to their apartments, something about him was different.

'Fiona,' she said.

With a grin, he opened the door wider.

'After you,' he said.

22

She used the short walk across the road to Rory's shop to try and learn a fraction more about him. Not that she really knew much to start with.

'So, you run both these places?' she asked, as they waited for a break in the traffic. 'That must be a lot of pressure.'

'Not really. They complement each other. Besides, it gives me the chance of a bit of respite now and then. If the café is driving me mad, I can always change the rota and do a couple of days behind the till in the shop. Although I do have a pretty good team. They make the job a lot easier than it might be. Most of the time anyway.'

'And your flat?'

'Is above the shop.'

'Very convenient.'

'Isn't it just?' He grinned. They crossed the road side by side, her head whirring with preconceptions. With his long hair and currently ripped clothing, she felt anything could be awaiting her. Marijuana plants. That one sprung straight to mind. She contemplated it for a moment. It had been a long while since she'd been stoned – before meeting Stephen, even. But it was hardly going to make her week any more bizarre. Perhaps it was what she needed, in fact. There would likely be lots of hand-made rugs and throws around the place too. Batik patterns, or else tie-dyes that he'd collected on his journey around Asia. He certainly looked like the type of person who went travelling as opposed to holidaying.

'Okay, just let me grab some stuff from here.' He unlocked the door and held it open for her to step through. 'Then we'll go upstairs.'

After a minute selecting things from the shelves, he led her through a door at the back and up a staircase.

'Next floor I'm afraid,' he said on the first landing. 'This one's all stock.'

When he reached the top, he turned the key in the lock and pushed the door open.

'So, welcome to the man cave,' he said.

The apartment that she entered was about as far from a man cave as she could possibly have imagined. So much so that she could barely stop herself from staring.

'You live here?' she asked.

'I do indeed.'

With the grin of someone who knew he had made an impression, Rory closed the door and took her coat. 'Come on. I'll give you the tour. Although there's really not that much to it.'

It was both the complete truth and an utter lie. She stared around her, mesmerised. With its minimalistic style, it reminded her of the entrance to the Marine Life and Conservation Institute, although it felt much warmer than that. Far from cold and uninviting, as such an open space should be, she found herself immersed in the glow of pink-tinted sunlight diffusing through the windows, causing everything it touched to shimmer slightly.

'I'll be honest,' he said, leading her into the combined kitchen and living area. 'It's been a long time getting here. Sourcing this glass for the windows was an absolute nightmare for a start and the Council delayed approving it for ages, but I think it's worth it.'

'You designed this?' she said, moving past a worktop to look through an entire wall of glass. The view was of rooftops, hundreds of them, and tiled terraces. It reminded her of a scene from *Mary Poppins*: a whole secret world that no one down below knew about, stretching out for miles.

'I would say I had the vision,' he replied, in answer to her question. 'It was a genius architect friend who designed it. Drink?'

She nodded. A minute later, a glass appeared. Breaking her gaze for the first time since she'd arrived, she turned to thank him. He grinned sheepishly.

'What?' she asked, feeling that she'd missed out on a joke somehow. His smile broadened. 'What?'

'You haven't even seen the best bit yet.'

* * *

'You have an allotment!' She found herself amazed yet again. 'You have an actual allotment on your roof!'

'I do.'

'And you can grow things here?'

'It certainly appears that way.'

She had seen plenty of roof gardens in her time. Some of her friends from the golf club days had lovely balconies which they decorated with planters and fairy lights. Even her mother, in the flat she'd lived in before she went into the home, had always had begonias and pansies on her terrace. But this wasn't a few terracotta pots or ornamental roses. By the look of it, nothing was ornamental.

'I'm going to be honest. It's taken a lot of patience to get it this way. And I started a fair-few things off in the greenhouse at the café first.'

'The café has a greenhouse?'

He shook his head and laughed. 'Did you not read anything about the place before you came?' He picked a leaf from one of the herbs and rubbed it between his fingers, inhaling the scent. 'Lemon balm,' he said, holding his hands out to her. The citrus aroma filled the air between them.

'So, what have you got up here? Tomatoes, right? What else?'

'Yeah, the tomatoes have been great this year, so have the carrots. Courgettes are always a winner, although my potatoes have turned out a bit lacklustre. Not sure why. Need to look into it.'

'And you use all this down in the shop? This is what you sell?'

'No,' he said. 'I take down some herbs occasionally, when we're running a bit short but, mainly, this is just for me. My little indulgence.'

'It's hardly little.'

He looked at her pointedly, raising his eyebrows.

'Really?' She slapped him on the shoulder and shot him a look that caused him to erupt into laughter.

'Right, I'm starving. You okay to grab me some salad bits while I sort out what's in the fridge?'

Without waiting for an answer, he disappeared back into the

flat, leaving her alone on the roof top, apparently with a job to do.

It was hardly the first time she had picked food straight from a plant. When Joseph was younger, they would often head out in the summer to a pick-your-own place. She'd never found it the most practical use of her time. Not to mention the fact that they could get all the food they needed, chopped and freshly prepared, thanks to Stephen's job at Alton Foods. Still, picking strawberries and raspberries was something Joseph had enjoyed, and she had indulged him. Salad was a whole other matter.

'How do I know if it's edible?' she called into the flat, her hand around what she thought was a lettuce, but could just as easily have been a variety of poison ivy. She would have had no idea either way.

'If it's out there, we can eat it,' he shouted back. 'Except the Monkshood.'

'How do I know which that is?' she asked, quickly letting go of the bundle of leaves.

A burst of laughter was followed by his head appearing through one of the glass doors. 'I'm pulling your leg. Everything's fine. The rocket is in that one.' He pointed to a wooden planter on the edge of the terrace. 'And there are mustard leaves in the next one along. Just grab a couple of tomatoes. I've got a few things from the café that need using up too, so that should do us just fine.'

Until the comment about the café, and that fact that she was about to eat food that had come from it, she had forgotten all about the menu with dumpster-diving credentials. She swallowed nervously as she gathered the rest of the things and headed back inside.

'When you say from the café,' she said, placing the items in the colander waiting in the sink, 'are you talking about leftover food, in the sense that it's perfectly fresh, but unwanted? Or are you talking leftovers in a past-their-sell-by-date-and-pulled-out-of-Tesco's-rubbish-bin-probably-going-to-give-me-food-poisoning kind of way? I feel I should be warned first.'

On the hob, a pan sizzled with oil. Turning the dial down, Rory looked at her.

'Okay, if you and I are going to be friends then we need to get a few things cleared up first, because you obviously have a bee in your bonnet about this whole waste-food thing.'

'I just don't want to be eating something dodgy, that's all. And who said anything about becoming friends?'

This time, the hob went off entirely.

'Right, sit down,' he said.

'But—'

'Sit down. You are going to have a lesson, right now.'

Pouting at the assumption that she needed lessons in anything, particularly from a man who looked like he probably still owned a skateboard, she placed her hands on her hips.

'Hold o—'

'And there's to be no interrupting—'

'But—'

'I mean it. No interrupting. You can speak when I ask you a question. Or you can wait for me to finish. But I mean it. You need to listen. God knows I listened to you enough yesterday.'

Her mouth fell open and then snapped shut. 'Fine,' she said. 'But if I don't like what I hear, I'm not going to eat.'

'I don't expect you to like what you hear, and if you don't want to eat my food, just don't expect a second invitation.'

While she sank down onto the grey sofa – feeling remarkably like a child who'd been scolded at school for merely speaking their mind – Rory busied himself in the kitchen.

'What are you doing?' she asked when, two minutes later, he was still bustling away, pulling items out of the fridge and placing them onto plates. 'I thought you were going to give me a lesson?'

'I am. Right now. So come and sit at the table,' he told her.

An audible growl came from her stomach as she crossed the room to what wasn't exactly what she would consider a dining-room table, by any stretch, more like a small piece of patio furniture. Although there wasn't really room for much else and it did suit the place, in its own unique way.

'Okay,' he said, pulling out a seat and indicating for her to do the same. 'Your personal lesson in waste food. Now, first, I want you to take a look at one of those peaches,' he indicated four sitting in a small bowl, 'and I want you to tell me what's wrong with them.'

'There's something wrong with them?'

'That's what I want you to tell me.'

Sensing there was more to this game than he was letting on, she ignored the one on the top and instead went for one that was tucked away underneath.

'Okay, what's wrong with it?' he asked.

Trying to pay no mind to the grumbling in her stomach, she turned the peach over in her hand, absorbing the smell that rose from it. Her mother had always adored peaches. Whenever they came into season, she would buy them by the dozen. In fact, when Fiona had moved out, she determined never to eat one again. Now, as the soft flesh yielded beneath her fingers and her mouth watered at the aroma, she wondered why on earth she would have done such a stupid thing.

'So, have you spotted what's wrong with it?'

Drifting back from her daydream, she studied the fruit in her hand. It was certainly a perfect peach colour. There were no bruises or anything that she could see, but then she couldn't tell what the inside was like.

'Here,' he said, taking it from her and twisting it over. 'See that mark?' He pointed to a rougher area of skin, no bigger than a centimetre in length, that she hadn't even noticed.

'What does that mean?' she asked.

'Mean? Nothing. Absolutely nothing. But supermarkets won't take it, because it's not perfect.'

'You're not serious?'

'I'm absolutely serious. And these...' he put the first one back and picked another two out, '...were too big.'

'Too big?'

'Yup, you know those little trays that the fruit sit in, at the supermarket? It's shipped in them too. That means if a piece of fruit is even a tiny bit too big, they can't pack it properly with all the rest. Which means they can't sell it, which means in most cases it gets discarded.'

'You're kidding me?'

'I'm not. And we're not talking about throwing out one or two items here. We're talking two or three tonnes.

'Okay, how about this?' He handed her a pack of blueberries.

A familiar uneasiness crept in at the sight of their plastic container. Perhaps she'd developed an allergic reaction, she thought. Was that even possible? She sniffed and focused on the new specimen.

'Well, it's not the date. That looks fine.'

'Good, so you're happy enough that I'm not going to serve you rotten food.'

'I wouldn't say that.'

His grin returned. 'Okay, come on then. What is it?'

Having lost on the peaches, she was determined to spot this one. She turned the package over and over, hoping for a clue.

'The weight?' she asked. It felt fairly light. 'Maybe it doesn't have enough in it.'

He cocked his head to the side, seeming impressed with her powers of deduction. 'Good try. I like it. But, no, you're wrong,' he said, dashing her short-lived hopes.

'Okay then, what is it?'

'It's the label,' he said. 'Notice how the ink's not clear on one side?'

'People would throw out food because of that?'

'Big companies do.'

'But surely you could just peel it off. Stick another label on.'

'You'd think, right? But it takes too much time. *Time is money*,' he intoned. 'I've got eight whole boxes of organic chocolate in the pantry at the café. That's a hundred and sixty bars, all thrown in the back of a dumpster because they forgot to translate the ingredients into English.'

'You're making this up.'

'I wish I was. It's horrendous. Like, crazy. I swear, you wouldn't believe the scale of some of it.'

'But, why don't people do something?'

'Who? Either people don't know, or they do know but ignore it, because it's too much hassle.'

She shook her head. Anger was building inside her. Plastic. Food waste. Everywhere she turned, it felt like people were determined to find another way to screw the planet. And she'd been one of them.

'So, this is where you get your food from, then? From companies who've messed up the labels?'

'Occasionally. Mostly, it comes from supermarkets and other restaurants. When new stock comes in and they're out of space, they clear the older stuff out. Or when one of the big restaurants overorders on something.'

'You just ring them up and ask?'

'I used to. Now I just drive around in the mornings. As places are opening up. They usually have stuff ready and waiting for me. Then I head back to the café and sort out the menu, depending on what I get.'

'What if you don't get anything?' She envisioned a menu board offering nothing but bars of organic chocolate.

He laughed at the irony of her question.

'Trust me, that never happens. Anyway.' He stood up, bundling the fruit from the table. 'We need to get eating. I'm starving.'

23

Had it not been for the darkening room, as daylight gradually faded, Fiona wouldn't have realised how much time had passed listening to Rory, more relaxed than she had felt in days. The home-brewed kombucha had helped. (She hadn't realised what she was drinking until after she'd finished the first glass and, by that time, she'd got a taste for it.) More probably it was the effect of being with someone who had no expectations of her.

'So, what do you think?' he'd asked, after they'd finished their meal. They'd had a burger with their salad, followed by a peach cobbler, served with home-made ice cream – made from surplus milk.

'Of the food?'

'Of everything. From what I remember, you were pretty dubious the first time you came to the café.'

'You don't remember that.'

'Really?' His eyebrows rose. 'Cappuccino with *milk* milk. No food. You were pretty hard to forget.'

'God, I must have sounded like an idiot.'

'Yeah, you did.' Sitting back in his chair, his eyes narrowed. 'So, come on then.'

'Come on what?' she asked.

'What about you? You've listened to me talk for hours. Literally. And you've said absolutely nothing about yourself.'

'That's not true.'

'It is. Other than the fact that you'd never had kombucha before which, to be honest, I could have guessed. So, what is it? There's obviously something going on. Something about you I should know.'

Avoiding his gaze, she fiddled with the tablecloth.

'Why do you say that? Perhaps I'm just the type of person who likes to listen.'

'No, you're not.' He smiled wryly.

'Okay, well, maybe I'm the type of person who is trying to be the type of person who likes listening.'

He angled his head to the side. 'Well, my intuition is usually pretty good. And I would say you're deliberately avoiding talking about yourself because you feel vulnerable.'

'Is that so?'

'Now if I were to hazard a guess, I would say that maybe it has something to do with your husband or perhaps with whatever I said about that whale.'

'Martha,' she replied reflexively. 'Her name was Martha.'

'Right. So whale trumps husband, does it? Interesting.'

She ran her tongue against her top teeth. As much as she hated to admit it, he was right. For the last couple of hours, since she'd arrived at Rory's, Stephen hadn't entered her thoughts.

'My husband and I are having difficulties,' she said, deciding to divulge what she was coming to realise was an understatement.

'But it's not over?'

'What makes you say that?'

'Well, you're still wearing your rings.'

She glanced down at her hand, as if surprised to find them there.

'The engagement ring was my mother's,' she told him. 'I wouldn't take it off because of him.'

'And the wedding ring?'

Pausing, she held the white-gold band between her fingers and twisted it around. There was nothing special about it, except for a dent, where she'd once caught it, painfully, on a door handle. She'd probably have a hard time telling it apart from any other of the same size and colour. But it meant something. It had meant everything. It meant that he had said forever.

'Sorry.' Rory stretched over and took her plate. 'I didn't mean to get so personal. Forget I said anything. You don't have to tell me anything.'

'It's not that I don't want to...' she surprised herself by saying. 'It's just... I don't know.'

He nodded understandingly. 'I get it,' he said. 'And the whale, is it too soon to talk about that too?'

She nodded. 'Like you said, whale trumps husband.'

They moved to the sofa for coffee and their conversation took a small detour through travel experiences and film culture. He had been to India, thus allowing her to feel vindicated in her earlier thoughts about tie-dyed blankets and batiks.

Just before nine, he stood up and picked up the cups.

'I don't want to appear rude,' he said. 'But I've got to be up at four.'

'Four? Why?'

'Supermarkets. Have to be there before any refuse trucks arrive, remember?'

'And that means getting up at four?'

'It does. Of course, you're welcome to join me if you'd like to?'

She cocked her head. 'Maybe another time.'

He smiled. 'Another time then.'

He fetched her coat and opened the door. There was no goodbye kiss, or lingering hug, merely a peck on the cheek, one side only.

She was two steps down the stairs when he called after her.

'Do you want my number?' he asked. 'You know, so you can ring me up the next time you're having a meltdown, rather than coming into my shop and terrifying all my customers.'

'Now where's the fun in that?' she asked. 'Besides, I know where to find you if I want you.'

* * *

The next morning, she awoke with a clear head. Something felt different as she stretched out, only to recoil at the cold, untouched part of the bedclothes. Opening her eyes, she stared at the ceiling until she realised what it was. The television. She must have forgotten to turn it on when she got home last night. Expecting the silence to cause another panic, she kicked off the duvet and made a grab for the remote, only to hesitate. Outside, a bird was chirping. Several birds in fact. It wasn't the most pleasant song: shrill and high pitched. But still, it was birdsong. She lowered the remote and continued to listen, until the clock in the hall told her it was time to get moving. Heading downstairs, she fixed herself a coffee. It was going to be a good day.

* * *

It was not a good day.

Still humming, with an air of optimism, she had barely stepped into the office when she caught sight of Annabel's ashen complexion.

'What is it?' she asked. 'What's happened? Is it VertX?'

Annabel shook her head, her glasses wobbling on her nose.

'No,' she replied. 'It's another one. One of the recruitment agencies.'

'Shit,' she said, heading for her desk to check her emails.

It was no surprise. One of Dominic's closest business associates and, if she remembered correctly, Octavia's godmother, had bailed. Still, she'd hoped she'd have a little more time. The chance to invite them in, explain her new vision and get them on side before they heard any rumours.

Naturally, there was a range of reasons given, none of which included the exact words, *you completely lost your shit with one of London's most-beloved socialites and for some reason also decided to sabotage your relationship with your biggest client*, but she could read between the lines. Instead, the message said things like, *taking our business in a different direction* and *cutting back due to other developments*.

'Wimps,' she told the computer. 'The least they could have done was be honest about it.' Still, it was only one company. She had a dozen more on her books.

By lunchtime, yet another email had arrived, from a second company apparently *going in a different direction*. She picked up the phone and began making calls.

'You need to eat something,' Annabel said when, at 3 p.m., Fiona was still busy talking to clients, informing them that while, yes, what they may have heard about the changes she was making was true, she was still there to service all their needs and more; in fact, they had the opportunity to be in at the start of something brilliant. She used all the best lines from her presentation to Dominic, which she honed and refined as she went and, by the fifth call, was even selling it to herself.

'How do you think it's going?' Annabel asked, when Fiona had ignored the question about food. 'Do you think it's making a difference?'

'Well, I definitely don't think it's hurting. So that's got to be good, right?'

'Right. And food? I was going to go to that noodle place. The one that does the mee goreng you like?'

Stretching her head back and then to the sides, she let out a groan.

'It's fine,' she said. 'I'm not going to stay here much longer. There's nothing I can do until I know whether people are staying with me or not.'

'Are you sure?'

'I'm sure. You might as well head off too. I don't expect tomorrow is going to be any more fun than today.'

* * *

Back home, Fiona sat down with a plate of scrambled eggs and went through the figures. She wasn't going to be immediately destitute. The issue was whether or not she would be pouring money down the drain, fighting to keep the business afloat. In which case, would she be better off just packing up altogether? She had to be realistic. Yes, when Stephen finally pulled his head out of his arse and came back, he would be able to handle all the household bills, and Joseph's university expenses too, but did she really want to be beholden to him? And did she even know who she would be beholden to? The way he had spoken to her before he left was like he was an entirely different person to the one she had married. Had he really changed that greatly, and if so, why hadn't she seen it happening? There were too many questions she simply didn't have the answers to and so pushing thoughts of Stephen out of her head, Fiona returned to mulling over the numbers in front of her.

At the end of the calculations, she came to the decision that she could just about afford to lose one more company from her list. That was what it came down to. If she lost more than one – or maybe two of the smaller ones – she wouldn't be able to keep her head above water, which would necessitate having to let Annabel go, too. She had to make sure that didn't happen.

24

'So, what does that mean?' Annabel asked.

It was just after eleven when the email Fiona had been dreading came through. This time from OnLearn, only a smallish company, but one of her longest-serving clients. All those years of loyalty, gone in an instant. Once again *restructuring* and *sincere apologies* had been offered.

She picked up her phone and messaged Holly.

Lunch?

A message consisting of six smiley-faced emojis pinged back to her.

Great. My choice?

* * *

'Why on earth are we meeting here?' Holly asked as she pecked Fiona on the cheek. 'I thought you hated this place.'

'You said the food was good.'

'When did you ever listen to my opinion?'

Chuckling, she pushed open the door. 'Besides,' she said. 'I need to pay for a coffee. So, tell me, how did the date go?'

An unabridged account, including details that she really didn't need to hear, came spilling from Holly's mouth. Fortunately, Fiona was only half listening. She'd deliberately walked straight past the shop first and, on seeing an older man with grey hair at the counter, had felt her heart flutter a little. If someone else was working there, chances were that Rory would be in the café.

A minute or so after taking their seats, the kitchen door swung open and he appeared, arms laden with plates. His faced cracked into a smile when he saw her.

'Here again so soon?' he asked, placing the plates behind the counter.

'I told you, I need to pay for that coffee.'

'And I told you, you don't.'

It was a ridiculous idea coming here, she thought, as she picked up the drinks menu. She didn't know what she was trying to prove. Or who she was trying to prove it to. Only that this was the one place she thought would help clear her mind of worry for an hour.

'Right,' she said, sitting up straighter in her chair. 'We came for food. You want to eat, right, Holly?' Then she turned her attention back to Rory. 'What would you recommend for us today?'

He frowned and looked around the café. There were two other people working out front that she could see: once again, the man with the neck tattoos and the girl who looked like she'd just heard her dog had been run over. Together they were dealing with the dozen or so customers, half of which were already eating.

'It's pretty quiet,' he said. 'How about I make you ladies something off menu?'

'Off menu?' she asked.

'Yeah. Something a bit different to our normal fare.'

'And you are going to let us pay for this.'

'Well, I'm—'

'It wasn't a question,' she interrupted.

His smile spread.

'Okay then, sit tight.'

With a grin firmly in place, he headed back through the kitchen door.

'Okaaay,' Holly drawled. 'What the hell was that?'

'What was what?'

'What do you mean, *what was what*? You? And him? And that? You refused to eat here only a week ago.'

'Well, I've learned a lot since then. Besides, he cooked me dinner last night. In his flat.'

The expression on Holly's face as her jaw literally dropped was enough to make Fiona laugh out loud.

'Not like that. I'd had a bad day. He was there.'

'And he cooked you dinner last night? Fiona, what is this? Who are you? What about Stephen?' She paused, eyes widening even further. 'Tell me you got his name first this time.'

Fiona swiped at her across the table.

'It wasn't like that. It isn't. And as for Stephen...' She considered how to word the feelings that had been swimming around her head all morning. Instead, she simply lifted her shoulders and dropped them with a sigh. 'Last night, Rory and I just talked. We talked for hours and I didn't even notice the time passing. I didn't feel the need to check my phone or reply to an email, or think about the hundreds of other things I should be doing instead.'

'So, you actually *like* him.' Holly was having more and more difficulty believing what she was hearing.

'No. Well, yes. Maybe. I don't know. That's not the point. The point is, I can't remember the last time Stephen and I were like that together. I really can't. Even when we went on holiday, we were always rushing about. Yacht trips, fancy restaurants, you name it. And all the while, he would be on the phone to that damn boss of his. It was all about seeing things and doing things and ticking boxes, never just sitting and enjoying each other's company. I've finally come to realise that maybe our relationship has been gradually dying for years.'

'And you don't want to try to – I don't know – resuscitate it?'

She tilted her head from side to side. Hesitation was all she could offer.

'Wow.' Holly sat back in her seat, looking both moderately impressed and shocked at the same time. 'You've thought a lot about this, haven't you?'

'It's amazing how much time you have when you sabotage your own company and lose all your biggest clients.'

'*What?*' This time, the expression was pure disbelief.

'I might as well tell you that story too. Everyone else seems to be finding out.' She waved the tattooed girl over for a *milk* milk cappuccino and started at the beginning.

She'd got to the part where Professor Arkell stopped her from being arrested when Rory appeared with two small plates, tendrils of steam spiralling up from them.

'Course number one.' He placed the dishes in front of them and stepped back. 'Roasted artichokes with sea truffle and saffron foam. Served with shredded baby pak choi.'

'Where the hell did you rescue sea truffles from?' Fiona asked in disbelief.

He tapped the side of his nose. 'All collected this morning,' he said. 'Well, most of it. Let me know what you think.'

As he left, Holly leaned in. 'Any chance the next person you start dating could be a jeweller?' she asked. 'Or a chocolatier? I'd definitely be open to a master confectioner.'

'Shut up. We are definitely not dating. Besides, you don't even know what it tastes like yet.'

'Like a mouth orgasm, I'm willing to bet.'

'That's the most disgusting phrase I've ever heard. Be quiet and eat your food.'

Despite the vulgarity of Holly's vernacular, there was no denying that her words were an apt description for the experience that followed the first bite.

'Good God. Did he say how much we're getting?' Holly asked, as she finished the food with her second forkful. 'Because, as amazing as it is, I'm going to need about thirty courses, if they're all this size.'

After the artichokes came a salmon raviolo – singular – with fennel cream and turnip gratin that, despite sounding horrible, was once again divine.

Next was braised duck, with baby shallots and asparagus.

'There's no way this is waste,' Fiona said to him, her knife and fork ready before the plate was even on the table.

'Big wedding at one of the hotels got cancelled. Bride changed her mind the morning of, apparently.'

'You know, I'd like to feel sorry for her,' Holly mumbled through a mouthful. 'But this is too good to waste on regrets.'

'So they just gave it to you?' Fiona asked, still amazed that what she was eating could be served up in a place called The Dumpster Dive.

'I paid them,' he said. 'But not a lot. What else are they going to do with it? There's no way they would get through it all themselves.'

Mouthful by mouthful, they finished their plates.

'Dessert's going to be a little while,' he said, clearing away. 'So, what do you think so far?'

'Marry me,' Holly replied. 'Marry me and we'll run away to a beach where you can spend all day foraging and cooking me scallops and coconuts to my heart's content.'

'It's a nice idea,' he laughed. 'Although I do have two businesses to run.' His attention came back quickly to Fiona. 'And you?' he asked. 'What did you think?'

She moved her gaze from Rory to the tabletop, to the blackboard and back again.

'Why aren't you offering this?' she asked. 'Why is this not on your menu? Why is it pasta and burgers and whatnot? People would pay a fortune for food like this.'

'Would they really?'

'Of course they would. I would eat this again in a heartbeat.'

'But a week ago, you wouldn't have. A week ago, you sat there, ordered a single coffee, and refused anything from that board.'

Her cheeks coloured. 'I know but—'

'It's not a judgement,' he added hurriedly. 'It's a fact. You might get a few people who'd come along for the novelty value; but food like this is not what my regular customers are looking for. They are mainly young and open minded, but they like things simple. I get that. It's not like I don't mix it up a lot. That duck has made an awesome green curry for the board. And salmon burgers are always a hit.'

'But you must love cooking like this?'

'Some days. Now and again. Mostly though, I'm content just the way things are.'

She was confused. No one was content with the way things were in life. Wasn't that the point? Everyone was looking for the next thing.

She was still mulling this over when a familiar ringtone came from her bag.

'Excuse me,' she said, reaching down and retrieving her phone. If it was another business calling, she was going to ignore it all together. They could call again later if all they wanted to do was fire her, rather than ruin her lunch.

Her brow creased.

'What is it?' Holly asked.

'Just a number I don't know. You don't mind, do you?' She indicated the need to leave to answer it.

"Course not,' Holly said. 'Go for it.'

'I'll see how your dessert is coming along.' Rory walked back to the kitchen.

She hurried outside onto the street.

'Fiona Reeves,' she said. 'Omnivents.'

'Hello, that's great. Fantastic. Good morning.' The accent was tantalisingly familiar, but she couldn't quite place it.

'Sorry, who is this?' she asked.

'Sorry, I should have said. It's Ben here.'

'Ben...' Nope. The name wasn't familiar to her. In fact, the only Ben she could think of was, '...Professor Arkell!' she exclaimed, suddenly realising who was on the other end of the line. Then, with more concern, added, 'How did you get this number?'

'I hope you don't mind. I've been trying to track you down for most of the week. I haven't been able to stop thinking about you,' he explained.

'Oh?'

'In a professional capacity, of course,' he added hastily. 'Anyway, I couldn't get out of my mind what you'd been through. What you'd seen and found. I wondered if you might be willing to talk about it?'

'Talk about it? To whom?'

He sniffed and cleared his throat.

'There's an eco-conference on Tuesday next week. I know it's incredibly short notice. I do realise that, but I hope you'll consider it. I'm presenting, along with other experts in their fields, to various different companies about the environmental impact they're having. It's normally just a lot of data, you know, pointing the way to simple measures they could take to reduce waste or lower their carbon footprint.'

'I'm not sure I'm going to be any good at that,' she said. 'My experience is pretty limited.'

'Exactly. That's precisely what I was thinking.'

'I'm afraid you've lost me.' She glanced through the window of the café. Rory was back at the table with Holly, laughing. No doubt she was arranging a date for next week. Or that afternoon. And he'd probably say yes. Biting down on her lip, Fiona turned her attention back to the phone.

'If what you give these people are facts and figures, how can I help?'

'Because you've got the human angle. You're the piece that we've been missing. These big companies pretend to listen to us, but it's just so much lip service. It's profit over planet for them, every time. Profit over planet, they seem to manage to justify to themselves and their shareholders. But profit over *people*? And people like you: hardworking, intelligent, personable? That's something to relate to. They won't just be able to push you to the back of their minds, the way they now have with Martha. You're a person with a voice. With passion.'

'Well...'

'And the press will be there. They're usually just interested in the bigwigs and ignore us, but you can bet they would lap this up. Maybe you'll even become a national figurehead. A reminder to everybody out there what's happening. You don't have to say anything different to what you said to me in my office. Perhaps just give a little more detail.'

'And without the hysterical tears?'

'Hysterical tears would be just fine.'

She pressed her lips together. 'Do you mind if I think about it?' she asked. 'There's a lot going on in my life right now. I'm not sure if this—'

'Certainly, certainly. I don't want you to feel any pressure. You've got my number now. Please just ring me if you have any questions. Any at all.'

25

When she returned to the table, a steaming chocolate sponge was waiting for her.

'Fiona, this is simply divine,' Holly mumbled, eyes closed, her plate already half empty. 'Honest to God, I don't think I'll ever need sex again. Hey, you need to eat it while it's hot.'

Fiona dug her fork in and watched as a cascade of molten chocolate poured out and onto the plate.

'Everything okay?' Holly enquired. 'That wasn't to do with Stephen, was it? Or the business? Don't tell me someone else has dropped you?'

'No.' Her fork was still embedded in the pudding. 'It was the scientist from down in Plymouth. He wants me to give a presentation at some big conference.'

'A science conference? What does he want you to talk about?'

'Martha.'

'How's it going?' Rory reappeared, resting his hands on the back of Fiona's chair. 'If you're not a fan of chocolate...'

'Oh, no I am. I am. Sorry. I was just thinking about something.'

'Looks serious,' he said.

'She was just saying some scientist wants her to do a presentation on something,' Holly told him.

'Really? Sounds cool. What on?'

'Oh, it's nothing. Nothing exciting.' Fiona flashed a look at Holly that told her, in no uncertain terms, to keep her mouth shut.

'It's just something that came up in a conversation once. About rubbish and plastic and stuff.'

Stepping around her, Rory looked at her with far more scrutiny than she was comfortable with. On the end of her fork, the melted chocolate cooled.

'What are you doing tomorrow morning?' he asked.

* * *

'I can't believe you got me to crash your date,' Holly whinged, as she adjusted her running top. 'This is ridiculous. You know that, don't you? He asked what *you* were doing today.'

'It doesn't matter,' Fiona replied, pulling the zip on her top up a little higher. 'It was just something he said the other day. And anyway, he meant 'you' in the plural sense.'

'He did not. And you know it's going to rain too, right? You're having me crash your date and get soaked into the bargain. This whole thing is preposterous.'

'I thought you liked exercising.'

'You can't tell me you actually want to do this. It's only because you want to get in Mr I-cook-amazing-food-out-of-left-overs-even-with-a-ponytail's pants.'

Ignoring the comment, Fiona cast her gaze up at the sky and

shuddered. Holly was definitely right about the rain. Grey clouds had been gathering since the moment she got up that morning. Hopefully, it would hold off until they got back.

'You know half of Asia is under water 'cos of flooding?' Holly asked, noting her gaze. 'Apparently, it's going to be us next. Just you wait. We're going to get some crazy storms over the next couple of weeks. It's probably going to start today, while we're out, and we'll all get washed away.'

'In Clapham Common?'

'It's not impossible.'

Wondering how on earth they'd managed to stay friends for so long, Fiona looked across at the gathering crowd. About fifty people stood around on the small, cobbled road, all dressed in running gear. A few of them looked like your average London joggers – latest gear, earbuds in, water bottles strapped to their belts, mobiles strapped to their arms. Some looked as if they'd taken a wrong turn on a road trip back from a belated summer-solstice camp. Several were wearing the same logoed T-shirt: lime green, with a picture of a bottle on the back. All of them had the additional accessories of canvas bag and thick gloves.

'Isn't that the yoga teacher you screwed?' Holly asked, squinting.

'What?' she asked, darting behind her back.

Holly chuckled. 'Nah, maybe not. But it looks like the type of thing he'd turn up at, don't you think?' Then, as if a penny had dropped, she turned back to Fiona. 'Oh my God, you have a type now! You have a man type.'

'What?'

'You like the new-age hipster men. That's your thing now. I mean, it makes sense that, after all those years of Stephen with his stuffy suits and tubs of cream cheese, you'd want to start dating someone at the other end of the spectrum.'

'I'm not dating anyone,' Fiona protested. 'This is not a date.'

'No. It's not.'

'Thank you,' she said, relieved by her friend's sudden acceptance.

'But that's only because you're too scared that people will judge you for going out with him, only two weeks after your husband left you, even though he'd been having an affair for a year and a half.'

'Why do I keep you as a friend?' Fiona asked.

'Because you're completely up yourself, enormously judgemental and annoying, and no one else wants to hang around with you.'

'Well thank you so much for those kind words.'

'You're welcome.'

The crowd had started to come together outside one of the shops. Fiona walked towards it.

'This Professor Arkell,' Holly persisted, 'is he a hipster type too? Any tattoos, long hair? I feel I should warn him if he is. Or maybe warn Rory, before he gets his heart broken.'

'I thought you said I was the annoying one?'

'Didn't say I wasn't too.'

They smiled at each other.

'Thank you everyone for coming. Everyone!' A woman at the front, wearing one of the lime-green T-shirts, was trying to get the crowd's attention. One or two adults, who had brought their children with them, pulled them back to their sides, as people slowly stopped talking and listened.

'Sorry I'm late.' Rory slipped in beside them. 'Had a mammoth pickup this morning. You found the place okay?'

'Wasn't too hard.' Fiona found herself smiling. He grinned back, causing a slight flutter in her stomach, which she tried to ignore.

'I didn't have any issues getting here either,' Holly said, leaning across to him.

Their attention was drawn back to the woman at the front.

'It's great to see so many new faces here today,' she said. 'We're delighted you want to come and make a difference and we hope you will enjoy *plogging* with us.'

Holly looked at Fiona and they both shrugged.

'For those of you who are seasoned *ploggers*, week in and week out, you obviously know the difference you have made. We've grown from a tiny group of four, simply wanting to do our bit, to this.' She swept her arm across the crowd.

'Okay, so, safety first,' the woman continued. 'Everyone should keep their gloves on at all times, please. Do not pick anything up without them, even if it only looks like a crisp packet. All we need is one accident for the Council to have an excuse to stop us meeting like this—'

'Despite the fact we're doing their job for them,' someone shouted from the back.

The speaker nodded sympathetically. 'I know. It's true, but they're starting to take notice. And the bigger we get, the more they will have to. So, gloves on all the time please, and do watch where you're treading if you step off a path. I know some of you are wearing hiking boots, but still. And those of you who have brought children, that is incredible. Thank you so much. You're raising your young ones to be true eco-warriors.' She stopped to acknowledge a group of youngsters wrestling at the front. 'Warriors' seemed a given. Fiona wasn't so sure about the 'eco' bit.

'If there's anything that looks remotely hazardous, and I'm talking needles here, folks, then call one of the supervisors over and we'll deal with it. Please don't touch that stuff yourself. If you're new and you don't know which of us are in charge, we're the ones wearing the green T-shirts.'

'Shit.' Next to her, Rory dropped his bag and started rummaging through it. A second later, he pulled out said T-shirt.

'Look, he's one of the guys in charge!' Holly hissed into Fiona's ear. 'I bet he'd like to be in charge of you too, if you asked him.'

Fiona elbowed her in the side.

'And last but not least,' the woman continued. 'Have fun with this. If you want to jog, jog. If you want to walk and chat, walk and chat. Don't worry about separating stuff into different bags, just pick up whatever you can and we'll do that when we get back here. See you all in an hour, everyone.'

A ripple of applause went round and people gathered up their belongings to start the short walk to Clapham Common.

'So...' In a few steps, Holly had managed to push through to the opposite side of Rory. 'Tell us about yourself. Hobbies, secrets, sexual preferences that any woman should be wary of, before considering starting a relationship with you.'

'Holly!' Fiona gasped.

'What? These things are important to know.'

Rory laughed. 'Actually, I should probably head up front, you know. I was a bit late getting here. Supervising and all.'

'Of course.' Holly nodded slowly. 'You are highly important.'

Fiona glared at her but either Holly didn't see, or she didn't care. Fiona was fairly sure it was the latter.

'We'll just be back here, bending over and picking up litter, when you're done.'

With a nervous laugh, he glanced at Fiona.

'I'm so sorry,' she mouthed, apologetically.

'I'll be back in a bit.'

'What the hell was that?' Fiona demanded, shoving her friend on the shoulder as he made his way forward.

'What was what?'

'The poor guy. You terrified him! He literally ran away.'

'I was only having fun. Besides, these things are good to know. He needs to be able to take a joke. Anyway, why should it bother you? You're not interested in him.'

'That's not the point.'

'And you've never been bothered when I wind guys up before.'

'Yes, but they've never... They are never...'

'Yes?' Holly's eyebrows rose, her tight-lipped smirk twisting, as if the whole charade had simply been to elicit this exact response. Which Fiona now knew it had.

Out of the corner of her eye, she spotted a chocolate wrapper. Changing direction away from her friend, she bent over and picked it up. When she stood back up, Holly was leaning over her.

'So?'

'Look.' Fiona sighed, knowing there was no way out of this without some form of discussion. She dropped the paper into her collection bag. 'This is important to me. I know it's hard to understand and everything—'

'Oh no, I get it. I completely get it. I was reading up on the whole whale thing and sea life yesterday. Man, that shit is crazy.'

Fiona paused, picking up another piece. 'You did?'

'Sure. I'm one step away from being a cat lady. What do you think I spend my nights doing? I'll be honest, I'm not sure this will make any difference but, hey, if you want to do it, I'll support you.'

'You will?'

'Always.'

The insults and innuendos of only a moment ago were

forgotten, as she stared at her friend. This was why she loved Holly, more than anyone else. This was why they'd been best friends for so long. Because, when it really came down to it, when it really mattered, she'd be there.

'Great, so you'll give Rory a break?'

Holly picked up a plastic bottle lid. 'Why would I do that?'

'I just explained why this is important to me. You just told me you were on board.'

'With the plastic stuff. Yeah. I get that. But the Rory stuff? No way.'

A couple, whose bags were already half full, stopped and glowered in their direction. As subtly as she could, Fiona slipped her bag down by her side.

'I need Rory,' she said. Holly's mouth curled into a grin. 'Not like that. He's the only person I have to talk to about stuff like this. The only person who's not going to think I'm a complete weirdo. He can teach me things.'

'I bet he can.'

'For crying out loud, Holly!'

Her friend nodded slowly. 'Okay. I understand. I'll stop winding you up—'

'Good.'

'I'll stop winding you up, as soon as you say you find him attractive.'

Fiona dropped her bag and planted her hands on her hips.

'You're not serious? What are we, eleven?'

'Fine then, don't.'

They'd stumbled upon a whole heap of rubbish, probably left over from a picnic. Holly began grabbing handfuls, leaving Fiona standing.

'This is stupid.'

'It's fine,' Holly said. 'I mean, if you can't even say it.'

'Why should I have to say it? What does it matter if I do or I don't?'

'It doesn't.' Her friend's voice remained infuriatingly cool. 'I mean, it doesn't matter at all, right? So, I wonder why it would be so difficult to say something that doesn't matter.'

'You want me to say I find him attractive, even if it's a lie?'

'Is it a lie?'

In spite of herself, Fiona's eyes were drawn across to where Rory was crouching by a bush, helping a small child extract a bit of rubbish she'd spotted inside. There was something so easy about his manner. So relaxed and comfortable. As if all of life's problems would just roll right off him.

'Fine,' she muttered, picking up a cigarette butt.

'Sorry?'

'I said, fine. Yes, he's an attractive man.'

'A man that you find attractive?' Holly pushed.

'A man that I guess is above-averagely attractive.'

'Good, now go and talk to him.'

'What?'

'Go and talk to him. I'll stop bothering you as soon as you go and talk to him. Why else would he have invited you here?'

Fiona pressed her lips together.

'I thought you had dinner at the guy's flat?' Holly questioned. 'Come on. How difficult can one conversation be? Either that or I'll go over there and get his whole dating history out of him, and you know that's not going to be pretty.'

With a reluctant sigh, Fiona glanced at the bag in her hand. 'Fine, I'll go. Just give me some of your rubbish first.'

'What?'

'You heard me. Swap bags. You've got way more than me. I don't want him to think I've spent the whole time just gossiping.'

'But you have.'

'Are you going to give me your rubbish or not?'

Two minutes later, after a mad dash to fill up the bag, she sauntered across to where Rory was continuing to help the little girl. Mastering a casual, chic look, while wearing gardening gloves and carrying a bag full of condom wrappers, was not as easy as she'd hoped. Particularly when every part of her felt like it was breaking out into a cold sweat.

'Hey,' he said, smiling when he saw her. 'How are you guys getting on?'

She raised her bag by way of an answer. 'I can't believe there's this much stuff. And when you look at what everyone else has collected too.'

'Yeah, you'll realise just how much there is at the end, when we go to sort it all out. This is pretty average. You should see what it's like when there have been concerts and stuff in some of these parks. Seriously. That takes some beating.'

'I can imagine.'

Something glinted in the hedgerow. A metal bottle top by the looks of it. She reached in to get it.

'Thank you for inviting me. I didn't even know people did this.'

'You're pretty new to the whole thing.'

'You could say that.'

'That business with Martha. I mean, it hit a lot of people hard for a while, seeing her like that. But it seems to have had a more lasting effect on you.'

'It has.'

With that area looking clear, they began walking up towards a wood, where they landed upon another gold-mine of detritus. Lifting her head, she saw that Holly had joined a small group of women. When she noticed Fiona looking at her, she mouthed,

'Number,' holding out her hand as if she had a mobile there and pretended to dial. 'You need his number.'

She swallowed. Did she really?

Getting someone's details was easy enough to do in a professional situation, with an exchange of business cards. Even socially, it wasn't usually a problem. But he had already offered her his number and she had brushed it aside. Asking for it now would be embarrassing. But would that matter, even if he rejected her? She was still married. And planning on staying that way. Wasn't she?

'Are you free for dinner?' The words flew from her mouth before she could stop them. It was a full leap past exchanging phone numbers, but it was out there now and there was nothing she could do about it. A surge of regret flooded through her, as she watched the surprise register on his face. 'Sorry. I mean, you're probably busy. Or with someone. Or busy with someone.' *Just talk coherently, for crying out loud!* she screamed at herself. She tried again. 'Sorry, what I meant to say was—'

'Sure.' The look of surprise was replaced by the infuriating smirk she was becoming so used to. 'How about tonight? I could cook again?'

'You've already cooked for me, twice. How about I do it this time?' she offered, another unexpected idea escaping her lips.

He smiled. 'That sounds good. I'm looking forward to it already.'

A moment later – and with his number in her phone – she fled back to Holly, who was ready and waiting.

'Well that looked pretty smooth,' she said. Then, seeing the look on her friend's face, added, 'What's wrong? Is he seeing someone?'

'Worse,' Fiona replied. 'I just offered to cook him dinner.'

'Oh shit.'

26

When Stephen and Joseph had been there, weekends always felt very similar to weekdays, except Joseph would normally be in and out of the house. A lot of the time, Stephen would head to the office to work – or had that been his excuse? Fiona wasn't so sure any more – and she would use the time to catch up on the mountain of emails she received. With that task now substantially reduced, the upside of losing half her clients, she found herself at a bit of a loose end. The Stephen-induced cleaning spree, combined with the fact that there was no teenager making a mess, meant that a quick vacuum and wipe down in the bathrooms was all that was needed to get the house in order. She even called and cancelled the ironing lady, on account of the fact that most of it had consisted of Stephen's things.

Her sense of cabin fever wasn't helped by the fact that the rain, which had been threatening all morning, had well and truly settled in by the afternoon. Having initially dismissed Holly's talk of flooding, she now felt that perhaps her friend had been more on the mark than she'd expected. She had learned over the years that the *idea* of being tucked up inside, while inclement weather raged outside, was far more appealing than it actually turned out to be.

Even now, with her diminished to-do list, she felt there were so many other things she should be spending her time doing. She picked up the current book she was reading, skimmed through it for a while, and then put it down again.

It had been a week since Martha had passed away. One week since the poor creature had met her undignified end, watched by crowds of photo-happy sightseers. Wondering if there might be any more updates, Fiona flicked on the news.

There were reports about the situations in Iran and Syria, along with a rail strike that was threatening to affect the Tube the next month, if the unions didn't come to an agreement. The next channel offered the same headlines, along with additional coverage of the American presidential race and some divorcee who had just received the largest settlement in history, after being married for only two-and-a-half months. There was nothing on Martha at all. Frustration bubbled. She moved to her laptop, to check there. *Martha sperm whale death,* she searched, filtering her results to only those from the last twenty-four hours.

No Martha, but four more whales washed up on the shores of British Columbia, she learned. She scanned the article, a deep ache swelling in her chest, as she moved down to yet another on sperm whales.

There was a video clip attached to this news report, although the write up was scant.

Mother sperm whale dies attempting to rescue her baby from a fishing net, off the coast of Italy. Baby also dies.

She shook her head. It was unbelievable. How could that have happened, so soon after Martha? She had been world news. The photo of her in the Thames had been on the pages of newspapers all around the globe. Photos of *her* balloon had been there, too. And here she was, only a week later, reading that people had killed another mother, and her baby too. She clicked to the next article. Another sperm whale, dead in Thailand. Plastic bottles in its stomach. Next, Portugal: another grey whale. Emaciated. Early signs pointing to the same cause.

She closed her eyes. Her body temperature was inching upwards, second by second. It was happening again. Another panic attack, goddammit. At least she was on her own. Not standing in the street outside someone's shop. She attempted to refocus her attention away from her body and onto the screen.

A stingray had been found with a camera in its stomach. A whole camera.

Still trying to control the hammering in her chest, she looked at the time on her computer. Three-fifteen. Rory was coming around at six, after he'd finished up in the shop. He was the only one in today, apparently. Three hours until he was due. Three hours until she didn't have to be alone with these thoughts and nightmare images any longer. She could manage that, couldn't she? Of course she could.

'Screw you,' she said and slammed her laptop shut.

* * *

She didn't even notice the rain streaming down her face as she paced up and down the street waiting for her Uber.

Thunderclouds had transformed the sky and it could almost have been evening, as she climbed into the taxi, ignoring the driver's gripes about how she was going to soak his seats and what the hell was wrong with her, had she never heard of an umbrella?

Ten minutes later, she was dripping on the tiled shop floor.

'Fiona!' Rory dashed towards her, grabbing a towel as he did so. 'What's happened? Are you all right?'

He wrapped the towel around her and tried to pull her against his chest, to rub her dry but she held him back and tilted her head up towards him, feeling a trickle of water running down her forehead. She could smell him, his earthiness, his warmth and, at that moment, it was all she needed.

'You should know,' she said, pushing herself up onto tiptoes, her lips brushing his. 'I'm a terrible cook.'

* * *

A distant roll of thunder echoed, as he traced a line on her skin, from her elbow to her collarbone. 'It was a good job I didn't have any customers in the shop,' he murmured, speaking the first full sentence since they'd arrived in the flat.

She laughed. The storm continued outside but, wrapped in his arms, she paid it no attention.

'Just so you know, this wasn't planned,' she said, pulling the sheet further up over them.

'No? Then what did you have in mind?'

'To be honest, I'm not exactly sure.'

'Don't take this the wrong way,' he pushed himself up onto one of his elbows, 'but am I part of some midlife crisis you're going through?'

'Quite possibly. Yes. Or a complete mental breakdown.'

He laughed, stroking her cheek softly. 'Do you want to talk about it?' he asked.

She bit her lip.

'You don't have to,' he reassured her. 'Really you don't. I just want you to know that you can, if you want. I'm here for you.'

Closing her eyes, she breathed in.

'I think it's probably time I told you,' she said. 'I think it's time you knew the truth.'

* * *

'Jesus, that's a hell of a lot to go through. A hell of a lot,' he said.

They were sitting up in bed. He had brought them both coffee before she started.

'I don't blame you for reacting like you have. Christ, what do you do when something like that happens? Jesus.' Sensing that his reaction may have been a little too strong, he hurriedly tried to backtrack. 'Of course, you don't know it was yours. It's more than likely it wasn't. That supplier may have gone bust, but you know they'll have sold hundreds of them in China or India or wherever they were made. The chances that that particular balloon was actually yours are miniscule.'

'But there is still the possibility,' she replied. 'That it was mine. And I can't ever do anything to get change that. All I can do is make sure that it's not me again.'

He took her mug and placed it on the bedside table. 'I know what you are saying, but you're putting too much pressure on yourself too quickly. The sort of adjustments that you're going through, that you are trying to make, they take time.' He paused, studying her.

She looked away, a hot flush colouring her cheeks. 'That's enough about me,' she said, her skin prickling from the attention. 'Tell me about you.'

'Didn't I tell you everything about me the other night?'

'No, you didn't. You told me about food waste.'

'I can talk about that a lot.' He grinned.

'I noticed. So, tell me something about you. Why did you set up the shop, for starters? And which came first, the shop or the café?'

'Did I not cover that?'

'No, you didn't.'

He shifted over, creating a space beneath his arm for her to slide into.

'It's a terribly dull story. Are you sure you want to hear it?'

'I'm sure.'

With the rain beating outside, she snuggled down against his chest and closed her eyes, her head rising and falling in time with the rhythm of his breathing.

'There isn't much to it. I'd reached a certain age, experienced a bit of life and started seeing what was going on in the world. It wasn't like you. I didn't have a sudden epiphany.'

'Is that what I've had?'

'Is it not?'

'Maybe.'

'Well, anyway, it just kept adding up, you know. There were so many things I couldn't control.'

'Like what?'

'Life. So many things wrong with the world. So, I started up the shop, which is how I ended up learning about waste food, and then I decided to open up a café too, to try to do something about that as well.'

Everything he said was spoken with overwhelming ease and simplicity. She gazed up at him, wondering what it must be like to be able to approach life that way.

'What do you think about this presentation for the professor?' she asked, hoping to tap into his ability for calm and logic. 'Do you think I should do it? Or would it be hypocritical?'

His brow furrowed. 'Hypocritical? Why?'

'Well because, you know, I'd be saying all this stuff is bad, and they shouldn't be using all these plastics and yet I must have bought tonnes of it in the last few years alone.'

'Are you still buying them now?'

Had she bought anything in the last week? Mainly she'd been living off Rory and coffee. 'Not really.'

'Then there you go.'

She mulled it over. It sounded so simple, but she still wasn't convinced.

'Look, this professor guy,' Rory said. 'He wouldn't have asked you without a good reason. He must have thought you could make a difference. And I agree. If the press pick up on this, it could be just the sort of thing that strikes a chord with people who need that extra push.'

'Okay,' she said, nodding her head slowly.

'So, you're going to do it?'

'I think I am.'

She imagined that he would be grinning now, the way he did when he knew that he was right about something, but she had her eyes shut and his lips were already closing in on hers.

27

Fiona had never been one to believe that a positive outlook made a difference to the success of your day. That wasn't to say it didn't have any effect. Being in a good mood did mean she was a little more tolerant of some of the idiots she had to deal with – always a good thing in her line of work. But positivity alone wasn't responsible for success; that was all down to efficiency. Efficiency and hard work.

Monday morning somewhat altered her views on this.

'You're in a good mood,' Annabel observed, as she placed a strawberry and caramel Frappuccino on the desk in front of her.

'I am,' she said. 'And look. I got you a reusable cup. You need to use it a hundred times to compensate for its carbon footprint though. So, drink up.'

Once in her office, she'd barely sat down when the telephone rang.

'Oh,' she said, surprised by what she was hearing. 'Well yes, brilliant. That's brilliant.' She hung up and swept back through to Annabel. 'Now *that's* a bit of good news,' she announced.

'What is?'

'I've just got off the phone with The Truncton Recruitment Group.'

'I thought they dropped us.'

'They did. But that was last week. Now they're saying that they've read through the manifesto I sent them, about our new ethos and direction, and had a rethink about their *restructuring* – their word, not mine – and that they're hoping we can continue to work together.'

'Fantastic!'

'It is. It really is.'

Annabel's enthusiasm, as she sat there biting her lip, wasn't up to its usual level, though.

'What is it?' Fiona asked, sensing that something was wrong.

'Do you think I could I have a look at our new manifesto too?' her assistant asked.

'Oh shit! Yes, of course!'

For the next two hours, Fiona proceeded to talk her through a slightly abridged version of recent events. (Annabel was a good friend, but she was also an employee and some things had to remain private.) She also told her about Rory, in terms of the things that he was doing and all that he had taught her – once again from an environmental standpoint only.

'And now you're going to talk at this conference tomorrow?'

'Yes,' she said, feeling for the first time a frisson of excitement at the statement. 'Yes I am.'

After that, the day only got better. Two more companies had a change of heart and did an about turn on their decision to leave her and, when she went around to Rory's that night for dinner, they retired to the bedroom for dessert.

'I just hope I do her justice,' she said, eating sticky toffee pudding, propped up against a pillow, something she would never have considered in her own house, yet now felt like the only way to do it. 'Martha, that is. It sounds stupid, I know. She was an animal, for crying out loud. But it's like you said to me before, if I can make even one of those companies listen, if just one of them changes their mind about wrapping everything in a double layer of plastic, that's got to make a difference, hasn't it?'

'That would make a whole world of difference.' He moved in for a lingering kiss.

'Will I see you tomorrow?' she asked, separating so she could finish off the last of the sauce. Sex or pudding? Sometimes, it really was a tough call. 'The meeting isn't until the evening. I could text Ben. See if you could come too.'

'It's Ben now, is it?' he smirked, moving their dishes away before flopping back down on the bed and pulling her against him. 'I wish I could, but I'm going to be busy all day. I've got to do pickup in the morning and then I'm on my own in the shop.'

'I could pop in?'

He wrinkled his nose. 'That's going to be a bit difficult. You don't mind, do you? Only I have a load of deliveries coming in too, and they'll need to be sorted and—'

'It's fine.'

'I don't want you to think that I don't want to see you.'

'Honestly, it's fine.'

With a relieved smile, he brushed a strand of hair behind her ears.

'Wednesday? I can see you on Wednesday though. And you can let me know how it went.'

'Sounds good.' She nestled in against his chest. 'Sounds very good.'

* * *

The advantage of Rory's early mornings was that she felt under no obligation to stay the night. In fact, it was better that she didn't. At half-past eight, she gathered up her things and headed home, with time for a little more fact checking and research ahead of her presentation.

How this project had swept her away was unlike anything she'd experienced before. Of course, she was always absorbed in her work, often to her detriment, but this was all consuming.

There would be a projector available, if she wanted to show photographs or illustrations. And she did, one thing in particular. She would lay herself bare for Martha.

When she woke the next morning, she hadn't expected to be such a bundle of nerves. Neither her first coffee nor a shower did much to alleviate them and, by the time she reached the office, she was a quivering wreck.

'Can I make you another coffee?' Annabel asked, perturbed by her employer's inability to sit down for more than fifteen seconds without jumping back up again.

She shook her head. 'No, I don't think I should have any more. That damn cafetière has already got me drinking double my normal amount.'

'Do you want me to fetch you something to eat, then? Maybe food would help.'

'Honestly? I don't think I could stomach anything.'

It had been a mixed morning. To Fiona's disappointment, no more of her clients had decided to return to Omnivents' fold. On the plus side, no more had left. That meant she was just at the break-even point she'd calculated. It wasn't ideal, but it was sustainable, if no costly surprises came along. What she needed to do was find a way to pare back her costs, the biggest one being rent.

By midday, she'd had enough searching for possible new premises and needed to get out of the office.

'Actually,' she said, despite her reaction to Annabel's earlier offer, 'I think I'll head out and grab something to eat myself. I'll see you back here in a bit.'

She had almost been on automatic pilot, heading towards The Dumpster Dive. Shawarma was no good; she needed to go further, to stretch her legs, and sushi was a nonstarter – just the thought of eating fish, after her last few days research – put paid to that. Besides, she could swing by and see if Rory had managed to sort out all those deliveries and, perhaps, spare half an hour for a quick lunch together after all. Calm her nerves. So, it would make sense, she thought, to head to the shop first.

As she arrived, she anticipated his surprise and pleasure at seeing her there. She pinched her cheeks and stepped inside.

'Welcome to The Hive, can I help you?'

'Oh.' She was taken aback, as a woman in a grey apron stepped out from behind the counter.

'Were you looking for something in particular?' she asked.

'Actually,' Fiona leaned to the side, peering towards the staircase. 'I was looking for Rory. Is he in?'

The woman's smiled broadened, as if it was a question she was frequently asked. 'Sorry, no, my dear. He's not working here today.'

'Oh,' she said again and frowned.

Most probably she'd got it wrong and he'd said he'd be working in the café. Why would a person do that? she wondered, run two businesses at the same time? Would they not realise how infuriating it would be to track them down when someone wanted them?

'Not to worry then. I'll catch him later. Thank you,' she said, and went back out onto the street.

Lunchtime was the worst time to head to the café. The road was a nightmare to cross, with crowds huddled together by the traffic lights, or else loitering in random places along the pavement. And a stream of people was already bustling through the café door. She wasn't going to stay, she told herself, just pop her head in and say hello. Maybe grab a quick bite if there was a free table.

She peered through the window. Three-quarters of the tables were already filled and both the normal members of staff – the scowling girl and the overly tattooed older man – were busy serving, with no sign of Rory, meaning he was most probably out back. Disappointed, but determined to stick to her vow of not disturbing him, she turned to leave, only to notice something out of the corner of her eye.

It was the familiar loose bun that had caught her attention: that flop of unruly hair that just begged to have her fingers pulled through it. A moment later and he came into full profile. It wasn't his hair that struck her now though; it was his hands. Placed in front of him, but not flat on the table. They rested on another pair. A woman's.

A tremor struck her knees and lungs simultaneously.

'No,' she whispered to herself.

It was a miracle they didn't see her, with her nose almost pressed up against the glass. But, from the looks of things, they were too absorbed in each other to notice anyone else. Every time the girl's mouth moved, Fiona watched as the creases around Rory's eyes deepened and dimples appeared in his cheeks. She had never seen dimples when he smiled at her. Her head buzzed, as the sounds of the street amplified around her. Car horns, people chattering. All at a volume that had become cacophonous and jarring. With her heart hammering, she tried to back away. But her legs seemed paralysed. Her feet were rooted to the spot and she couldn't take her eyes off this beautiful young woman. And she was beautiful. She was graceful too and her smile had a luminosity to it. And her face... well, if she was over twenty-five, it would be a miracle.

'Bloody prick. You're all the same,' she muttered, finally stepping back onto the foot of an unsuspecting passer-by. 'You stupid, stupid...' Even as she said the words, she had no idea who she was aiming them at – Rory, or herself.

28

'What's happened?' Annabel asked, jumping from her seat, dropping a piece of sushi into its container.

Fiona marched straight by without a word, slamming her office door, only to reopen it and stick her head out.

'That had better be a reusable tub,' she fired and slammed the door again.

What got to her most was that she'd fallen for it so easily. That Rory had somehow turned her into the exact cliché she'd been furious at Stephen for becoming. Three days into the relationship and she had already been wondering what the next weekend might bring, even the weekend after that. She was nothing but a sad, spurned wife who'd jumped straight into bed with any man who'd show her a bit of attention, ignoring every warning sign possible. The thing was – and this was what really got to her – she hadn't even seen the warning signs. Even now, she thought he genuinely enjoyed her company, among other things. And he probably did, just not enough to be faithful to her. Did he even genuinely care about Martha? At least the yoga teacher had. With a scream of frustration, she slammed her hand down on the desk.

Her mind flitted from Rory to the conference that evening. Professor Arkell wanted her to bring passion to the event. Well, if passion was what he wanted, passion was what he was about to get.

* * *

The feeling of nausea was genuine, no matter how much she tried to convince herself it was all in her head. The tightness in her throat, her stomach and every other part of her body was real. At first, she'd thought it was all to do with Rory. She assumed he was to blame for what she was experiencing. But as the room began to fill, a feeling of panic was added to the mix and she was forced to admit that he wasn't the reason at all.

'I thought you said it was going to be a small group of people?'

'Well, it is normally,' Professor Arkell replied. 'I guess with all the coverage about Martha, a lot of companies thought they ought to make an appearance, to show their concern. Or at least to make it seem that way.'

She took a moment to scan the room again. He wasn't joking when he said there would be some big names here. Catherine Laudel, the CEO of FIZD, the second largest soft-drink producer in the UK, was helping herself to a second glass of water from a tray. And she was fairly sure the Health Secretary was over by the door. She'd even spotted Stephen's boss, John Orbiten, tucked away at the back of the room on his mobile. Perhaps he was on the phone to Stephen, she thought.

Three weeks ago, this would have been a networking dream. She would have worked the room from the moment she stepped inside. Not today. And no one was approaching her. Maybe it was the vibes she was giving out – terrified with a hint of I've-made-a-massive-mistake-please-get-me-out-of-here. Or maybe the rumours of her split with golden girl Octavia Lovett-Rose had reached them. Either way, she was thankful for the wide berth she was getting.

'There are two brilliant speakers on first,' Ben told her. 'From the Sea Life Trust and Plastic Oceans. Then there's a presentation by one of the big companies attending, of course.' He paused and looked at the programme in his hand. 'To be honest, I don't know who he is. Must have been a late booking. It'll all be a load of smoke and mirrors, anyway. Someone called John Orbiten.'

'John Orbiten!' She pulled the programme out of his hand. 'Why's he speaking?'

'You know him?'

'Yes. No. Sort of. He's my husband's boss. My ex-husband's boss. Well not officially yet. He's just been going through some —' She clamped her mouth shut before any more drivel could emanate from it. 'Sorry. Nerves,' she said, as if it wasn't obvious.

Ben smiled sympathetically.

'I thought someone in your position would be used to speaking in front of large groups of people like this.'

'Well you thought wrong. I'm very much a small group speaker, or in the background.'

It was true. The thing about her job was that it had never involved addressing crowds. She *watched* people doing it, like Dominic, for example. She'd organised several of his seminars over the years. And other large companies'. After Stephen had got his first big promotion, she'd listened as he'd spoken in front of all the senior managers and employees and had felt such a surge of pride for the man she'd married. At his confidence. His eloquence.

That wasn't her forte. Not since secondary school, when she'd foolishly decided she was going to take part in the school production of *Annie*, had she been expected to perform in front of more than twenty people. And back then, she'd only had a single line.

'So, after him, it'll be you, and then two more speakers and then I'll close the meeting,' Ben was saying. 'Remember, you've got a five-minute slot, but don't worry if you finish sooner. Or go on a bit longer. It's just a guideline. Most of these people will just be waiting to get to the bar, ply themselves with free drinks, and hobnob. They'll probably have forgotten every single thing we've told them by the time they reach their cars, unfortunately,' he finished, gloomily.

'Wow, you make it sound so worthwhile.'

He smiled. 'Now, you're sure you're okay with us using the birthday-party photo? We don't have to.'

'Yes, we do,' she said with certainty. 'Without it, I'm just another crazy fanatic.'

* * *

At ten to six, people began to move towards their seats in the large auditorium. Fiona, under Ben's guidance, took one on the front row. Four chairs down, John Orbiten took his place, and she suddenly became engrossed in her programme.

Despite doing her best to listen to what was being said before it was her turn, she passed most of the time going over in her mind what she had prepared and wiping sweaty hands on her skirt. Every now and then, something did catch her attention, usually something she'd come across in her Martha research binges. Nearly ten million carrier bags used globally per minute. More microplastic particles in the ocean than stars in the Milky Way. An estimated 1.1 million seabirds dying each year due to plastic. Countries claiming they were doing their bit for recycling by sending their rubbish to Asia, only for it to be piled up into small mountains on the coast of some previously unspoiled island. *We are being lied to. We are lying to ourselves.* That was what the activists said. Of course, big business held a different point of view. She'd read it all before, but that didn't stop her blood boiling once again.

If what Professor Arkell said was true, then the people in the room who could make a difference would forget what she told them the minute she finished her speech. How was that even possible? How would they not go racing out and start stripping plastic from the shelves of their shops, vowing never to use it again?

Seeing John Orbiten take the stage to loud applause, she stifled a laugh, thinking of Holly's comment about him and Stephen sharing a yogurt bath. At five feet four and bald, he was hardly the most attractive man in the room, but there was still something about him. Probably the allure of money and power.

'What we have heard today is heart-breaking,' he told the audience in his most sincere voice. 'These images, which I'm sure we've all seen before, are understandably emotive. No one enjoys this happening to our planet. No person or business should be responsible. That's why we, at Alton Foods, are taking steps to become the most environmentally conscious, mass-produced food retailer in the UK.'

More applause.

'We, at Alton Foods, promise that, by 2050, half our packaging will be made from renewable materials.'

Even more applause.

Next to her, Professor Arkell snorted.

'Renewable resources,' he muttered to her. 'Oldest marketing ploy in the book. It's still plastic. Still screws up the ocean. Just means they put a green label on their tubs.'

'And,' John Orbiten continued, 'we will commit to a nation-wide buy-back scheme for a further 10 per cent of our products.'

Applause.

'We at Alton Foods will lead the way when it comes to helping this planet, and we will support anyone who wishes to join us on the journey. This is our pledge, which we make in front of you all, today.' He nodded his head, picked up his papers and left the podium to thunderous applause.

'Smarmy git,' Professor Arkell spat. 'It's the same bullshit every year. Set inadequate targets they have no intention of meeting. And, whatever we show them, whatever we say, they know they can pretty much ignore us. We're in their pocket; they provide us with half our funding and without that, we couldn't even exist.'

'They do?' Fiona was appalled.

'They do. They provide us with money so that they can pretend they're working with us. It's why I have to be so bloody polite up there.'

A whirlwind of thoughts raced through her brain as John Orbiten received several slaps on the shoulder as he sat back down.

'You might have to watch what you're saying. But I don't.'

Whether it was her turn or not, she didn't care. Without waiting for the applause to die down, or to be introduced, she marched up onto the platform to the podium.

'Ladies and gentlemen.' She tapped the microphone, partly

to make sure it was still on, partly to gain everyone's attention. 'You don't know me, at least not in this capacity.'

She glanced around the room. A few people were frowning, as if there was something vaguely familiar about her.

'My name is Fiona Reeves and, a couple of weeks ago, I would most likely have been found among you lot at the back of the room. You know the ones I'm talking about, in your suits and cocktail dresses, grabbing the free booze and canapés, arranging your next meeting or round of golf, only half listening because, let's face it, you're only here because it would be bad for businesses if you didn't show up to at least one environmental conference a year.'

The room had gone suddenly quiet. At least she had their attention, that was for sure.

'It's tough for me to judge you,' she said, changing her tone to one that was slightly less aggressive. 'It is. Like I said, a few weeks ago, I would have been there with you. I would have thought how sad it was that all this was happening and hoped that someone would find an easy, scientific solution to fix it all, so that my newsfeed didn't have to be swamped with pictures of dead animals. I like pictures of holidays. The occasional cat in a flowerpot. Not a bird with a razor stuck in its beak.

'But that's beside the point. First of all, you need to know I'm not a doctor. I'm not a professor. I haven't made any great strides in scientific research. I can't tell you how many turtles have been killed by rubbish this year. But I can guarantee that when you saw that picture of the stomach contents of the whale that died in the Thames, you didn't think for a second that it was actually your plastic bag that had killed the creature, did you? Your rubbish wouldn't do that, would it?'

Already eyes were starting to roll. She looked down at Ben

and nodded. A moment later, her presentation lit up the giant screen behind her. He handed up the remote to her.

'Two weeks ago, I didn't care about the environment. Well, I cared that my water was clean. That my air was breathable. That people didn't use my rubbish bins, because I needed all the space I could get. But that was it. And I'm sure some of you can relate to that too. But then, something happened in London.'

The screen changed. Martha appeared. It was the first day, when she'd just been sighted in the Thames. Back then, she'd looked almost healthy although, given how she ended up, any look was healthy compared to that.

'Now, I'll admit, I was hooked pretty much straight away. She was a mother, you see. I'm a mother. She was away from her babies, and my baby had just left home to start university. It's a tenuous link, maybe, but I felt as though we shared something, on a maternal level.

'Then we all know what happened. She died. We saw how our plastic and rubbish killed her. Humans put this in the ocean, no one else. Now I'm fairly sure that lots of you switched off at that point, just like you're switching off now, because you don't want to hear it all again. But believe me, you haven't heard what I'm going to tell you next. I promise you.'

She pointed the remote at the screen and triggered the next image.

'This,' she said, 'is a picture of my son Joseph's sixth birthday party.'

Given the size of the image, everyone, herself and Joseph included, was more than life size.

'I was good at party planning. I still am actually, although one or two of my former clients aren't so sure any more.

Anyway, if you look closely at the top right-hand corner, you might notice something.'

She clicked the remote again and a red circle appeared around the balloon. Another click and it enlarged to fill the whole screen. She turned back to her audience. Most looked perplexed but, gradually, their expressions turned from confusion to realisation, as they whispered to those on either side of them. This was what she had been hoping for. By the time she moved to the next slide, they all knew what was coming.

'This is a picture of the contents of Martha's stomach,' she said. 'And there it is. My balloon. My wonderful little party accessory, a disposable trifle, there... lodged in the digestive tract of one of the most spectacular creatures on Earth, slowly starving her to death.'

Mouths were open. The buzz of the delegates had grown louder.

'You see, you lot out there are lucky. You still live in the delightful bliss of wilful ignorance. You can believe that your recycling is actually being recycled. That your plastic is somehow different to all these other plastics you see floating around in documentaries that you switch away from. But I don't have that luxury any more. I lost the right to it.

'The thing is, I'm not any different to you. To those of you who continue to peddle this stuff. But I'm personally responsible for so much less than what you are doing, corporately. So much less. And I if I have to live with my burden, then you sure as hell should have to live with yours.'

She took the mic from its stand and moved to the edge of the stage.

'The targets they're talking about.' She spoke now directly to the group of press, seated to one side. 'They don't mean a thing. They really don't. 98 per cent of companies do not meet their sustainability targets. *98 per cent*. That means, if a hundred of them were talking to us here today, impressing us with their ethical stance, only *two* of them would have any intention of actually sticking to their promises. Their vision for the future? What the hell does that mean, anyway? No, actually, we all know exactly what it means. Words like vision, targets, pledges, they're just one more marketing ploy, to distract us from the fact that they didn't honour the last one. Because... did you?' Her gaze turned on John Orbiten, sat there in the front row. She held it just long enough to watch his jaw tighten, before looking from one person to the next.

'How many of you out there actually did meet your last target? If you're sincere about achieving something, stop *telling* us about it and start *showing* us what you're *actually doing*. Stop giving speeches and start giving us action. Not this recyclable plastic nonsense, which is just marketing speak for you've found another method of trashing the decent things this planet has given us. Tell me the number of lives, animal and human, that have been improved by what you're doing. Show us how you removed all the waste from Tanzania, by building a brand-new recycling plant. One that can actually cope with what we've dumped on it. Tell me how you've banned single-use items with your name on. Start proving you care, by showing that you're willing to risk a year without your million or billion-pound profit margin, or any profit at all, for that matter because, for crying out loud, you can't put a price on saving the planet and it's more important than lining your pockets. How are your yachts going to float on an ocean full of plastic? Ask yourself that. Stop pontificating, get off your corporate arses, and do something!'

29

The press descended on her the moment she left the stage, phones out, ready to record. What was her name again? Where was she from? What did she do when she first saw the photograph? How did she end up speaking here today? She smiled the best smile she could manage, given the adrenaline that was still coursing through her. Of course, she had been devastated. Yes, she'd substantially reduced her use of plastic and, no, she couldn't be entirely certain the balloon was hers. When she finally broke free, she made her way to Professor Arkell.

'I thought there was supposed to be someone else speaking after me?' she queried, picking up an abandoned programme. 'Yes, there were. Two.'

He shook his head. 'You really think anyone was going to try and follow that? Are you kidding? No way. Believe me, what you did up there was incredible.'

Pride positively radiated from her.

'Do you think it will make a difference?'

'If it doesn't, I don't know what the hell will.'

A number of shocked and angry people were beginning to filter past her, only to be confronted themselves by members of the press, John Orbiten being among them. Good, she thought, they deserved to stew. The lot of them. And it felt so good to watch.

'Look,' Professor Arkell cleared his throat. 'My train isn't for another two hours. I don't suppose you'd like to get a drink? Purely platonically of course.' He raised his left hand and displayed his wedding band. 'Just two environmental crusaders sharing a quiet victory celebration?'

She sighed with relief at the sight of the ring. The last thing she needed was more complication in her life but she did need to unwind. 'Yes. That would be wonderful.'

Turning to leave, she found her path blocked by a petite woman in a short, grey dress. 'Ms Reeves, my name's Catherine Green. I work for the *City Times*. I'm sure you're incredibly busy right now, but I was wondering if you might give me a call, later in the week perhaps, and we could get together? I'd love to talk to you about doing an article regarding what you had to say tonight.'

She held out her card for Fiona to take.

'That would be great,' Fiona said, exchanging a look with Professor Arkell. 'That would be fantastic.'

It wasn't until Ben had left for the station, and Fiona was on her own, that her thoughts turned to Rory. Looking at her phone, she began scrolling through her new text messages. There were a number from him, all supportive and caring, and then asking how it had gone. All bullshit, she thought. She ignored them, went to contacts and rang Holly.

'How was it? Are you an eco-warrior queen or something now?' her friend asked.

'You know what? I feel like I might be.' Fiona smiled to herself. 'Don't suppose you've got room for a very late dinner, have you?'

'I sure have,' Holly answered without hesitation. 'You want me to pick something up and bring it over to yours?'

'Are you all right with that?'

'See you in an hour.'

'Perfect.'

Given that Holly was almost certainly going to be late, she had run herself a bath and switched on the radio. For a short while, she'd attempted to read, but the music and her thoughts – most predominantly, now, her thoughts about Rory – kept interrupting her concentration. What hurt so much was how quickly she'd imagined herself slipping into his life. They had seemed perfect together. With everything that was going on, she'd felt she'd found a soulmate, someone who could understand her, who would guide her on her newfound journey.

'Screw it,' she said, dropping her book onto the floor and twisting the tap on again with her toes. It was her journey. She would do it on her own. First London, then the world. This newspaper interview was the next step, she could feel it. If that was what it took to get her message to a wider audience, then she would do it.

She heard the door open downstairs and a voice call out.

'I'll be down in a second!' she yelled back. 'Just in the bath.'

'Don't worry,' Holly's voice came back up. 'I'll dish up.'

Fiona was wrapping a towel around her head as she walked down the stairs.

'Smells good,' she called.

'I got Indian. I hope you don't mind; I just really fancied a biryani.'

'Sounds perfect.'

It was as if a lightning bolt had hit her, or a bullet slammed into her chest. She gasped as she set foot in the kitchen.

'What the hell is this?' Her stomach plummeted as she stared at the scene.

'I got a little carried away, didn't I?' Holly grimaced. 'I was just starving, and I didn't know what you'd fancy.'

Fiona could barely breathe as she stepped towards the table.

'Why did you do this?' she whispered. 'Why?'

She couldn't even start to count what was lying in front of her. She wanted to, but there was just too much, and her hands and head were shaking too much to focus. A plastic bag for the poppadum, plastic boxes for the curries, rices, samosas and pakoras. Small tubs for the sauces – lots of those – and a large one for the dhal. Two more plastic bags were on the table and one, in which something had leaked, was on the draining board.

She rushed to the table and began grabbing things, forcing lids onto containers, only to spill their contents everywhere.

'You need to get this out. Get this out of my house, now!'

'What?'

'You heard me. I said *get it out*.'

'Fiona, stop!'

Holly reached for her arm but she flicked her hand away.

'I don't understand. You asked me to come over and bring food. I told you I was getting takeaway and you love curry!'

'Not like this. Why would you do this?'

'Do what?'

Her heart was pounding. She'd splashed curry on her top,

the table, even on the wall, where it would probably leave a stain. She didn't care though. She just wanted it gone.

'Fiona, you're being ridiculous.'

She stopped.

'Pardon?' She turned slowly to face her friend.

'This can't be about the plastic?' Holly said. 'It's just a few tubs. If it is, then, like I said, you're being ridiculous.'

A new wave of heat engulfed her.

'That's what you think, is it? That's honestly what you think?'

Holly's jaw set. 'I do understand, Fi. You've had a traumatic experience. I guess I didn't realise quite how badly it's affected you. But you can't expect everyone around you to suddenly change their whole way of life just because you've had some kind of epiphany.'

'Why not?'

'Why? Because they're *our* lives. You can't dictate how we live.'

'But can't you see how wrong that is? Have you been listening to anything I've told you? Didn't you see what Martha went through?'

'Of course, I have. That's why I bought a reusable cup at the coffee shop yesterday. And I said no to a plastic bag in the paper shop.'

'Wow, one paper cup and one plastic bag. You're really going to save the fucking planet at this rate.'

Holly stepped back.

'Why are you doing this? Why are you being such a bitch? I'm sorry this upset you but—'

'Oh, so telling you the truth makes me a bitch now, does it? I thought that was your go-to line, that you can't offend people if you're telling them the truth, right? That's all I'm doing.'

'Is this to do with Rory?'

'This has *nothing* to do with him. Or Stephen. Or anyone. This is to do with you. Waltzing through life in your little bubble, not giving a toss about who or what you destroy in the process.'

The colour had drained from Holly's cheeks.

'Fiona, you need to stop this now. You need to stop.'

'And you need to get out,' she replied. 'And take all your rubbish with you.'

* * *

Several drinks were consumed between Holly leaving and Fiona finally dragging herself to bed. It just didn't make sense, any of it. How could her friend claim to be supportive and yet behave like that? Was she completely blind to everything going on around her?

She pulled off her shirt and headed to the bathroom. Maybe she had been a bit harsh, but she'd been right. It was people like Holly who were screwing up the planet. People like her thinking they could do just as they liked, without a second thought. They were no better than the John Orbitens of the world. Well, sod the lot of them. Holly would come round, see that Fiona was right. And if she didn't, well, did Fiona even want someone like that in her life anyway?

When she finally fell asleep, it was fitful. Every hour, she would wake in a hot sweat. Twice, she got up to get a glass of water. Twice, she struggled to fall back asleep.

When she awoke and found that morning had finally arrived, memories of the night before and the row with Holly hit her.

'Shit,' she muttered to herself.

That feeling of gloom soon gave way to another, as the image of Rory with his golden-haired beauty crept into her mind. One step forward, two steps back. That was what yesterday had been. Although it *had* been a big step forward, she reminded herself. For Martha and for herself. The business was safe. People were listening. The rest she would deal with in due course.

Feeling like hell, she pushed herself out of bed, thinking about all the things she had to do. That was, at least, the bonus of no boyfriend, or midlife crisis toy boy: plenty of time. Without the added distraction of Rory, she would be able to focus completely on work. And Holly would come round. She was the one in the wrong, after all.

* * *

'So how did it go?' Annabel was bouncing on her seat at an impressive pace, even for her. 'It went well, didn't it? I wanted to call you last night, but I didn't know where you'd be—'

'You mean the presentation?'

'Of course I mean the presentation. Did you ace it?'

'It did go well.' She smiled a little, finding Annabel's crazy grinning infectious.

'Yay!' Annabel flung her arms into the air. 'I knew it would. And now what? Eco events, here we come?'

Despite it all, Fiona couldn't stop herself from grinning.

'I feel like we should celebrate.' Annabel had stopped her bouncing to get the sentence out. 'Get cakes or something. I could go downstairs. Head to the shops. No plastic, obviously.'

The ache in her cheeks was starting to build. This was what saving the planet was meant to be like. This is how she'd expected people to behave. Fun. Happiness. Not like Holly with her dozen single-use tubs in one takeaway.

'I wouldn't say no to one of those artisan pastries,' she said, reaching for her wallet.

'Don't be silly. I've got these. We're celebrating. It's a sign of good times ahead. Things are going to sort themselves out, you'll see. Sod Dominic. Sod Octavia and those other clients. Sod the lot of them! You're going to come back bigger and better than before. I can just feel it.'

As Annabel skipped out of the room, Fiona ambled into her office and gazed out of the window.

It was peculiar, she reflected. Things were all up in the air yet, somehow, she felt calm. She'd weathered the worst of it. She'd bounce back. It wasn't like it was the first time she and Holly had argued. That was the whole point of true friendship, wasn't it? That you survived things like this. And to hell with men. What was she even thinking about, screwing around while she and Stephen hadn't even managed a single proper conversation? Maybe counselling would be the way forward.

She was still pondering this when she heard footsteps at the top of the stairs.

'That was fast, or have they already sold out?'

On receiving no reply, she turned and poked her head round the door.

'Stephen?' Fiona said, taken aback. 'What are you doing here?'

'That's exactly what I'm wondering.'

If the saying, *you're only as old as the woman you feel*, held any truth at all then, judging be the frazzled state of his hair and the bags under his eyes, he must have spent the last year-and-a-half in bed with an octogenarian. His tie was pulled loose around his neck in a manner he would most certainly have judged someone else for during working hours, but it was his eyes that were most alarming. Bloodshot and red and absolutely furious.

'What the hell have you been playing at?' he demanded.

'What are you on about?'

'What am I on about? Are you serious? Your stunt at the World Wildlife Conference or whatever the hell it was.'

'You've heard about that?' she replied, a glimmer of pride in her voice.

'Of course I've bloody heard about it. I've had John Orbiten on the phone since last night, asking why the hell my wife was trying to sabotage his company!'

'I wasn't trying to sabotage anything,' she sniffed. 'I was trying to open people's eyes. Get them to see what they're doing to the planet.'

'Since when have you given a shit about that? Oh wait, that's right, something to do with that stupid whale. That's what he said.'

She tensed.

'Stephen. I can see that you're upset but—'

'Upset? He thinks you did it because of me. Some kind of revenge, which I have to say rings true. Why else would you do something like that?'

'Why else? Did he listen to anything I said? Or is your ego so huge you think that everything revolves around you?'

He ground his teeth.

'Well, thanks to your little stunt, I had to explain our current situation. He put two and two together and now he's fired Penny.'

'Penny?'

'My secretary.'

'Oh.' She struggled to keep a smirk from her face. 'Well, I'm sure you'll give her a wonderful reference. *Goes above and beyond. Very versatile, ambitious.* Does that sound about right?'

He glared at her and was about to launch into another tirade when the sound of heels clicking on the stairs announced the arrival of a third party and he closed his mouth again. He couldn't say what he wanted to her now, she thought, and she certainly wasn't going to let him ruin Annabel's day. Not the wonderful mood she was in, after all the worry of possibly losing her job.

'Look, I'm sorry that things have gone tits up for you but, let's be honest, he couldn't have sacked your secretary for screwing you, if you weren't screwing your secretary. That's the truth. And everything I said at that conference, every single thing I said, was true too.'

Annabel appeared in the doorway. She blanched. Fiona nodded reassuringly. She was putting a stop to this.

'You need to go now,' she said matter-of-factly. 'If you don't mind, I've got a business to run.'

'Oh no you don't. Not any more.'

His voice was a mixture of hiss and whisper, low and resonant, sending a chill down her spine.

'What did you say?'

'I said, no you don't. You do not have a business to run.'

'Pardon?'

He straightened and locked eyes with her. It was impossible to believe that those same eyes had ever looked at her with anything close to love. All she could see now was a dark, malevolent bitterness. More hatred than she'd ever encountered in her life.

'Why do you think The Truncton Group came back to you? Why do you think any of them did?'

'You know about that?' She was starting to feel decidedly uneasy.

'Everyone thought you were off the rails. The only reason you've still got any clients is because I convinced them to stay with you, reminded them of how innovative your ideas had been in the beginning, when they first started with you. I reassured them that you were working on something special, something brilliant—'

'I am!'

His eyebrows rose.

'If you didn't believe that then why would you say it?' she demanded, rubbing her temples as she tried to fit the pieces of the puzzle together. 'Why would you get them to stay with me?'

'Why do you think?'

It took her a few moments for it to sink in. When it did, she wanted to retch.

'You thought it was because of you? You felt responsible? That all of this was because you walked out on me?'

'Well, it was, wasn't it?'

She shook her head in disbelief.

'You arrogant, supercilious son of a bitch. No, it bloody well wasn't.' Her laugh was harsh and guttural. 'Just you wait and see.'

It was Stephen's turn to look confused.

'See what?'

'The press.' She hissed at him. 'The press were there yesterday. They heard what I said. They loved it. So did a whole host of other people. I don't need your misguided nepotism. I've got interviews booked and I'll soon have clients banging on my door.'

'The press? Seriously?' He laughed. 'You think they'll be your saving grace in all this? You have no idea.' He laughed again. 'People like John Orbiten *are* the press. They own it. Powerful people like him don't care about you little people, unless you're lining their pockets for them. You really think the papers are going to print something that jeopardises one of their biggest advertisers? You're deluded.'

She shook her head. 'They have to. It's the truth.'

'And the British press are well known for telling the truth? If they do interview you, I'd love to read it,' he mocked. '*The woman who turns to saving whales when her husband leaves her.* I mean, it's not exactly broadsheet material, is it? But it sure would do well in one of those trashy, real-life magazines your mum used to read.'

She could feel herself shaking now. Her mind was struggling to make sense of what was going on. It wasn't just what he was saying; it was the way he was saying it. A month ago, she thought she would spend the rest of her life with this man. She had loved him. Adored him. Now she didn't even recognise him.

'What did I do?' she asked, as a tear trickled down her cheek. 'You were the one who cheated on me. You broke my heart. What the hell happened for you to become so damn vindictive?'

'You shouldn't have made this personal,' he hissed back at her. 'You shouldn't have brought Penny into this.'

'I didn't!'

She picked up the nearest thing she could find on Annabel's desk – a pack of Post-Its – and threw it at him.

'You conceited, self-centred bastard.' She picked up the day planner and that went too. Next it was a mug, just missing him, hitting the wall and shattering in a ceramic explosion. 'How was I supposed to know she'd get the sack? I didn't even know about her. You were the one screwing around, not me! You!' She went for another mug.

'You've lost your mind!' he shouted back, ducking.

'You self-absorbed twat. You little prick.'

'You're crazy. You're an absolute lunatic.'

'You think I give a damn now who you screw? You think I was thinking about you, when I was up on that stage?' She picked up Annabel's keyboard, only to see sense and lower it again. 'You know what, though? I'm glad she got fired. Let's see how well this love of your life works out when you've lost all the fun of sneaking around. Why don't you see how much you enjoy chasing after a twenty-something-year-old then? When she wants to go out clubbing every night and you need to be in bed with your snore strips so your sinuses don't play up.'

'You will never stage another event in this city, if I have to see to it myself,' he snarled, retreating past Annabel and down the stairs.

'*Screw you!*' she shouted after him.

30

Shards of broken china littered the carpet.

'You should sit down. You're shaking,' Annabel said. 'Take my seat. I'll get you some water.'

The smell of pastries wasn't enough to tempt Fiona to take a bite. She wouldn't have been able to swallow anything. Her throat had seized up, stopped functioning, like the rest of her, every part of it numb. It was only thanks to Annabel's dash across the room that she hadn't ended up on the floor too.

'Here, drink this.' Annabel slipped a glass into Fiona's hand and pulled up a chair next to her.

She took a tentative sip before placing it on the desk.

'You don't believe him, do you?' Annabel asked, shifting in her seat ever so slightly. 'About our clients? You don't believe he'll stop them working with us, do you?'

Fiona stared at the glass of water, as if the answer lay in its calm surface.

'I do,' she said. 'It makes sense. We'd remarked ourselves how strange it was that the ones who dumped us suddenly returned. He's a powerful man. He told them to stay, and now he'll tell them to go.'

'But they won't. Surely, they won't. They liked your new ideas, didn't they? You said they liked the new direction you're taking.'

'Maybe they did. Maybe they were just using that as an excuse to save face. It won't matter either way. You scratch my back, I'll scratch yours; that's how these things work. And Stephen's going to do anything it takes to get back into Orbiten's good books after this and the affair with Penny.'

It felt peculiar, giving a name to his mistress like that. She wasn't just a random, anonymous person any more. She had a name and soon she would probably have anything else she wanted too.

'So you think he'd go so far as to destroy his wife's company, her livelihood?'

'Well, he was intent on destroying our marriage,' she reminded her. 'It's not a huge leap from that.'

The sentence drifted into silence.

'What do we do now then?' Annabel asked, attempting to be positive, yet failing to hide her worry. 'I mean, when will we hear?'

'I don't know. I guess we just wait.'

And that was what they did. They sat at their respective desks, staring at silent screens, awaiting the inevitable.

Thoughts of her mother came to Fiona's mind. Of that last day at the hospital. The waiting. She'd been admitted before, after her first fall and the second. And then after the awful incident, when she'd gone missing for nearly twenty-four hours and was found in such a state, they all thought she would die of pneumonia. She hadn't. The last time, when Fiona was fairly certain that the inevitable was going to happen, had seen it coming for months, she thought she was prepared. How wrong she'd been.

As it turned out, they didn't have to wait long. No doubt Stephen had urged them all to make their intentions known as soon as possible. He would want quick results. A short, sharp, focused attack.

One of the executives sounded genuinely regretful. 'We really have enjoyed working with you, Fiona. And the new direction you're taking sounds very interesting. We're just not ready for that sort of change yet. Maybe in a couple of years.'

'Thank you, Chris. I appreciate you calling me in person and I'm so sorry we couldn't work it out together. Like you say, maybe down the line somewhere.'

By contrast, other clients sounded almost relieved. Not that it made any difference in the long run. Two didn't even have the courage to phone and sent emails. Dear Johns.

Different reactions, but the same outcome. Omnivents was dead in the water.

* * *

At midday, they decided to get some lunch. Fiona asked Annabel to head to King's Cross Market and grab a couple of tortillas there. She didn't actually want any food – she still hadn't touched the breakfast pastries and wasn't even sure if the tortilla man still had a stall over there any more – but she wanted some time alone. Even if Annabel didn't want to leave her on her own for long, she didn't have a choice.

It was absurd how a few hours could transform a place. This morning, her office had been alive, buzzing with opportunity. Now it felt dead. An empty echo chamber. There was nothing she could do. This was it. Then she remembered the card in her wallet.

Fishing around, she found it. She checked the name and dialled the number.

As soon as it was answered, she asked, 'Hello? Is that Catherine Green? It's Fiona. From the eco-conference. Fiona Reeves.'

'Oh, ah yes.' The voice at the other end sounded somewhat confused. 'Fiona and the whale.'

'Yes, that's right. That's me.'

'How are you?'

'I was just ringing to arrange that interview you talked about. I could come and meet you anywhere that's easy for you. I'm free all day today. Well, I'm free all week.'

'Oh, yes... thank you. Well... I spoke to my editor about it this morning and... well...' Short pauses punctuated her reply. 'At the moment, we're looking for something a little different.'

Fiona inhaled sharply. 'You mean something that doesn't upset your advertisers?'

Silence.

'You know you're supposed to be a journalist, don't you? This should be your job: telling the truth, letting people know what's going on out there. Your lack of balls is half the problem. You should hold people accountable, like you're supposed to...' She let the sentence drift.

'Look, I wish I could help. I really do. Maybe you could try one of the smaller papers? Or one of the online independents? Some of them have huge readerships. You can definitely get your story out there.'

'Just not with you?'

Another silence was all the reply she needed.

Fiona nodded. 'Of course.' She used the cheeriest voice she

could muster. 'I completely understand. Thank you for talking to me.'

'I really am—'

Fiona hung up before she could hear another apology.

So that was it. She placed her elbows on her desk and cupped her chin in her palms. Stephen was right. The ones with power keep their hold on it. That's the rule and damn the planet. Damn anyone and anything they hurt.

Deciding the debris from her fight with him had sat there long enough, she fetched a dustpan and brush from the cupboard. There was something more she was missing, she thought, flicking bits out of the carpet pile. Something that was making him act like that. Maybe there was already trouble in paradise with Penny. Maybe his plan was to make Fiona destitute, so that when he came crawling back, her only option would be to welcome him home with open arms. That would be twisted, for sure, but no more twisted than cheating on her for a year and a half.

She was still on her hands and knees mulling over the absurdity of the situation when a throat cleared behind her.

'Excuse me, sorry, is this a bad time? We're looking for Fiona. Fiona Reeves.'

Barely older than Joseph – although substantially less well dressed in a ripped band T-shirt – the girl stood a half a foot taller than the boy beside her, mostly due to the massive, wedged, knee-high PVC boots she was wearing.

'Is she in?' The girl spoke again. 'Fiona?'

'Oh, yes.' She pushed herself up from her knees and placed the dustpan and brush on Annabel's desk. 'Yes, I'm Fiona. What can I help you with?'

'Well, with planning an event, we hope.'

'I'm sorry if we've interrupted you,' said the boy, who she

felt was probably technically a man. 'We're not too sure how these things go.'

'You want to organise an event?'

'We've *got to* organise an event,' he stressed. 'A big one. And well, we, it—'

'We've been struggling and getting nowhere,' the girl interposed, 'and then you were recommended to us—'

'By whom?' she asked, wondering who on earth could have survived the Dominic, Octavia, and now Stephen blacklisting. 'Who was it that recommended me?'

The pair smiled. 'Jonas. He spoke ever so highly of you.'

'Said you have a real authenticity about you. A real positive energy.'

'Oh.' She racked her brain, trying to think of when, if ever, she'd known anyone by the name of Jonas. It didn't feel like a name she would forget.

'Sorry, which Jonas was that?' she asked. 'I know a couple,' she lied to cover her confusion.

'Of course, sorry. Jonas Oughton.'

Still nothing.

'He works at the Yoga Palace.'

'Ahh... ohh.' Her mouth dried and colour rose in her cheeks.

'He said he mentioned us to you? About the start up? With the big investors? You gave him your card to pass on to us.'

'Of course. Of course, I did.'

She studied the young couple. With *his* inability to make eye contact and *her* studded choker and belt, Fiona felt sure they were barking up the wrong tree approaching her, for whatever event they'd envisioned. Not to mention the issue of money. But beggars couldn't be choosers. In the worst-case scenario, she'd listen to their story, tell them she wouldn't be the right fit for them and send them down to Frolics and Fancies for their party needs.

'Well, why don't you tell me what you're after,' she said, ushering them to seats. 'Then I can tell you a little bit about me,' she offered.

It turned out to be one of those tech-company fairy tales you sometimes hear about. Two young kids design an app for fun, it's popular, attracts the attention of big business, but they refuse to sell. That attracts the attention of even bigger investors, at which point, they still refuse to sell, but agree to a partnership, still maintaining creative control. She had to admire their chutzpah.

'It's a catch twenty-two situation,' the girl said. She'd introduced herself as Jenny. 'We don't want to sell out to one of the big corporations,' she explained, 'but we want people to use our app. And to use it they have to hear about it, and to hear about it—'

'You need the backing of big investors to help you with advertising, development and everything else. I completely understand. So, what is it you want my help with, exactly? You have an event to organise, you said.'

'We do,' Caleb, the male half of the duo confirmed, looking overwhelmed. 'A launch party.'

'You don't sound too happy about that.'

With a reassuring hand on his shoulder, Jenny looked at her partner before turning back to Fiona.

'The thing is, you know those really geeky tech guys who spend all day shut in a bedroom, never see daylight and have no idea how to interact with humans in a real-life situation?'

'Not personally, but I get what you're saying.'

'Well, we're them. Like an extreme version of them.'

'We are not good at talking to people,' Caleb confirmed, picking at a hole in his jeans. 'Not good at all.'

'But you're talking to me just fine.'

Fiona sensed the overtones of motherly tenderness in her voice. She felt it too. Her thoughts flickered momentarily to Joseph; she needed to check in with him, see how he was doing.

'That's because we know what we need to talk to you about,' Jenny continued. 'And you are just one person.'

'And Jonas said you were a great listener.'

This surprised her. From what she could remember, very little talking or listening had been involved at all.

'Anyway, our investors said that the launch has to be big, make an impact,' Jenny told her. 'And they've given us a list of people that they want invited. Other than that, they said we were in control. We've got to come up with something really good.'

'We feel we've got to show that we are up it, to stand any chance of maintaining control of the business, you see,' added Caleb.

'I get it.' Fiona reached across her desk for a notepad. 'It makes sense. It's your launch and you want to have your mark on it.'

'Exactly.'

'Great. Okay. How big is the guest list?'

'Currently, around four hundred,' Caleb said.

'All right.' She wrote down the number, then circled it. 'That's doable. We can easily find a suitable space. When's the event going to be?'

There followed a fleeting exchange of glances and then both sets of eyes studied the carpet. It was, in fact, the very look of Joseph and his friend, before confessing to scraping her car on a bollard, only the second time of borrowing it.

'We just kind of let it get away from us,' Jenny finally spoke.

'Yeah, it's not like we weren't doing stuff, you know? We've been developing all these upgrades and building this new algorithm...'

'Okay, so when is the launch party meant to be?'

They still wouldn't make eye contact.

'It's got to be on Wednesday,' Caleb muttered.

'Wednesday? As in a week today?'

'Uh-huh.' Jenny's face was red.

'We didn't realise it was going to be so big though,' Caleb was becoming a little more vocal as he tried to justify their lack of action. 'We thought it would be, like, fifty people, you know? And we could have it a pub or something.'

'You wanted to launch your business in a pub?' Fiona couldn't hide her shock and disapproval.

'Like we said, we're new to this.'

Sitting back in her chair, she gazed at the page on her lap, which still contained only the three-digit number.

'This short notice, for a venue of the right size, you're really going to have to pay.'

'It's all right. We've got money,' Jenny assured her.

'Yeah, like crazy money,' Caleb added.

A seed of doubt crept into her mind. A newbie's idea of crazy money was very different to someone with experience, who knew just how expensive these things could be. She'd seen that enough times with start-ups.

'How much is your budget, exactly?' she pressed.

Jenny started flicking through her phone.

'There's the email. See.' She handed her phone to Fiona.

'Okay, so money is not going to be an issue.' She swallowed as she handed the phone back. 'What I don't understand is how you can have a guest list of four hundred and no venue. Don't these people already need to know where they're going?'

'No,' Caleb grinned. 'It's like one of those secret dining things. You don't find out until an hour before. No dress code, no venue. Nothing.'

'Okay...' That was something at least. Waiting for a venue to be announced had a much more positive impact than suddenly requiring it to be changed.

Had Fiona had a full client list, she would have run a mile from this, even with the size of the budget and the possible commission involved. She would have wished them well and given them the number of one of her solid – but inferior – competitors. But she hadn't. She'd a handful of clients left, at best. And this could be the exact thing she needed to give Omnivents a boost. Not to mention a few more contacts too.

'Okay, so I've heard what you need,' she said. 'But if I'm taking you on, this is what you need to know about the way I work...'

31

By the time they left, it was agreed. Fiona was going to take them on and find them – in seven days – a venue, including all catering, presentation facilities, the lot. In return, it was going to be a green event. No goodie bags filled with plastic crap.

'We are with you on that, man,' Caleb enthused.

'I'll need all your marketing material, any images or graphics you want included, ASAP.'

'I'll send them to you now,' Jenny replied. 'I'll give you everything we've got.'

'And I need you to know that this won't have all the bells and whistles I'm usually known for. I mean, I will do the very best that I can for you, I really will, with only one week to play with.' She exhaled heavily. 'But most companies would be talking to me at least three months in advance and even that would be pushing it.'

'Honestly, whatever you can do.'

Despite the spikey choker, Jenny looked a pitiful sight. *When did I become so sentimental?* Fiona wondered.

Standing, she signalled the end of the meeting.

'All right, I'll spend tonight and tomorrow seeing what I can pull together, and we'll catch up on Monday.'

'Thank you,' Jenny said, looking relieved. 'We just want to make a good impression. Shit, I feel like such an idiot! I mean, if this goes wrong, they could pull out, think we're not up to it and there goes all our backing.'

'Don't worry.' Fiona rested a hand on her shoulder. 'I'll handle this.'

She walked them to the stairs with a strange feeling of déjà vu, like waving Joseph off on his first school bus trip.

* * *

'So...' She turned around and faced Annabel who, returning with tortillas and drinks, had sat listening through a crack in the door. 'We've got a lot of work to do!'

It was good. Frustrating, but good.

At six o'clock, Fiona packed up her computer and began to head home, although her phone was still pressed to her ear as she walked.

'Honestly, that's completely fine. I quite understand. No, it's really last minute. Sure, maybe for the next one. I'll definitely keep you in mind.'

She had rung around close to thirty venue hotels already, all with nothing available.

'What about that old church on Hawkins Street?' Annabel had suggested.

'Tried it. There's an arts festival on next week that's booked up a lot of places. Then there are all the usual midweek weddings and I think someone said something about a fashion show.'

'And the hotels?'

'I'll have to try some of them again tomorrow. Half the events teams had packed up and gone home for the day.' She sighed. 'I just want something really special for them.'

'You'll do it.' Annabel had smiled reassuringly. 'I know you will.'

Dragging herself home, Fiona's hands, legs and every joint between her neck and her ankles throbbed. With over two weeks spent on, essentially, gardening leave from proper work, she'd forgotten how exhausting the job could be. The minute she stepped inside the house, she was going to kick off her heels and pour herself a large glass of something. That was the plan at least. However, when she reached her front door, it got unexpectedly derailed.

'What are you doing here?'

An icy sensation prickled across her skin.

Pushing himself up from the step, Rory looked at her.

'What do you think? I came to see you. You haven't replied to my messages. I thought something was wrong. You didn't tell me anything about yesterday; I was worried.'

'Well, there's nothing for you to worry about. You can go now. Come to think of it, how did you even know where I live?'

'You gave me your address, remember? You were going to cook me dinner.'

Huffing, she reached into her pocket for her keys and waited for him to move aside.

'Look,' she said, when he still hadn't budged. 'I've had one hell of a day. Seriously. And right now, I'm on the edge. I really don't need you here to be the tipping point.'

He frowned. 'What am I missing here? What's happened? I thought we were getting on great. Better than great.'

'Yeah, me too.'

'Then what's this about?'

Sighing, she pushed past him and jabbed her key into the lock. It wasn't a key that stuck, or at least it never had before, but she was having an unusual amount of difficulty making it work.

'Here.' He wrapped his arms around her shoulders. 'Let me help.'

'I don't need your help!' She shrugged him off as the key finally turned.

Once again, despite every part of her willing them not to, her eyes started to fill up. Looking at the sky, she attempted to blink her tears away. She didn't want him to think he was the cause. He definitely wasn't. It was exhaustion. Exhaustion from dealing with idiots. Exhaustion from battling every day and not just the last couple of weeks, she realised, but for years. Battling to be heard in a room where men's voices always got the attention. Battling to be taken seriously as a woman business owner, even by her own husband. Battling balancing being a good mum, a fair mum, one her son could turn to, with all the other demands on her. She was just exhausted.

'Fiona, please, just talk to me. I can see you're upset.'

Throwing her bag into the hall, she turned to face him.

'Do you know who should be upset?' she asked. 'Your girlfriend.'

'My girlfriend?'

'Or wife. Or whoever it was you were cosied up to in the café yesterday.'

This was like dealing with Stephen all over again. No denials, no excuses or explanations. Just his skin turning pale as the blood drained from it.

'See, not so easy to lie now, is it?' she demanded, stepping through the doorway, about to push the door closed.

He caught it with his hand. 'Fiona, please.'

'I popped by to say hi, that was all. Just thought it would be nice to see you.'

'Please, let me explain. It's not like that.'

'No, it never is.'

'I swear. It wasn't my girlfriend. I don't have a girlfriend. Or a wife. It was my daughter. I was with my daughter.'

The door was still wedged open, his foot now blocking it from closing.

'Please. I should have told you about her, I know now I should. But if you'll let me come in, I'll explain. I promise. I'll explain everything.'

What was it with her and falling for a sad face today? she scolded herself. Wife or daughter, she didn't want to hear any more. Yet, as she stepped inside, she left the door open behind her.

The need for wine was replaced by one for something stronger, for spirits. Pouring herself a vodka tonic, which she'd finished before even sitting down, an awkward silence hung between them. He was clearly waiting to see if she was going to offer him one too. She didn't.

'We got married young,' Rory started, realising that she had no intention of playing the hostess.

'How young?'

'Nineteen.'

'Jeez, that was young. Were you religious or something?'

He chuckled briefly, only for his face to fall again.

'No, we were not religious. We were just in love. We'd been together since we were fourteen. We were in love, and we thought we'd be together forever.'

'And you weren't.'

He scoffed. 'I was a kid playing at being grown up. I didn't know what responsibility meant. I thought I did. I was working in a kitchen and wanted to be a chef. And when Shelly – that's my ex – when she fell pregnant, I was so excited. Kept thinking about all these amazing things me and this kid were going to do together. We'd head out on hikes, go camping. Maybe we'd learn to ski or sail – all of those typically cheesy things.'

She allowed herself a small smile, despite her own growing sense of sadness at this description of young love.

'I was delusional. I didn't know what it was like to have a kid. Of course, I didn't. I was still one myself. And when Pippa was born, from day one, everything changed. I felt I'd had to give up my whole life, everything I'd dreamed about, you know, for this screaming child. It's tough to admit, but I did. And it wasn't as if Pippa even wanted to be with me, either. Any time I'd try to help, try to give Shelly a break, she would scream the whole house down, like I was the worst person that she could possibly be left with. She would go purple in the face.'

'All babies do that.'

'I know that now, of course. I know lots of things now. But, back then, I didn't.'

'So, you left,' she said.

'Deep down I knew that I was leaving for me. That I was leaving to get my life back. But I'd managed to convince myself that everyone would be so much better off without me. I packed up and I went travelling. Didn't look back. By the time I grew up enough to realise what a dick I'd been, Shelly had moved on, and Pippa had a new man in her life who she called Daddy.'

'I'm sorry.'

'Don't be. It's not your fault. It was my own doing.'

'So now? Are you and Pippa close?' She handed him a vodka of his own.

'We're working on it. I think we'll always be working on it, if I'm honest. For a while, I got angry, really angry. Decided I was going to fight for her. I wasn't going to have another man being called Daddy by my baby girl. It just wasn't going to happen. So I got myself a lawyer, went to court, the whole nine yards. Social service visits. Family counselling. God, I dragged them through everything I could. Honestly, I've done a few things in my life that I'm not particularly proud of. But the way I treated Shelly during those years... that's the worst of it.'

She could see the pain in his eyes, as if it were only yesterday.

'What happened then?'

With a small sniff, he reached down and lifted the glass to his lips. 'I was angry,' he said, after taking a sip. 'It went on for years. The court dates, the solicitors. And then Pip was about to start secondary school. You know, she was a proper person. Not just a kid any more. And I had visitation rights. I just didn't think it was enough. That was why I was still fighting. But I was starting to see a change in her. The resentment she had for me. She'd have never said anything – she's too much like her mum – but it was there. And then, one day, I was standing outside the courthouse, waiting to see the judge. And I saw them all: Shelly's family. And that was when it hit me.'

'What did?'

'All the pain. The pain that I was causing them. Me kicking up like that, it wasn't helping anyone. Especially not Pippa. I knew Shelly would be in the same boat as me, having to use up all her savings to keep fighting. I'd known that I probably wouldn't stand a chance, but if I couldn't take my daughter from her, then I'd at least take everything else: her money, her time, even her new relationship, if I could. And that was when I had my eureka moment.'

For the first time since he'd started, he looked from the ground, directly at her. 'I did lie to you. I said this whole lifestyle thing was a gradual change. That I wasn't like you. But the fact was, it was exactly the same. I watched as Shelly kissed Pippa goodbye and then kissed this guy – Ted, his name is – and Pippa took his hand. She had a brother by then as well – two, now. And they were all there together. And they looked like such a perfect family. They are a perfect family. No matter what I was putting them through, they were sticking this out together. And I was trying to ruin it all for them. And why? Because I screwed up. Me. It was all on me. Ted hadn't done anything. Shelly hadn't. God knows, Pip couldn't do anything bad if she tried. And yet there I was doing my best to tear their lives apart, to make myself feel better.'

'So, what happened then?'

'I apologised.'

'Just like that?'

A sad, but coy, smile appeared for the first time.

'Let's say I grovelled. A lot. Promised to do things on their terms. If that was leaving Pippa alone, then that was what I was going to do. Believe me, it's taken us a long time to get where we are now. And things are still far from perfect, but Shelly's a great mum. Puts Pippa first no matter what. She'd never wanted me out of her life.'

'And where does the shop fit into all this?'

'My dad. He died only a couple of months after that day. It was part of the reason I changed so much too. I decided to do something good in this world, so I took all the money he left me and ploughed it into the business. Every last penny. That's why it was so important to me that it worked.'

Fiona lifted her glass back up to her lips and held it there a moment, before remembering it was empty and lowering it back down again.

'You could have told me all this.'

He nodded slowly. 'I could have. I should have, but I just didn't feel ready. You seemed to see me like some kind of rock, and I liked that. Honestly, it was the first time in a long time that anyone had looked at me like I was the one who had it all together. I liked being this stable person you could rely on. I didn't want to ruin that illusion and disappoint you.'

She fought back the urge to reach out and touch him.

'So, you lied?'

'I know. I know I did. I guess I just wanted you to get to know the good parts of me, before you learned about all the screwed-up bits.'

'Ah, yes,' she smiled. 'I went for the same approach too. You may have noticed. I definitely showed you my best side first.'

His small smile became somewhat more substantial.

'Yeah, I definitely noticed that.'

This time, her hands didn't hesitate. They reached across and took hold of his.

'And now?' she asked.

'And now it's whatever you want it to be.'

And at that moment, she knew exactly what that was.

32

'So, what happened today?' Rory asked as he lay back and patted to the point on his collarbone where she should nestle in. Fiona sank her head down against him. A pleasant warmth radiated through to her.

'When you came home,' he clarified. 'You said you'd had one hell of a day. What happened?'

'A lot,' she answered.

'Such as?'

'Well, for starters, my husband heard about the speech I made at the conference.'

'Shit.' He sat up, dislodging her from her comfortable resting place. 'The conference! That was the reason I came here. How did it go? You spoke, right?'

'Oh, I spoke all right.' She pushed him back down onto the bed. 'And it went well. Well enough to ruffle a few feathers.'

'That's good.'

'Not exactly.' She shifted around a little to see him better. 'My husband's boss was there. I might have laid into him and companies like his a little too much.'

'And I'm guessing your husband wasn't too happy about that.'

'That's an understatement. He rang around all my remaining clients and got them to drop me.'

This time, she caught him before he could spring back up. 'You're kidding? You have to be kidding?'

'Nope. Apparently, he felt that my speech was a personal vendetta against him and his girlfriend, so he decided to trash the one thing I had left going for me in my life.'

'Honestly? And you were married to this guy?'

'I still am,' she said quietly. She could hear his heart thumping angrily in his chest.

'Jeez.'

Tinkling wind chimes played somewhere outside.

'I got a visit from some kids though,' she said, her fingers moving in circles around his chest. 'They need me to set up a launch party for their start up. A very lucrative launch party.'

'That sounds good.'

'It is. The only thing is, I have to somehow find a venue that can hold four hundred people, by next Wednesday. It will have to be able to adhere to my new ethically sustainable manifesto too.'

His hand caressed her cheek. 'You're going for a sustainable business?'

'It would be easier if I could just forget it all and go back to how things were. But I can't. So I have to.'

'You know what?' he said, raising her face to his and kissing her softly on the lips. 'You sure know how to win a guy over.'

* * *

'I was thinking,' she said, watching Rory conjure up a feast from the random tins and packets gathering dust at the back of her cupboard. 'If I found the right venue, would you do the catering for it?'

He stopped stirring and twisted around to her. 'Are you serious?' he asked.

'Yes, completely.'

'No,' he said, firmly, and turned back to the hob.

She fixed them both a drink and carried his across to him, placing it on the countertop beside him.

'Why not?'

'You want me to list the reasons? It's a terrible idea.'

She stepped back, sipping her drink and trying to work out what she'd missed.

'It would be perfect. It would fit in with everything I'm trying to do.'

'Have you ever worked with someone you're in a relationship with before?' he asked, stirring in some spices she didn't even know she had.

'No,' she said, smiling. 'So, we're in a relationship?'

Sighing, he balanced the spoon on top of the pan and twisted around, taking hold of her by the hips.

'Whatever we are to each other right now, do you really want to risk ruining it before it's even started?'

'Who said it would ruin it?'

'Besides, if this thing is as big as you say, you really think you're going to manage to get them on board with the idea of waste food?'

'If I can persuade anyone, it would be these guys.'

'Okay, then what if I couldn't source enough food?'

'You said you always get plenty.'

'Yes, but that's to run a café. You're talking about four

hundred covers, plus enough for The Dumpster Dive too. I couldn't risk it. It's too hit and miss.'

Disappointed, she slunk back to her seat. She could see his logic but that didn't mean it wasn't annoying.

'Although,' he said, switching off the hob and turning around. 'I may have an idea for your venue.'

* * *

It was a peculiar feeling, kissing him goodbye at her front door. Part of her wanted him to stay the night, fill that side of the bed that had been cold and empty for so long. But she knew he had to go. She also needed some time by herself. Time and space to assimilate; there had been a lot going on. Besides, there was something she needed to do. Something she must see to without delay.

A phone call would have probably been the most mature way to deal with the problem, second only to going round and apologising face to face but, no matter how much she knew she owed her friend an apology, it didn't make it any easier. After starting to dial and then chickening out at least half a dozen times, she took the coward's way out.

> Sorry. I messed up. I miss you.

Three dots appeared only to disappear again. The message had been read. She waited. Nothing.

> Please forgive me.

Still no reply.

'Goddammit, Holly,' she muttered, glaring at her phone, willing it to beep. Five minutes later, she was still glaring.

After showering, drying her hair and setting up a work schedule for the next day, she still hadn't received a reply.

This is stupid, she told herself, desperately nervous about ringing her best friend. But she was going to have to swallow her pride and make that call. Scrunching up her face, as if in agony, she opened the screen and pressed call. It couldn't have been more than one ring away from going to voicemail when Holly finally picked up.

'Yes?'

Her pulse soared. Part of her was expecting Holly not to answer at all – that they would eventually get back to messaging and the whole thing would be resolved that way. She was soon wishing she hadn't.

'You can slap me if you want to. I probably deserve it,' she offered.

Her initial apology had been met with nothing more than a derisive snort.

'Can't say I disagree.'

Silence. There was no way Holly was going to let her get away with it without grovelling. Well, if that was what she wanted, that was what Fiona was going to have to do.

'I messed up. I'm sorry. I'm so freaking sorry. I just got caught up in my own little bubble.'

'You think?'

She ignored the sarcasm.

'Look, with everything that was going on... with Joseph moving out, and Martha, and this thing with Stephen and Penny. I guess—'

'Wait, did you say Penny?' Holly's previous bitterness had

suddenly evaporated. 'Does that mean you've found out who she is?'

Fiona sniffed. 'The secretary.'

'Honestly? That man is a fucking cliché.'

'Well if it helps, I got her sacked.'

'You did *what*?'

Fiona smiled to herself. They were getting back to their old selves. There was nothing like gossip to draw Holly in. Bit by bit, she could feel the barrier crumbling. Soon the silences became natural ones and, with each remark, a little more of the hurt and anger was whittled away and laughter replaced it.

'So, lunch on Friday?' Holly asked. 'You up for that?'

'I think we should make it every Friday, don't you?'

* * *

'You look good,' Annabel commented when Fiona arrived at the office the next morning.

'Thank you. I feel good too. I don't suppose any of the possible venues have got back to us, have they?'

'Not with anything useful.'

'Okay, well, we'll keep trying. If we don't find anything by the end of the day, I've got one more avenue I can explore.'

'We'll find something. I'm sure of it.'

Although Fiona had pretended otherwise, she was more than a little hesitant to go along with Rory's suggestion. It wasn't that she didn't think the place would be great; she was sure it would be. It was the idea of needing to rely on him for this make-or-break moment in her career. This had unpleasant echoes of what had happened with Stephen and she wasn't going to take that route again in a hurry.

But by Thursday evening, she was struggling.

* * *

'Look, we'll just go and take a look at the place. If you don't like it, don't use it. But it's crazy not to even consider somewhere that might be perfect. You never know.'

'What is it called again?' she asked.

'The Camellia House. The restaurant opened up about a month ago, but it's a great venue too. Lots of space.'

'So, why isn't it already booked?'

Rory slid a homemade burger onto her plate.

'They had some issues with licensing. Fire regs and stuff. Don't worry,' he said, seeing the reaction on her face. 'It's all good now. They got the clearance to start holding events over the weekend.'

'You know this how?'

'Let's just say I have people on the inside. We'll go after the lunchtime rush tomorrow?'

'All right then,' she reluctantly agreed.

* * *

Getting Holly to approve her choice of The Dumpster Dive for lunch had been incredibly easy, given her penchant for trying to embarrass Fiona.

'So, you and him, this is a thing now?' she asked, eying Rory over the top of her kombucha.

Fiona did her best to act dumb. 'He's taking me to see a venue as soon as we've finished. That's all.'

'That is clearly not all.'

'Well that's all you're getting here.'

'I'll be two minutes,' Rory mouthed, as Fiona and Holly said their farewells.

'No worries,' she mouthed back as she gave her friend one more squeeze goodbye.

'And I'll see you over the weekend?' she asked.

'I'll check my schedule.' Holly smiled coyly. 'I may have a free hour.'

Less than two minutes later, Rory appeared again and took her hand, ready to leave.

'Don't take this the wrong way,' she said, half a mile down the street. 'But you look nice. Have you brushed your hair or something?'

'Maybe.' He grinned in a way that made her stomach flutter.

'You did that for me?' she asked, reaching and tugging gently on his man bun.

'Not exactly,' he said.

A quick Internet search before she'd left the office had told her that The Camellia House was one of the trendiest new hangouts in West London, perfect to launch a tech company. It also told her that the restaurant was fully booked for the next month and a half although, when she mentioned this to Rory, he seemed somewhat dismissive.

'Don't worry. They know we're coming,' he said. 'And besides, we're not eating there.'

For the entire journey, her hand stayed in his, fingers entwined, quite unlike the way Stephen used to hold her hand. She felt his grip tighten when they crossed a road, or he manoeuvred them past people. And when he did let go, when rounding a lamppost and on the escalator in the Underground, her palmed tingled, waiting for the return of his warmth. She could get used to this, she thought.

'I can never work out whether I like places like this,' she said, when they stopped on the other side of the road to their destination.

'Trust me, you're going to love the inside.'

'You think you know what I like already?' she asked, a questioning grin on her face.

'I'm getting there.'

The grey stone of the building was accompanied by grey, metal window frames. The drainpipes were oversized, giving the place an industrial feel. It was stark, modern for modern's sake, in her opinion. Her first impression was that it would suit her young clients down to the ground.

'We should get inside. They'll be waiting for us.'

They crossed the road and he stepped forward to push the door open for her. Still holding his hand, she was part-way through when she ran head on into the person coming out.

'Sorry, I—' She stopped and did a double take. 'Stephen!'

A layer of sweat formed between her hand and Rory's which, reflexively, she held onto even tighter. A reassuring squeeze came back.

There were several ways this could go now, she realised. Several choices available to her.

'After you,' she said, looking her husband straight in the eye and stepping back onto the pavement.

His face was a picture: pinched, eyes narrowed on Rory with a look of confusion. Without waiting for a reply, she dropped Rory's hand and reached across her husband.

'And you must be Penny.' She smiled at the young woman with the overly bronzed face. 'I've heard so much about you. It's great to finally meet you. I hope the job hunting's going okay.'

The woman's mouth opened and shut like a fish. 'Oh, yes. Thank you. Well, we've met before, actually.'

'We have?'

'At last year's Christmas party? You had the most amazing dress. The blue backless one.'

Fiona was agog at the pure innocence with which the girl spoke.

'Ahh yes, the Michael Williamson. Well, I probably won't wear it any more, so I'd be delighted to pass it on to you.'

'Really?'

'Of course. You're fine with my cast offs, aren't you?'

'Oh well, only if you don't mind.'

'No, not in the slightest. Be careful, though. It's a bit flimsy. I wouldn't plan on getting too much use out of it, if I were you.'

She waited, lips pressed together in a perfect smile as her eyes fleetingly met Stephen's. She would have liked some sort of reaction. Something reminiscent of the scene in her office. But he had too much sense for that.

'I think Penny and I should be going,' he said, glowering at her.

'Yes.' She stepped back even further and made room for them to pass. 'And Penny, good luck with the job hunting again. I'm sure you'll find something out there.'

She watched as Stephen pressed his hand against the small of Penny's back and hurried her across the road. Only when they were safely out of sight did she fall back against Rory, trembling.

'That was Stephen. My husband,' she said.

'Yeah, I got that,' he said with a small smile. 'You okay?'

'Well, it could have gone worse, I suppose,' she replied.

'I thought you handled it beautifully.'

'You did?'

'Well, you were absolutely horrible.'

'But funny, right?'

'Oh, very funny. But evil. Utterly evil.'

'I can live with that.'

Reopening the door, he once more held it for her to pass through, but she stayed where she was.

'It's not actually true,' she said, her eyes on the patch of ground where her husband had stood only moments ago.

'What's not?'

'About her taking my cast offs. I'm the cast off. I'm the one who was no longer wanted.'

A wave of sadness rippled through her.

'Well, it's a good job you've found a man who likes saving things from the rubbish pile then, isn't it?' he replied, and kissed her on the lips. 'Cast offs are my specialty. Now, are you going to stand here all day and mope, or do you want to see this place?'

33

'This is perfect!' Fiona turned in a circle, trying to take in everything the space had to offer and then strode over to a corner and, pacing it out, started planning where things would go. Then she headed over to the other side of the room to do the same, before returning to Rory.

'It's industrial yet inviting. Stylish yet unpretentious.'

'Which is exactly what you were going for, isn't it?' he asked.

'How do you know me so well?' She stretched up on tiptoes and kissed him on the lips. 'And why did they just let us in here on our own? I thought you said the Events Manager was going to meet us?'

'Let me ring her.'

While he took out his phone, she continued to look around. The room was ideal. The clever use of wood, together with metal in soft, copper shades, gave a warmth to the place. It was wide, with plenty of open space for people to gather together in for the presentation, yet had enough little nooks and crannies which Jenny and Caleb could hide in, if the need arose.

'She's coming over now.'

A minute later, the door opened. The woman who walked towards them had a distinct familiarity about her. She was young – substantially younger than Fiona – with loose, wavy hair and an easy smile. Fiona tilted her head, trying to work out where she recognised her from.

'Fiona, this is Pip. Pip, Fiona.'

'Pip, as in... Pippa?'

'Yes, as in my daughter.'

The change in her pulse was immediate, as she stepped away from Rory. He laughed.

'It's fine. I've told her who you are.'

'All good things, I promise,' Pippa said, as she moved forward and kissed Fiona on the cheek – one side only – which was currently glowing pink.

'Well.' She hesitated, quite mortified by the situation. 'I've eaten at your father's café a few times. We have a professional interest in recycling. I mean we're only... I am actually still ma—'

'Okaaay,' Pippa said, trying hard to suppress a smirk, in a way that was uncannily like her father's. 'I'm going to ignore whatever's obviously going on here. Rory just said he had a friend who was looking for a venue.'

'Oh, yes.' Fiona breathed a sigh of relief, then realised that she'd probably just made the whole thing look even worse. She momentarily wished that the safety checks had missed something and the floor would conveniently open up and swallow her. 'I'm the friend. The friend who needs a venue.'

Pippa laughed. 'It's fine, honestly. Let me show you the place.'

After discreetly glowering at Rory, she followed Pippa around, making notes as she went.

'The speaker system has just been installed. The PA is state-of-the-art although, even without it, the acoustics in here are great.' She had the same easy manner about her as her father. 'I assume Rory told you we'd had a licensing issue?'

'He did, and that's all sorted now, isn't it?' she asked. Running an illegal event would definitely be the final nail in her coffin.

'Yes, the paperwork came through yesterday. We've started taking reservations today.'

'And Wednesday? Do you have anything booked here for Wednesday?'

'Not yet.' She grinned.

'Then, in that case, I think I've found myself a venue. Now, I guess we should talk about food.'

Pippa grimaced. 'I wish we could do that, but I'm afraid we can't,' she said. 'The restaurant is already booked to capacity. If I'm honest, the Manager wasn't quite expecting that. They're looking at getting more staff in, but there's no way that's going to happen in time for your event.'

Fiona cast her eyes pleadingly towards Rory.

'Nope,' he said. 'Not doing it.'

Pippa laughed. 'I could have told you he'd say that. Hates anything with big numbers. But from what he's been telling me, I might have an idea that would be right up your street.'

* * *

At 9 a.m. on Monday morning, Caleb and Jenny were sitting in her office, in identical clothes to the week before. Not that she judged them. Less washing was good for the environment, she'd discovered from Rory's sniff-and-air approach. Secretly, however, she'd vowed to grab anything of his that started to smell a bit dodgy and slip it in with her wash at home. She was taking this sustainable-living drive one step at a time and clean clothes were still pretty high on the list of things she wasn't willing to forego.

'It sounds amazing,' Jenny said.

She was sucking a lollipop, one of those hard, round ones, entirely designed to rot teeth. Fiona was having a hard time not snatching it from her and throwing it in the bin. She was a client, she kept having to remind herself. An immature one, sure, but one she currently owed a lot to.

'I mean, we trust you and everything and if you say this is the best choice, then we'll go with it.'

'There won't be any problems,' she assured her.

'Well, we're with you, Captain.' Caleb offered some strange form of salute, which the women decided best to ignore.

'All the invitations are set to go out at five o'clock on Wednesday, just as you asked,' Annabel said. 'You're sure you don't want us to put out anything beforehand? Like a sort of teaser, with the post code or something?'

'No.' Jenny removed the lolly from her mouth and shook her head. 'This'll work, trust us.'

* * *

The next morning, Fiona rolled over in bed. Something felt different. Shifting around, her foot dropped over the edge. Her eyes pinged open and a small smile crept across her face, where she let it linger. For the first time since Stephen's departure, she had spread herself out across the whole of the bed. Both sides, including his. The feeling of satisfaction was soon replaced, however, with one of nerves.

In her office, she paced up and down. She came out to reception.

'This just feels all wrong, you know? Like we should be doing something. We should be filling bags, or stuffing envelopes.'

'I know,' Annabel agreed. 'I've used up a whole notepad drawing little stick men, just to be doing something.'

Fiona frowned.

'It is a recycled notepad,' Annabel added quickly.

Ten minutes later and Fiona was back again.

'I think I should go and check that no one's moved the screens,' she said.

'Did they say they were going to move them?'

'No, but you never know. Pippa's great and everything, but... maybe I'll pop over there.'

'Why don't you just ring her?'

'Then she'll think I'm checking up on her.'

'And that will be different if you turn up, how?'

It was a valid point, Fiona conceded.

'Perhaps I'll just head home. Get an early night. You should go too. Go home. Read.'

'Are you sure you don't want me to stay?'

'What, and draw even more flick books? No, you go home. Waste your own paper.'

Together, the women packed up their things and headed out onto the street.

Back at home, Fiona fixed herself a meal. Her fridge was currently filled with a plethora of freshly bought produce and Rory's leftovers. Sunday, she'd gone to the farmer's market and made Holly a meal from scratch.

'I'm worried you're not even my best friend at all. I think your body's been taken over by an alien,' Holly had laughed as she helped herself to seconds.

'Would it surprise you if I said I had Joseph on video call as I cooked?'

'Thank God he was. I can't imagine what we'd be eating, otherwise.'

'What do you mean? I think I've found my metier.'

Holly had grimaced but then burst out laughing, reminding Fiona how important this friendship was to her.

Tuesday evening found her eating the last of the leftovers from that meal.

'How are you feeling about tomorrow?' Rory asked, the sound of pans clattering in the background, as he talked on speaker phone. Outside her own window came the gentle rumble of thunder, with the accompanying patter of rain, a counterpoint to the quiet of the house around her.

'I'm good. I think. As long as everything's still the way I left it, I'll be fine.'

'It will be. Pip's on top of things. I was thinking maybe we could all have dinner together, once this is out the way. I'd love for you to get to know her better.'

She put her fork down on her plate and reached for her glass.

'I don't know. Don't you think that's a bit soon? To introduce me as, whatever I am? I still haven't told Joseph anything about the last couple of weeks.'

'There's no rush. Take as long as you want.'

She was about to say something else, about the fact that it didn't mean she wasn't happy with the way things were going, she just needed a bit more time to make adjustments, when her thoughts were interrupted by more loud clanging and several grunts from his end.

'What is going on there?' she asked. 'Do you want me to call back?'

'No, it's fine, it's fine.' His voice sounded further from the phone now. 'This new juice store has just opened up in Covent Garden. I've made an arrangement to take all their veg pulp off them. Let's just say it was a little more than I'd bargained for.'

'Why? How much have you got?'

'Today? About twenty kilos of beetroot and the same again of carrots. It's going to be burgers and carrot cake on the menu for a while. I think we might have to come to a different arrangement.'

She laughed.

After another twenty minutes or so of chat about their days, she hung up the phone and ran a bath. She wouldn't sleep well tonight, she never did before a big event, so anything she could do to keep her mind distracted was a bonus.

But it was going to be great, she could just tell.

Once in the bath, she dipped her head under the surface and considered Rory's proposal again. Pippa was lovely, and she'd been right on top of everything with regard to the venue, but things had already moved far faster than she'd anticipated. Lunch with his daughter, without even having talked to Joseph first, didn't seem fair. It wasn't that she didn't think it would happen eventually; she just wasn't willing to go by anyone else's timetable but her own. Besides, there was the small matter of still being married. She just hoped Rory hadn't taken it too personally, that was all.

Realising there was one thing she could resolve straight away, she sat up in the bath, spraying water onto the floor as she reached over for her towel. Five minutes later, she was downstairs, in her dressing gown with a pen in her hand.

Even after everything he'd put her through, it still wasn't easy to write her name. She thought back to the good times. Summer drinks in pub gardens, when they had just got together. Their wedding day, so full of happiness that in almost every photo of her at the reception, she was creased up laughing. Joseph. Joseph being born. Joseph growing up. All those precious moments the three of them had shared. It was hard to finally sever all of those links.

She shook her head to clear the images from her mind. She would keep those memories for ever, but she had new ones to make now. Exciting ones. The spark between her and Stephen had faded as the years had progressed. Now she had the chance to ignite a new one. Wiping away a tear that had somehow strayed onto her cheek, she brought the nib of the pen back down to the divorce papers and signed.

EPILOGUE

The event ran like a dream.

Thanks to Pippa's and Rory's contacts, the food was brilliant and turned up on time, without a single piece of plastic in sight.

Jenny and Caleb, dressed in suits, worked the room like pros, managing to contain their nerves and chat with people who, only two hours before, hadn't even a clue where they were heading.

Annabel was there too, bubbly as ever, enthusing to anyone who came near about their new, ethically minded approach to business and how everyone can do something to help the planet.

And Fiona? As she handed out business cards, she felt the small flame of hope grow stronger. Maybe she'd finally found her calling. But the thought that lingered in her mind, long after that evening was over, was that she had made a start, to help all the Marthas out there. She wasn't going to change the world overnight. Perhaps even a hundred events down the line, she would still be fighting to see the changes she wanted. But she would still be fighting, because that was what Martha deserved.

AFTERWORD

Dear Reader,

Yay! You made it. Thank you so much. I knew I could rely on you. You looked like one of the good ones when you started reading this.

So, first of all, you should know that there's a lot of nonsense in the book. A lot. As authors like myself are often inclined to, I have used a bit of artistic licence in one or two places. For starters, a giant sperm whale has never, to my knowledge, made its way into the Thames. Also, the Institute of Marine Life and Conservation is a made-up organisation but, even if it did exist, I suspect they would probably keep all their data and photos stored on a computer. But you never know. Maybe they'd need to print them off for presentations or some such.

It is also unlikely that a whale dying in the Thames would be driven all the way down to Plymouth. It would probably be dissected where it washed up, before its body was carted away and dumped in a landfill.

I have tried to be as accurate as possible with facts and figures but, with so much contradicting information regarding waste production, recycling, etc., in the end I had to go with an acceptable average.

Sorry to those of you who maybe found the romance a little sappy but, deep down, I know you love a good old happy-ever-after, even if you try to deny it. I'm with you there. It just makes the day feel a little bit brighter, when someone's story ends well. And it was a book themed around a dead whale, remember. It did need a little bit of light relief in there too.

So that's it. The book I tore my heart apart to write. Seriously. You try researching something like this and still feel the same at the end of it. You won't, trust me on that.

Now, obviously, you're an intelligent person. (You finished this book, didn't you, after all?) You might just have sensed my ulterior motive for writing it in the first place, between all the talk of friendship, love and dirty dealings. I hope I didn't ram it down your throats too much though. If I did, I genuinely do apologise. It was really tricky, seeing how far I could push it. How many facts and figures could I slip in there, without you tossing the book aside like all the bloody circulars that get posted through your letter box? But you didn't.

Despite my inspiration for this story, and determination to try and make a difference, I do need to admit that I'm not the person I want to be. I am so many miles from it. I still buy a cucumber wrapped in plastic, if there is no alternative, for my daughter's school lunch bag. I still forget to check whether something like a cardboard box of chocolate chips I've bought for baking, has a secret plastic liner inside. (I did mention I talk about food a lot, didn't I? Sorry, it's an issue.) I'm nowhere near perfect. But here's the thing about perfection – it's unattainable. It's a high-protein, low-fat, raw vegan diet. It's thinking only kind and rational thoughts, when you're faced with that idiot at work who insists on mansplaining something to you, despite the fact that you've been doing the job a darn sight longer than he has. Attempt either of these things and, one day in, you realise that they're unsustainable. What's the point? Perfection is not possible. Trying is.

In the course of writing this story, I read a lot of reports, a lot of statistics and I've dropped a few of them in – sorry if it was too many but, believe me, there are hundreds more on the cutting-room floor – but here's one more. From me to you. For all of you who've got this far and didn't feel I was preaching to the converted. But, before I share it with you, you should know that I'm not some big-time author. I'm indie. Small fry. I don't sell a hundredth of the books that many out there do. Or that I'd like to. I have some amazing people following me and I'm continually grateful for their support, but the success I'm looking for here is not just based on how many sales I'm hoping it might make, but how many people it touches.

If I sell a thousand copies this year, I would be thrilled, particularly if a thousand people get this far. I don't doubt for a moment that a fair few will abandon the journey along the way, but play along with me for a minute please; I'm being optimistic. Say a thousand of you reach this point and make the decision, with me, to cut down on two pieces of plastic a week. I don't care what they are. Wrapped vegetables. Balloons – God, don't get me started on balloons. Plastic earbuds. I couldn't care less, but let's pick something. Let's pick the earbuds. Say you used two less a week. Say you all do the same. That would be two thousand less a week. That's over one hundred thousand less a year, not to mention the plastic boxes they come in. I'm just going to write that in figures: 100,000. That's more bits of plastic, that we could stop going into landfills or the ocean, than there are words in this book. That's the difference we could make, with that one, tiny change. You and I together. That's why

I had to write this book. Why it's so much more important than anything I have ever written before, or probably will do again. Because I honestly believe that we can make a difference.

Okay, that's the preachy bit over and done with. You should go on and read the acknowledgements. (It won't push you over the 100,000 mark, just in case you were worried.)

Hannah

Edit: A week after this book was originally published, a real sperm whale got stuck in the Thames and sadly died. Since then, there have been at least two more cases.

ACKNOWLEDGEMENTS

I must confess that writing acknowledgements is my least-favourite part of writing a book. I'm always so worried about forgetting someone that it completely stresses me out. I also worry about being too gushy, or not gushy enough. But with these acknowledgements, for the first time, I'm a little excited.

First of all, I need to thank a lot of people I've never met.

Jen Gale. When I first started making a conscious effort to minimise my unnecessary consumption of plastic and other goods, many years ago, her Facebook group was there with invaluable ideas. It's been through some name changes since then, but it continues to be an inspiration.

Rob Greenfields, whose journey could not have been more inspiring. Each year, he makes me want to do more and more.

Hugh Fearnley-Whittingstall, you are amazing for opening so many people's eyes to what is going on, mine included.

All those people who take the time to put information out there, like Sisters Against Plastic, who aren't afraid to share their journey, so that the rest of us can learn. The world needs people like you.

Okay, now onto people I have actually met.

My team at Boldwood, thank you for taking a chance and giving this book a second lease of life.

To everyone at The Hive for my first experience of a zero-waste shop and one of the places I miss most, now I no longer live in Kuala Lumpur. You were so patient, so willing to teach. Thank you.

To all the people involved in the process of getting this book out there. Particularly Carol, whose commitment to making this book its best version was tireless.

The amazing TBCers, Book Connectors, and Bloggers. You lot are incredible forces. Thank you so much.

To my daughter, Elsie, who makes me work that little bit harder. (Literally. That girl loves plastic toys.)

And of course, as always, my husband Jake. No man enjoys hearing about things like how many whales washed up dead in a certain twenty-four-hour period over their breakfast, but he had to do so for quite some time. To have you support me in everything I do is the most powerful thing of all. Thank you my darling.

Lastly, to you, my readers. Thank you for being part of my journey.

ABOUT THE AUTHOR

Hannah Lynn is the author of over twenty books spanning several genres. Hannah grew up in the Cotswolds, UK. After graduating from university, she spent 15 years as a teacher of physics, teaching in the UK, Thailand, Malaysia, Austria and Jordan.

Sign up to Hannah Lynn's mailing list here for news, competitions and updates on future books.

Visit Hannah's website: www.hannahlynnauthor.com

Follow Hannah on social media:

facebook.com/hannahlynnauthor
instagram.com/hannahlynnwrites
bookbub.com/authors/hannah-lynn

ALSO BY HANNAH LYNN

The Holly Berry Sweet Shop Series

The Sweet Shop of Second Chances

Love Blooms at the Second Chances Sweet Shop

High Hopes at the Second Chances Sweet Shop

Family Ties at the Second Chances Sweet Shop

Sunny Days at the Second Chances Sweet Shop

A Summer Wedding at the Second Chances Sweet Shop

Snowflakes Over the Second Chances Sweet Shop

The Wildflower Lock Series

New Beginnings at Wildflower Lock

Coffee and Cake at Wildflower Lock

Blue Skies Over Wildflower Lock

Standalone Novels

In at the Deep End

The Side Hustle

Hannah Lynn writing as H.M Lynn

The Head Teacher

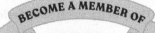

Boldwood

Boldwood Books is an award-winning fiction publishing company seeking out the best stories from around the world.

Find out more at www.boldwoodbooks.com

Join our reader community for brilliant books, competitions and offers!

Follow us
@BoldwoodBooks
@TheBoldBookClub

Sign up to our weekly deals newsletter

https://bit.ly/BoldwoodBNewsletter